Kinky Bones

Wildcat Wizard Book 7

Get deals and new releases notifications first via the
newsletter www.alkline.co.uk

All Gone

"Hey, Vicky, sorry to jump right here with the Teleron, but this is an emergency. Something's up with my computer and it's making..." I trailed off as the full horror of what I was confronted with sank into my shocked, squirming brain, much as I was trying to stop the images registering with all my mighty wizard powers.

"Arthur! What the hell do you think you're doing?" screeched Vicky as she scrambled for her clothes and covered herself up ineffectively.

It wasn't the image of her tiny naked body I was trying to banish from my brain though, it was the sight of a very naked Steve, including his hairy bottom. As if that wasn't enough, which it was, I also saw his... Ugh, anyway, let's just say the whole scene was gross, and brought to mind words fraught with imagery. Words such as moist, and rod, and bouncy, and dare I say it, thrust! I'd seen Vicky naked more times than I cared to remember, and once it was even nice, but this was beyond uncomfortable. It was too early, or late, as I hadn't gone to bed yet, for such shenanigans.

"Not cool, dude," muttered Steve, giving me a piercing stare as he slipped his jeans on casually, unconcerned by his nakedness, then sat on the sofa with his hands behind his head, looking bemused by Vicky's panicking.

"Sorry, guys, really sorry." I nodded an extra apology to Steve, and fair play, he took it well and nodded back. We were cool, all forgiven.

"Arthur, bugger off," snapped my diminutive sidekick, now dressed in child's jeans and a tight red sweater, as she attempted to pull her ponytail tight whilst simultaneously glaring at me and trying to put her hands on her hips for extra intimidation.

Like that would work on me, a wizard of over forty years. Scarred, battered by life, grizzled of hair, tired of body, mind, and soul, and not in the mood for any of her crap. She was still scary though, not that I'd ever admit it to her.

"I can't, my computer's beeping at me all the time and I can't remember any of my passwords. That's your fault," I accused, thinking it best to go on the offensive. "Are those your knickers?" I asked, pointing to something impossibly skimpy clinging to the arm of the sofa.

"Can't it wait?" asked Vicky as she grabbed the frilly red material and pocketed it, exasperated. She flung Steve's shirt at him and said, "Fun's over, lover boy," then bent and kissed him. So nasty.

Steve growled at me then finished dressing. Vicky straightened herself out properly then checked the time on the clock on the mantelpiece. "Arthur, it's still only half nine in the morning, what are you doing here?"

"I told you, my computer. More importantly, why are you two getting up to no good in the living room so early?"

"Why? I'll tell you why. Because I have children, and currently they are in school, and I have three loads of washing to do, I have to clean the house, go shopping, pick them up later, take them to their karate lessons, then I have to make them dinner, clean the—"

"Okay, I get it." I held up a hand to stop her as this could go on for hours. She loved recounting, on a very regular basis, the joys of having young children.

"Men!" Vicky stormed over to a cupboard covered in photos and garish things she liked to call ornaments and I liked to call junk, and grabbed her laptop. She slumped with a huff onto the sofa and lifted the lid. It immediately began to beep at her.

"Why's it doing that? Is it because of my computer? You have access to mine, right?"

"Yes, so you could have just called."

"I did. You never answered."

"I was busy. Idiot."

Vicky glanced down at the screen. Orange light reflected in her eyes, eyes which began to widen, and then it looked like they were glistening. Tears? She gasped, then typed furiously.

"What is it? Some kind of bug? I hate using the bloody thing, it's always going wonky. I just wanted to move money as a surprise for George, but I usually let her or you do the banking stuff. It doesn't make any sense. Then I couldn't log in and the screen began flashing and all this beeping and—"

"Will you shut up!"

"Have I broken the Internet? Did I ruin my computer putting in the wrong password? Can you do that? Can you?"

"I said shut up. What is wrong with you?"

Vicky typed furiously, looking increasingly panicked by the second. She was often like this when in virtual mode, lost to reality as cyberspace took over. Couldn't see the attraction myself. Technology was not a wizard's forte, and I hated being unable to understand it all. Vicky on the other hand was a genius with this world, was one of the best hackers in the country, although to look at her you'd assume she would struggle with anything more complicated than a toaster.

"How's things, mate?" asked Steve as he buttoned up his shirt.

"Usual. Knackered, taking it easy after that nonsense with the Hangman and Martha. Keeping a low profile to ensure my head remains attached to my shoulders. You?"

"A few small jobs, but same as you, keeping my head down, and intact. Been seeing Vicky quite a lot."

"Yeah, I'm happy for you guys. And we should catch up, it's been a while."

"Definitely. How about later on?"

"Will you two be quiet! This is serious." Vicky glanced up, looking about as stressed as I'd ever seen her.

"What is it? You can get rid of a virus, can't you?"

"Arthur, I haven't even accessed your computer yet. I'm more concerned with the alerts I've received. I'm in the accounts, your accounts, and my accounts, and they're empty."

"Well, that's good, isn't it? We never keep money in them for long. You always transfer the cash right out so we're safe."

"I don't mean the accounts we funnel payments through for jobs, I mean our private accounts, our separate ones. The ones where we do keep the money. They're empty."

"Haha, very funny. There's a fortune in them, in mine anyway as I don't waste it on crap like you do. And even with your spending, you should have a decent amount by now."

"I did, as the life insurance came through. It's all gone."

Vicky had finally got a large payout because her husband had died in a car accident. She kept quiet regarding the bit about it being a cover-up because she'd murdered him outside their front door. Still, he deserved it. Kind of.

"Haha, that's not funny. You said those accounts were unhackable, that they had the best security ever and you chose them precisely because of that. And you said you'd spread the money out, use a few accounts, just in case."

"I know all that," she snapped, sweat running into her eyes, her forehead a sheen of stress.

"Well?"

"Well, it's gone. From all accounts, large and small."

"You're screwed, mate." Steve rose and came behind the sofa to stand beside me as we looked over Vicky's shoulders at the worrying lack of numbers on the screen.

Vicky's computer began to beep manically. "That's what mine did. I just closed the lid and came here. Should I have turned it off then on again?"

"Shut up." Vicky typed angrily, battering the keypad like she always did, but whatever she did wasn't working, as next thing we knew, a series of 0's and 1's appeared on the screen. They danced around like jittery ants then formed an image. It was of a fist. Slowly, a middle finger rose then snapped into place.

Vicky's computer whirred then the screen went black.

"Fuck," she moaned, pressing the on/off button like it would dispense chocolate. "It's dead."

Hi, I'm Arthur "The Hat" Salzman. Gangster. Wizard. Suddenly very poor.

Some Perspective

Vicky sank even lower on the sofa and sighed deeply as she rubbed at her eyes. "It's all gone, all our money. Mine, yours."

"What about George's?"

"Hers was fine, all still there. And yes, I made sure to be careful accessing her account."

"Phew, that's good news."

"Not for us it isn't. Someone stole all our money, Arthur. We're skint."

"Oh, come on, don't be dramatic. It's just computer stuff, right? Just numbers on the screen, someone messing with us."

Steve sat beside Vicky and put his arm around her, while I tried not to breathe through my nose. Sex smell is all fine and dandy, but only when it's been you making it. So nasty.

"Arthur, are you being dense on purpose, or are you really this stupid?" asked Vicky.

"Hey, no need to be like that. I'm just saying, it's all virtual, someone screwing with us, messing about. It's not like the actual money is really gone, right? Just the accounts look empty. You know, virtual numbers."

Vicky and Steve both stared at me until I felt rather uncomfortable. I twiddled the Teleron nervously in my hand, wondering if I should jump back home and try to get some sleep. I certainly needed it. I'd been up all night, wandering about the land by my country home in Cornwall, many miles away from the city where Vicky lived and most of my work was focused. Mainly because it was where so many of the dangerous guys lived and did their business.

"You're serious?" asked Vicky.

I shrugged, being as non-committal as possible as I was obviously missing something here.

"So how do you think the money got into the accounts? That someone lugged millions in cash into a bank and then it got put on a computer but the actual money is still there really?"

"Obviously not, but we put that money in, so it can't have been actually taken. It's there somewhere."

"No, it isn't. It went in virtually, just numbers, and now it's gone, just numbers. You're joking, right?"

"Haha, of course I am. Just trying to take your mind off it. Haha." I wasn't, I really wasn't. Must have been because I was tired. I knew this stuff, but I was addled, as usual.

"It isn't helping. Okay, you two, bugger off, I need to solve this."

"No way," I protested.

"I'm staying too," said Steve. "I know how you get when you're working on that bloody computer. You forget to eat, you lose track of time, and you get, er..."

"Get what?" Vicky gave Steve a glare and he shrank away. Guess he was getting to know her quite well.

"Er, um..."

"You get bloody mental is what he's trying to say. Loopy-loo. Bat shit crazy. Off on one. Loco. So while you sort this mess out, and it is your mess as this is your job, why I let you in on this, be my partner, we're staying so you don't burn the house down, give the kids away, or forget to have a pee. You remember that time when we had to spend a few days on the security system for that place up north and you got the sofa so wet because you wouldn't get—"

"I told you, it was an accident." Vicky glanced at Steve nervously and smiled. "I drank too many fizzy drinks, okay?"

"Sure, babe. But Arthur's right, we'll stay, just in case."

And so it was, much to my chagrin, that we became embroiled in one of the worst, dare I say, capers of my career as a wizard thief. Mainly because Vicky was so grumpy.

By late morning she looked skeletal and had lost some hair because she kept tugging it. By dinner time, after I'd picked up the kids and got takeaway, she was screaming at a screen and using the PC as she'd broken two laptops.

By bedtime, after I'd helped the girls brush their teeth and Steve had read them three stories and been plastered with make-up and I'd had to figure out how to get young girls to put on their nighties without me having to help in any way or even be in the room, Vicky was losing the plot.

Steve and I marched into the dining room together, thinking there was backup if we went together, and stood in front of Vicky nervously.

We coughed discreetly; Vicky carried on typing and scowling, dark bags under her eyes. We called her name; she continued to punish the keyboard. We shook her; nothing. So I sat beside her at the table, grabbed the flat screen, and turned it away from her.

"Hey, what are you doing?"

"It's seven in the evening."

"What? Really? Oh."

"Aren't you forgetting something?"

Vicky stared at me blankly. "Like what?"

"Like your children? We made them dinner, because you didn't even say hello when I picked them up from school, Steve played with them, read them stories, and now they're ready for bed. You need to get a grip. You always do this and it isn't healthy. It has to stop. Chill out."

"Oh my God, I'm so sorry. Those poor girls. I thought I was better now, but I can't help it. But it's our money, Arthur, your money. This is my fault."

"Yes, it is."

"Dude, c'mon."

"I haven't finished. It's your fault, Vicky, and yes, you were meant to keep our cash safe, but it's just money. The girls are more important. This can wait, and if you can't figure this out without making yourself ill, then don't do it. Actually, I won't let you. You either eat, take care of yourself, look after the girls properly and stop making them feel upset, or this whole thing is off. Permanently. I mean it. If you don't get a grip then there will be no more jobs, no more working with me, and I'm done. You hear?"

"I do. And thank you. Both of you. I needed that. But I'm sorry, I don't know how this happened. Forgive me?"

"Sure. Like I said, it's just money. It's not like we're homeless. You have this place, I have mine, we have most of our money well away from the banks, so we'll —"

"Wait, what?"

"I said, we have our houses, and most of our money is well away from banks. Yours is, right? You did what I told you back at the start of all this?"

"Um, what was that again?"

"That you never, ever, leave more money in a bank than you are willing to lose. That you treat it like a gamble, and most gets converted to hard currency, preferably gold, and you dig a hole and hide it. I have mine somewhere safe, guarded by wards, a place nobody can get it. You said you did the same, that you were on it. I remember."

"Um, I did?"

"Hell, you had it all in the bank?"

"Most of it. Just got a little bit in a safe here."

"How little?"

"Few thousand."

"You muppet."

"I thought you were joking," protested Vicky, close to tears she was so exhausted and upset. Guess this wasn't helping.

"Why would I joke about that?" I asked, perplexed.

"Who the hell buries gold? Who even owns gold?"

"Wizards, for a start. All of them. Plus, people who don't want their entire fortune stolen with the press of a button."

"Oh."

"Look, just go put the girls to bed, they're waiting. We'll figure something out, don't worry. I have every faith in you. You'll find where it is and get it back."

Vicky staggered off like a hunchback, looking seriously depressed.

"Did you really hide most of your money in gold?"

"Yup. Why?"

"You are one weird dude, Arthur."

"But I'm not broke."

"True. You think she'll be okay?"

"As long as we watch her. You know she's got an eating disorder, right? That she goes through phases when she doesn't eat, sleeps worse than me, and gets manic with it."

"She told me, yeah."

"It's scary to watch, so be aware. She has to eat. She's small enough as it is, if she misses meals she wastes away really fast and it gets dangerous."

"Don't worry, I'll look after her."

"So will I. I'm happy for you, both of you."

"Hey, it's early days yet, but it's going good, yeah."

"Your funeral. Vicky's a, shall we say, handful."

"Haha, you got that right. But that's how I like my ladies, nice and feisty."

"Then you chose well, my hairy friend. You chose very well indeed."

Steve scratched at his full beard, full of product and not what I thought men should do to their hair. Different times I guess. Shifters went for the hipster look, and Steve pulled it off effortlessly. He was a good guy. Hopefully it would work out for him and Vicky.

There was a scream from upstairs. For some reason, I wasn't surprised. Something was starting, and this kind of crap was always part and parcel of another wildcat adventure.

Damsel in Distress

Steve and I bolted out of the room and dashed for the stairs, the going awkward as we kept getting in each other's way.

Wand was out of my pocket and shouting, "Yippee," as I took the lead and raced up the stairs. For a sentient stick, he sure got excited whenever he got pulled from the customized pocket that provided easy access to the hard wood.

"Hold your horses," I told Wand between pants.

"Been ages. I feel like letting off some steam."

"Yeah, well don't go nuts. The kids are up here, so whatever it is, wait until I give the go-ahead."

"Spoilsport."

Steve caught me up on the landing as I slowed and he gave me a strange look. He knew about Wand now, but it still took everyone a while to get used to me muttering to a stick.

Without forethought, we both entered the girls' bedroom—they liked to stay together even though they were old enough to have their own rooms if they wanted. Have I ever mentioned they were twins? I don't think I have. Well, they were. Two pale, blond, perfect children, taking after their father in hair color, thankfully not in girth. They were slight, like Vicky, already almost as tall as her though, so they'd buy clothes from grown-up stores when they were older, unlike their mum.

"What is it? What's happened?" I asked, half expecting to see either a maniac wizard, an elf, a faery, or something else annoying and magical.

"Mummy collapsed," said one munchkin.

"There," said the other, like we'd missed the figure of Vicky out cold on the carpet in between the two beds.

"Did anything happen? Was anyone here?" I asked.

"No, Mummy just keeled over. I think she's tired."

"I think you're right."

"Hey," said Steve, "why don't I read you your story while Arthur takes Mummy downstairs? Sound cool?"

"Yippee."

"Hooray. Uncle Steve's going to read to us again."

And with that, both girls hopped onto a bed and snuggled up together. Steve read a story while they cuddled in tight, their mum seemingly forgotten.

I slung Vicky over my shoulder and marched downstairs, then set her down on the sofa. Vicky murmured and came around a few seconds later.

"What happened?"

"You zonked out because you haven't eaten all day and you got too stressed. I've told you about this in the past." And I had. She'd been good for ages, but I guess we hadn't needed any serious hacking work done for a while, so she was out of practice plus this was more personal than it usually got.

"Sorry. Are the girls okay?"

"Fine, Steve's reading to them. Look, take it easy, okay? We'll sort this out, I have every faith in you. Just look after yourself and the girls first. Don't rush, or panic. You can do this but only if you're in control and focused."

"I know, guess I overreacted because all the money is gone. What am I going to do if I don't have any money?"

"You'll get it, and if you don't, then I'll give you some. Not too much," I added, "because this is your fault."

"Arthur, you are so mean sometimes."

Vicky began to cry. I went to make her a sandwich before I began patting her on the head and saying stupid things like, "There, there, good girl." Women seemed to hate that, even though I was only trying to make them feel better.

I entered the large kitchen of Vicky's Georgian house and nearly jumped a mile.

"I've got a job for you," said Ivan, looking about as vampiric as it's possible to look without blood dripping from your fangs.

"You can go fuck yourself," I said, then went to the fridge to get cheese.

"That's not very nice."

"I know. I told you, no more vampire work. I don't owe you anything, and after that Mikalus shit we are more than square. No more work for vampires. We're friends, you're Vicky's brother, but that's it."

"Arthur, this is important. Wasn't my little display enough for you? This is serious, you have to help. Actually, you have no choice if you want your money back."

"You motherfucker."

I believe this was the first time I tried to strangle Ivan. Or was it the second?

Family Fueds

"What's all the racket?" asked Vicky as she came running into the kitchen.

"Nothing," I said from my position on the floor, straddling Ivan with my hands around his throat.

"Get off him. What are you doing?"

"I'm strangling your brother because he's the one who nicked our moolah."

"What!? Is this true?" Vicky stared down at Ivan as I continued to throttle him.

Ivan nodded.

"See?"

"Fine." Vicky sighed. "Carry on."

I continued my pursuit of a dead Ivan but it wasn't going so well. However hard I squeezed, I couldn't seem to get a good throttle going. It was like squeezing steel, no give at all. Ivan stared up at me, smiling, not resisting in any way whatsoever.

As my fingers began to hurt he said, "Are you quite finished?"

I nodded and rolled off him then got up.

Ivan sprang to his feet, full of vitality, the vampire juices obviously flowing now it was dark outside and the call of the wild was upon him. I bloody hate vampires.

"Go on, tell her," I said, thinking of ways to kill him slowly and painfully.

"I was just telling Arthur that I need his help, yours too. Maybe yours even more than his."

"Tell her the bit about you stealing all our money."

"You didn't really? Tell me it wasn't you." Vicky's tears fell again, this time with a deep sadness born of betrayal by family. Nothing cuts deeper than that.

"I may have had your accounts moved, just to show you what we're up against. Have you got the money back yet?" Ivan brushed imaginary dust from his suit jacket, the black material spotless. Vicky kept an immaculate house, no dirt or dust on her kitchen floor. He ran his slender hands through slick black hair, as casual as if we were discussing the weather while Vicky cried and I plotted his demise. I hate vampires, did I mention that? I do, I really do.

"I can't believe you did this, to me. To us." Vicky began sobbing too much to talk.

"Everything all right here?" asked Steve as he sauntered into the kitchen and took in the standoff.

"No, Ivan was just leaving, weren't you?"

"No, I wasn't."

"Vicky?" Steve put his arm around her and whispered in her ear. She shook her head. He glared at Ivan and looked at me questioning what was happening. I shrugged, not knowing how much Vicky wanted to involve Steve in our business. Damn, why do things get instantly complicated when it involves family?

We remained like that until Vicky got herself together and wiped her eyes. Then, without warning, she approached Ivan, looked him in the eye, and slapped him hard across the cheek. The sound was surprisingly loud, and it took all of us by surprise, especially Ivan. He recoiled in shock, a hand to his cheek.

"Sister?"

"You dare call me sister after what you've done? You stole from us, our money. Do you know how stressed I've been, how bad I feel? I let Arthur down, I let the girls down, I let Steve down, and you did it. Why?"

"Because he wants us to do something for him. I already told him, I don't work for vampires any more. We're quits, no favors owed. Done and dusted."

"And what about you, Vicky?" asked Ivan, his cheek red.

"We don't work for you now. If you'd asked me, I would have done whatever you needed, even if Arthur refused. You're my brother. But now? No. We won't do it."

"I thought showing you a little of what we're up against was a good idea. This is serious, very serious, and I need your help. Everyone does. This could get very messy very fast if we don't contain the problem. Maybe I misjudged. I'm sorry."

"Too late. Get out. Get out of my house. I don't even want to look at you." Vicky stepped up to Ivan again, and we all held our breath. Vicky may have been tiny and pretty harmless to look at, but she was still scary. She had this way about her, an inner confidence even when up against the nastiest gangsters, and this was a family matter so it wasn't like Ivan could have her bumped off.

She didn't slap him though, she did something much worse.

"You betrayed me. You know I get stressed about money and the future for the girls. You took that away from me so I'd help you? That's not what brothers do. Get out, and don't come back."

Ivan flinched like she'd hit him, the words stinging much more than a slap. "Please, let me explain."

"No. Get out!" hissed Vicky as she shoved Ivan in the chest.

"Time to go, mate." Steve stepped forward and squared off against Ivan.

"You heard her," I said, annoyed and disappointed with how Ivan had handled this.

"As you wish. I'll be in touch."

"Don't bother."

Vicky walked Ivan to the front door and shut it behind him. She came back into the kitchen and the tears fell in earnest. I left her in Steve's capable hands and went into the living room.

Some time later, Steve popped his head around the door and said goodbye. After Vicky saw him out she came and sat beside me on the sofa.

"So, what's the plan?" she asked, a little sparkle returning to her eyes.

"The plan? Get our money back and then go to bed."

It was a long night.

All Sorted

By early morning we were both destroyed. I hadn't slept in days, had only been popping in the day before because of the tech problems, and Vicky was already perilously close to a meltdown before Ivan had shown his ugly mug.

But we persevered, or Vicky did. I was mostly tasked with making coffee and giving moral support. Initially, we got nowhere, so Vicky became anxious and stressed all over again. I told her to relax, because obviously that was the right thing to say, which, perplexingly, led to a massive argument resulting in more tears and several pats on the head.

Then I had a brilliant idea. If Ivan had done this to teach us a lesson, that meant he'd probably got someone local involved. Maybe even got them to do the deed from his home or workplace. Vicky was dubious, but nonetheless she began trawling through nodes, boinking dongles, fracturing fireproof walls, routing serving staff for some reason, and regaling me with useless information about backdoors and IP addresses and other nonsensical gobbledygook until I became convinced she was just making things up. Every now and then she'd look up, say something about onions that work, which I took to mean she was on the right track, then get back to keyboard assault.

She chased down the source of the hack, but it took almost all night. Credit where credit's due though, because by early morning she'd managed to not only discover how it was done, but get the money back.

Turns out it hadn't even been stolen. I won't even try to understand how it worked, but the gist of it was that the hacker Ivan had hired hadn't actually transferred the money out of the accounts—they really were that well safeguarded—but instead had gone down a convoluted route where they'd set up fake sites, clones of the originals, and done some tech wizardry to make it seem like we were accessing the accounts when in fact it was all just looky-likeys.

Seemed like utter madness to me, but Vicky said it was incredibly clever and hard to do, tougher than hacking the accounts in the first place. I wasn't impressed with any of it, but Vicky was happy, and slightly jealous, so all's well that ends well.

It was with great relief that Vicky finished her work and sat next to me on the sofa. She looked awful, but she was smiling, and so was I.

"Nice job, grasshopper," I said, patting her head.

"Will you stop doing that. I'm not your pet."

"No, but you look like one. You want your brekkie for being a good girl?"

"Arthur! Why did he do it?"

"Ivan, you mean?"

"Of course."

"He said it was to show us what we were up against, what he and everyone else was up against, and that it would affect us all. Dunno. He's nuts. You know what he's like. Hmm, actually, that's not right. He never does stuff like this. Usually he just comes and asks for a favor or finds another way to get us to do his crap."

"Exactly. So why do this? And to me? His own sister."

"You'll have to ask him, but I want nothing to do with any of this."

"Wonder what's going on?" mused Vicky, with a look that was all too familiar.

"Don't go getting any ideas," I warned. "The vampires have been keeping a low profile, he's running them smoothly, I'll give him that, but I don't want to get involved in their nonsense. We did what he wanted before, wiped the slate clean. I am not interested."

"Okay, okay, just wondering."

Vicky's phone rang so she reached over and grabbed it. "It's Ivan."

"Do what you want."

She tapped the screen, said, "It's on speaker," then answered with a sharp, "What?"

"That's a rather abrupt way to answer the phone," said Ivan.

"What do you expect after last night?"

There was no reply for a few seconds then Ivan said, "Sorry, you have me at a disadvantage. What happened last night?"

Vicky frowned at me and I shrugged.

"You know, the hacking, stealing our money, or making it look like you had. Coming here and trying to force Arthur to do a job for you. That."

"Um, I have no idea what you are talking about. Is this a joke? You know I'm not good with jokes. I was calling to see if I could visit this evening, see the girls, and you of course. Are you feeling okay? Sorry it's so early, but I'm going to bed soon."

"Are you winding me up?" shouted Vicky, standing and waving her arms about theatrically like Ivan could see.

"Vicky, my dear sister, I don't know what you are talking about. I was in meetings all yesterday evening. What time are we looking at?"

"A bit after seven. Maybe half past. What is this? Why are you being so mean?"

"I swear to you I did not come to your house yesterday. I'll see you this evening. I don't know what kind of joke this is, but I am not amused." Ivan hung up.

"Mummy, what's all the shouting about?" asked a bleary-eyed sprog as she came dashing into the living room, closely followed by another angel in a pink nightie. "We were sleeping."

Vicky and I exchanged shocked glances. The call was odd, this was odder. We'd been so caught up in our work we'd forgotten how lucky we'd been to have the chance to work uninterrupted.

And so it was, for the first time in history, the kids were up after everyone else.

Back Home

Two tiny tots running about screaming, begging for cereal Vicky said was unhealthy, stomping their feet about needing to watch TV, whizzing from room to room in search of faery princess outfits, and tugging on a poor wizard's clothing made it seem like a good idea to leave, so I did.

Phew. Fighting evil overlords of the black magic variety is draining, but I hold my hands up to the parents of the world and admit, they have it worse.

After a kiss from the terrible twins, and a scowl from Vicky for leaving her in the midst of such early morning carnage, I beat a hasty retreat by stepping into the hallway and pretending to go out the front door. I figured it best not to let the girls see me use the Teleron as I'd never hear the end of it. I'd be on a non-stop trip to the theme parks of the world.

I'd grown accustomed to using it a little more of late, but still found it disconcerting bordering on utterly terrifying, yet I couldn't be bothered to call a taxi.

I adjusted the Teleron, pictured the field beside the farmhouse where George, my darling daughter, and I lived, and then off I went only to appear there instantly. I checked I was still me, and not standing in the middle of a cow or something, the main reason why I hated using this thing, and then with a spring in my step I walked across the soaking ground to the farm.

George was already up and exercising one of the horses, which was weird, as she liked to lie in until a more respectable time. Guess the fact she had to care for the horses meant she was becoming accustomed to early mornings. She had help most days, but some mornings she was on her own, running her business, giving riding lessons, and offering stabling for an exorbitant amount. Here's a tip for you. If you want to keep hold of your money, never get a horse. George had done remarkably well, had a good business head on her shoulders. But I was still inordinately pleased to not have to tell her the family fortune was gone and all she'd inherit was my hat.

In need of coffee and breakfast, but wanting to see her beautiful face first, maybe even get a hug as there was nobody about so she couldn't feel embarrassed, I trudged across the fields, went through a gate, and walked past the stable block. The horses whinnied their protest at my passing; for some reason they hated me, and the feeling was mutual.

George was resplendent in a Barbour jacket, obligatory horsey leggings, riding boots that shone with oil, and her long auburn hair streaming behind her more gracefully than the horse she was running beside.

She ran it around and around in circles in the sand where they got their exercise and people could fall off, hopefully without breaking any bones.

Every day since she came into my life I counted my blessings. However tough things got, whatever nonsense went on, I always tried to put things into perspective and remind myself that I had a charming, sensible, independent, warm, kind, beautiful daughter in my life now. She'd appeared from nowhere—I had no idea she existed—after her mum had died and with nowhere else to go she'd come to me. It was weird to start with, as I was used to living by my own rules, coming and going as I pleased. But although she was old enough to look after herself, we both found immense comfort in each other's company and being part of each other's lives.

Hopefully she would stay forever, never leave her poor old dad.

Sadly, she was growing older, was close to being a true woman in every sense, but for now, and maybe a few more years, she would remain with me, share my life and allow me to share hers.

"Morning," I sang as I watched her slow, then release the reins to give the horse, a midnight black beast that looked like it belonged to the Devil himself, the chance to move at its own pace.

"Morning, Dad. Where you been?"

"Huh? I called you, told you."

"Sorry, been a bit scatty lately."

"Um, okay." She sounded weird, but I guess we all had things going on. "Had to go see Vicky. Someone, namely Ivan, played a nasty trick on us. It looked like they'd emptied the bank accounts so I spent the night there trying to get it sorted."

"You mean you made the coffee while Vicky did all the work?" George said with a twinkle in her eye, and a smile.

"Yeah, something like that," I grumbled.

"You said Ivan did it? Why? How?"

"That's the strange thing. He came to the house last night, said he did it to show us what we were up against, then Vicky threw him out and she got it sorted. But he called this morning, and acted like he knew nothing about it. Said he didn't do it, wasn't at the house yesterday. Dude's weird."

"Maybe he's stressed with work. He's got a lot of responsibility now."

"I don't care, that's his choice. He took on the role of heading up the vampires, and he bloody enjoys it anyway. Plus, he's got the old ones to run their business. He focuses on the gangster stuff like always. I don't know what's got into him. Maybe he's still pissed because I refuse to work for the vamps after all that crap with Mikalus."

"Or maybe it was a cry for help. Maybe he wants to be close to you guys again. What was the job?"

"Didn't ask. Hey, want some breakfast? We can eat together."

"Sure, sounds good. I'll be in soon, just finish off here."

"Okay, no problem." I put my arms out for a hug then checked to see none of George's girls were here to work. "All clear."

"I'm not embarrassed to hug you if there's people around. Why should I be?"

"Cause I'm old and wrinkly and look like a scarecrow but with a nice hat."

"Haha, I'm used to it."

We hugged. George smelled funny, different. Must be the horses and whatever she used to clean the stables out. It didn't matter, the hug made everything right in the world, and it was with a happy heart that I walked across the field to the house.

After taking my boots off, I wandered down the hall, but stopped dead in my tracks as I heard a noise from the kitchen.

Slowly, I crept forward, Wand at the ready. At the doorway to my uber amazing barn conversion that was now officially the best kitchen in the whole world, I gasped.

"George?"

George turned and smiled at me. She was in her pajamas, hair tousled, looking like she'd just got out of bed and was making her first cup of coffee of the day.

"Morning. Fancy a coffee?"

"Um, yeah, I think I'm gonna need it."

Spinning Head

I crept across the tiled floor, watching my reflection in the shiny black surface, feeling numb. Was I hallucinating? I did that sometimes when the insomnia got out of hand. That must be it. It had felt so real; we'd even hugged. Sitting at the table, I watched George shuffle about like she always did when she was up relatively early. She was hunched over, dragging her feet, performing tasks on auto-pilot, needing coffee to kickstart her day.

She brought two mugs over, set them down, then sat.

"Um, so you aren't out doing the horses then? You didn't do them then rush in and put your pj's back on?"

"Huh?" George sipped her coffee, hardly listening to me. "Hey, where were you? Been out all night?"

"Yeah, I already told you. Um, I was at Vicky's. Look, something odd is going on here."

"Haha, isn't it always?"

"No, I mean now. I just talked to you in the field."

"Yesterday you mean?"

"No, just now. And I've just come from Vicky's because someone hacked our accounts. Ugh, I've already told you all this. And I'm sure I called you to tell you where I was."

"Nope, you didn't call. At least I don't think so. Sorry, the days blur. Tell me again. You're acting weirder than usual, you know that, right?" George put her mug down and stared at me. "You look awful too, super tired. You want to have a lie down?"

"In a minute." I went on to explain what had happened with the money and Ivan, and seeing her outside. Obviously, the two were connected. What I didn't think to do was go outside and take another look. I needed coffee for that. And I had the feeling the other George would be long gone. Plus, well, she couldn't have been there. Magic was afoot, spells to make us see people who weren't there. Or something else I couldn't think of right now.

"Wait here," said George after I'd finished. Before I could muster the energy to stop her, she was gone.

I sighed deeply then rested my head on the table, too tired to bother using my neck to hold it in place.

"Dad! Dad!"

"Huh?" I jerked awake to find George shaking my shoulder and leaning over to stare at me.

"There's nothing there. Nobody about. But Satan was sweaty, so he's definitely been out. You weren't imagining it, someone's been here."

"Goddamn! Okay, so somebody stole our cash, pretended to be Ivan, said we had to do a job for him, now they turn up here. What's the game plan?" I rubbed at my face, trying to get some clarity, but I was too befuddled.

"I guess they hoped that you'd say yes yesterday and go along with whatever it was. Keep pretending to be Ivan. Maybe they don't know all the history."

"Or maybe they do and that's why they chose Ivan to impersonate."

"Maybe."

"But why be you? How did they know I'd be here when I was?" That was worrying. I'd used the Teleron, so it wasn't like I could have been followed and they'd know when I was arriving.

"Maybe they're just screwing with you now? Maybe they know they've blown their cover, after you spoke to Ivan this morning."

"Maybe. Ugh, be careful today, okay? Don't believe anything you see, and don't—"

"Don't trust the buggers. I know. Same old, same old."

"That's my girl."

And with that, I drained my coffee, forgot all about breakfast, and staggered up the stairs then collapsed on my bed.

I lay there with my hands laced behind my head, attempting to understand this unwelcome intrusion into my life. Things had been relatively quiet for a few months, no drama after the kidnappings, and it had been nice. Easy.

Such is the life of a wizard though. If you aren't making the trouble yourself, someone else will make it for you. Could be worse. I just wasn't sure how.

Weird Goings On

You know when you wake up and feel like something's wrong? Almost as though you're misplaced, out of the loop somehow? Just an uneasy feeling in your belly, your body aware of something you aren't?

No? Maybe it's just me then.

That's how I felt as I opened my eyes cautiously, like there was something terribly amiss. My stomach churned, my body ached like I had the flu, and something was screaming at the back of my mind but I couldn't figure out what. Clearly my senses were more aware than my head, as I'd picked up on something and it had brought me out of a fitful slumber.

Glancing at the clock, I noted with dismay that it was only eleven in the morning. Guess this was all the rest I'd get for the day. The Hat's peace was well and truly shattered. Still dressed, I got up and decided to ignore the warnings until I was at least semi-conscious. I relieved myself in the bathroom—even wizards in stories of their own telling need to pee—scowled at myself in the mirror, then stripped off and showered, letting the hot water turn my skin pink, wash away the tiredness, and ease my aching bones.

Refreshed, unsullied of body if not soul, I dressed in clean clothes and wandered downstairs.

There was nobody about, and I somehow knew George was fine, but I couldn't shake the feeling of something being wrong, like a brick in the pit of my stomach. Coffee made, I pulled aside the glass doors at the far end of my awesome kitchen, glanced around just to admire the huge island, the worktop running the whole length of the converted barn, the awesome tap, the fact it was clean and tidy, the old wooden beams that gave it a homely yet very stylish look, then stepped outside into the frigid late morning air.

I sipped the scalding coffee and stared at the woman standing at the bottom of the lawn, my guts relaxing, telling me this was the reason I was so edgy. She was too far away to make out properly, but she had a shock of pink hair cut into a bob, and by the looks of it was keen on leather and exposing her flesh no matter the weather.

Whoever she was, this woman was the cause of the recent upset, so I ignored her and drank my coffee. Never chase trouble, it'll find you soon enough.

And it did.

As I drank, and watched her silently, she turned from staring at the fields beyond where sheep grazed contentedly, and faced me. She wasn't surprised; she knew I was here. With a nod, she wandered casually up the garden as if she'd been invited and we were old friends.

As she got close I made out more detail. She was neither skinny nor fat, just a tad on the curvaceous side, with a sexy walk and a deep-seated self-confidence. She wore your typical alternative gear. Heavy on jewelery and ear piercings, leather trousers, Doctor Martens, and a leather waistcoat over a tight vest full of holes.

Late twenties by the looks of her, caught in a student attire time warp she would probably now remain in. But all that was just superficial, everyone was part of one group or another regards their dress, it was merely a way of reflecting your stance with the world and how you approached it. She wasn't a citizen, wouldn't conform, and you had to admire that.

Plus, she was obviously a witch, and witches are rare in these here parts. There was George, her teacher, and not many others. Rural villages on the coast aren't known for attracting magic users, which was exactly why I had chosen it as a place to live.

"Hey," she said brightly as she stopped several feet in front of me.

"Hey," I replied, watching her carefully as I gulped coffee.

She stood, relaxed, smiling a little, waiting.

Two could play at that game, so I continued drinking, and tried not to shiver with the cold.

Cryptic Bullshit

The girl studied me casually, as though she were watching a TV program she was only half interested in. She was utterly chilled, and I half expected her to yawn. As I sipped my coffee slowly, just to have something to do and to hide my smile at this show of forced calm, she remained focused on me. She was certainly confident, and I could sense the power inside her, what she was capable of. I gotta say, I was impressed.

But for all her bravado, it was just that, an act. She may have been sure of herself, but studied disinterest was for show. She was dying to talk, and I could tell she would be a blabbermouth once she got going. It was almost like a pressure cooker ready to blow a gasket and let forth a torrent of chatter. She reminded me of someone. A tiny person with a mouth too big for her face. Vicky and her would either love or hate each other.

"What you smiling at?" she asked, as I couldn't hide my grin at the thought of the two of them trying to get a word in edge ways when locked in a room together.

"Oh, just thinking about someone."

"Ah, the badly dressed tiny person?"

"Actually, yes," I said, surprised.

"She's your partner."

"No, she's my annoying sidekick. The comedy, the light relief. The one that screws things up and almost gets us killed."

"But she got you out of this latest mess, right?" The girl, although I suppose she was a woman, cocked her head to one side like a bird listening for danger.

"She did. But it damaged her. Whoever pulled this crap," I paused to stare at her hard and show my disapproval, "harmed my friend. Vicky has, er, issues, and stressing about money, meaning, her children and their future, sends her spiraling. Believing her brother would treat her like that, do her harm in such a mean, nasty way, drove her close to the edge. Not nice at all. In fact, I'd go so far as to say I'm royally pissed off with the joker who dared put a friend of mine at risk."

"Oh, um, that's terrible. I, er, I'd have thought she would have enjoyed the challenge, found it exciting. Someone to pit her wits against, that kind of thing. I'm sure whoever did it, they didn't mean for her to make herself ill, or worry about her children. Maybe they thought seeing her brother, thinking he was involved, was a good idea and it would get her and you to perform a little job for them. Whoever they are. I'm sure they didn't mean to upset anyone, just wanted to show that they were capable, that they could help."

"Is that right?" I copied her movement, cocked my own head to the side, tilted Grace back so this woman could see my eyes. I was not a happy camper, and she knew it.

"Um, yes."

The cool exterior was crumbling, and her eyes shifted, breaking our gaze. She'd got it all wrong, that was obvious, and was now realizing that The Hat was not impressed with someone screwing with his finances and upsetting his sidekick, let alone involving the most powerful gangster in the country who happened to be a vampire.

Then it hit me. If she'd impersonated, or had someone else, impersonate Ivan, she knew a lot about him. Not that his vampire status and the extent of his criminal enterprise was a secret in the magical underworld, but still, the conversation with him proved she knew plenty. She had the advantage, and that wasn't good.

I continued to stare at her, wondering what she wanted, why she'd gone to this much bother to get my attention. She could have just got in touch via the usual channels if she had a job. But then, I turned down most work, was selective, so maybe she thought this would help. It had certainly put her on my radar.

"Tell me," I said, and she snapped to attention.

"Yeah?"

"Is there any reason why I shouldn't just kill you right now? Do you think impersonating Ivan, or my goddamn daughter, was a good idea?" I shouted, and she jumped back, eyes wide, looking if not scared then certainly shocked and a little worried.

"What!?"

"My fucking daughter. You dare play games with me? You pretended to be my daughter, at my home. This is where I live, with George. You have no right to come here and trick me. I've killed people, men and women both, for insulting my friends and family yet you think you're better than that? That you can play your games and screw with those I love and not reap the consequences? You want to play games, little girl? I'll show you things you couldn't even dream of. You do not fuck with my family. Understand?"

Wand was out of my pocket and flaring dully at the tip as I loomed forward, putting on my best scowl and furrowing my brow to look extra old and wizardly. My heart wasn't in it, but I think the drama paid off and she was convinced. Truth be told, I just wanted to go back to bed and cry into a cold pillow.

"She looks nice," said Wand.

I just grunted in reply.

"Be a shame to blast her to goo, but if you're sure?" Wand flared bright purple, not his usual color but it was more dramatic and looked pretty cool.

"I'm sure," I grumbled in my best pissed off wizard voice.

"Wait, wait," screeched the no longer brimming with confidence young witch.

"You," she pointed at Wand, "don't need to blast me. I just wanted to offer your master a job. Please, wait a minute, okay?"

"Nah, I'm gonna blast her," said Wand, sounding extremely happy about the whole thing.

"Oi, talk to me, not him. I have a job, an important job, please, just wait."

The sigils flared down Wand's length. He was doing great playing along with this, although a small part of me really did want to blast her for what she'd done. "You can hear Wand?"

"Huh? Yeah, sure. Sentient wizard wand, of course I can hear him."

"That's quite unusual. Not many magic users can hear him. He's linked to me."

"Like a familiar. I know. Got one of my own. I told you, I'm pretty good, and I'm sorry for messing you about. Not my usual style. Thought doing something cool and being all menacing would make you want in. Guess I blew it." Her whole demeanor changed. Gone was the cocky witch who had the upper hand, in her place was a woman who was certainly confident, but who also knew she was out of her depth.

"Go away," I said with a sigh. "I'm not in the mood for juvenile games. Don't mess with me again, or Wand really will blast you. Now, bugger off."

I turned and walked back towards the kitchen.

"Hey, if you change your mind, meet me tonight at Inferno."

"I said go away." I closed the glass doors behind me and didn't turn around to look. She was gone, and good riddance.

Too Old for This

It was bloody freezing, and we both had our coats wrapped tight to keep out the autumn chill. Seemed we were the only ones though, as everyone else was either unaware it was frosty verging on glacial or had forgotten to bring anything to keep warm.

The line to get into the club was long although moving at an okay pace, but it would still be ages before we got in. Kids chatted excitedly, immune to the weather, older men and women conversed quietly, although several were obviously off their heads on one chemical compound or another and were either in semi-comas or more animated and excited about being out than the youngsters.

"Right, that's it," I grumbled after getting knocked in the back by some numnuts in a ripped t-shirt and a kilt. Yeah, a guy.

"Arthur, where are you going?" asked Vicky as she stepped out of the line and followed me.

"To the bloody front. I don't stand in line, it isn't the wizardly way."

"You can't just jump the queue."

"Why not?"

"Because if everyone did that it would be chaos."

"We aren't everyone else. We're us. Gangsters don't act like citizens. What if somebody saw? I've got a reputation to maintain."

"Yeah, or you just don't want to wait."

"Whatever." I winked at Vicky; she knew me only too well.

We marched to the front, acting like we were on a special guest list, VIP to the max, and stopped the other side of one of those ridiculous red ropes strung across two cheap looking three foot high brass poles.

The two bouncers who were checking people over then letting them in or telling them to bugger off, based on secret bouncer knowledge or maybe just to relieve the boredom, ushered a giggling couple in then turned to stare at us.

"What? Go stand in line."

I lifted my hat to reveal my face and the guy who'd spoken said, "Oh, sorry, didn't realize it was you." His face lit up and he asked, "How you doing, Mr. Hat?"

"Pretty good, Mike. You?"

"On the grind, same as always."

"No more bother with the thing?"

"None. Thanks for that. Mum said to pop around any time. She talks about you a lot but you haven't been by."

"You know how it is. Busy."

"Yeah, I know, but she'd appreciate it."

"Sure, maybe next week, okay? I'm in the middle of something at the moment."

"Ooh, need any help?"

"Nah, not on this one, Mike."

"Hey, what's the hold up?" asked a young kid with spiked hair, wearing a Ramones t-shirt with the sleeves cut off. "It's bloody freezing out here."

"Should have worn a bloody coat then, you stupid fuck," said Mike. He turned back to me, rolled his eyes, and said, "Kids, eh?"

"You know it."

"Coming in?" he asked.

"If you don't mind?"

"No problem. Allow me." Mike dropped the rope on one side and we moved forward. The other bouncer nodded. I knew his face, but not his name.

"Hey, that's not fair," whined the young kid again.

"Shut it," ordered Mike. "This is The Hat, you numpty."

"Who the fuck is The Hat?"

"A man who saved my mum from a bloody loan shark, and if you don't shut your mouth I'll ram your—"

"Thanks again, Mike. Say hi to your mum."

"Will do."

We stepped inside as Mike made good on his promise to the kid.

There Are Worse Places. Maybe

Neon screamed, the seemingly timeless Nine Inch Nails blasted through the speakers so loud I couldn't hear myself think, lights strobed, bodies thrashed, and I couldn't take my eyes off Vicky.

I don't know where she got it from, or how on earth she got into it, but Vicky was wearing an outfit so tight it was like a second skin. A very shiny, very revealing, very PVC skin. Her face was expertly made up with bright red lipstick, thick eyeliner, and her hair was out of its ponytail and hanging straight and oiled past her shoulders, dripping down her upper chest and tickling the top of her tiny, but surprisingly juicy looking breasts. Now I knew why she'd kept her coat buttoned right up until she'd handed it over at the cloakroom.

She wore an all-in-one cat suit, black and shining plastic that hugged every contour of her body. There was a zip from crotch to neck, but it was only done up as far as her breasts that were pushed together like two small melons in a plastic bag. Damn, I'm focusing too much on the breasts, aren't I? To be honest, it was hard not to, and the sweat already forming on her exposed skin didn't detract from the allure.

"What?" she screamed, looking at me funny.

"You look hot," I shouted.

"Thanks." Vicky smiled, clearly enjoying every minute of this. It wasn't often, make that ever, that she wore anything but her usual Stepford Mom outfit, so she was making the most of it. I swear if she'd had a tail she would have been purring.

I felt underdressed, and a little out of place with my usual attire. Hat, threadbare sweater, jacket of many pockets, combats with even more pockets as wizards need them for stuff, and scuffed boots. As I glanced around the club, aptly named Inferno, I noticed we were getting a lot of approving glances. I'd assumed it was Vicky drawing all the attention from the other similarly attired men and women, Vicky looking tame by comparison, but I realized I was getting as many approving nods as she was.

Guess the grizzled wizard look was something they thought was cool. Then it hit me, and my smug grin was wiped away, replaced with a growl and a frown. They thought I'd dressed up, that I'd taken time to make myself look like this to come out clubbing. They thought I was wearing a costume and they approved because I looked, well, I guess I looked like an old wizard who was pissed off with the world. I hadn't dressed up, put any thought into it. This was just me. The Hat.

Mood darker than Vicky's eyeliner, I took her hand and waded through the steaming mess of bodies, trying not to poke people with Wand who was being rather insistent about being released from his pocket prison.

We had a silent conversation that went something like this.

"Let me out."

"No."

"Why not? You're such a spoilsport."

"Why do you need to be out? You can see everything from in there. You're a magic wand."

"It's not the same," he whined. "I want to experience it all properly. It's not fair. You get to rub up against all this flesh, feel women's bouncy bits pressed against your back. Feel men's crotches pressed hard against your thigh and—"

"That's enough!" I warned. "Um, I didn't know you swung that way."

"I don't swing any way. I'm a stick. But if I could, and I would if I could, then I'm not choosy. The human body is so interesting, and don't forget, I'm a manifestation of you, an extension of the person who made me, brought me to life. I am you, you are me."

"Am not."

"Are too."

"Shut up."

It went on for a while longer, but you get the idea. Yeah, bloody annoying. And so for the rest of the evening I was very conscious of the blokes pressing up against me, and couldn't help wondering about... Anyway, that's for another time. Maybe. I also cursed

Wand repeatedly for putting funny thoughts in my head. I didn't like men, did I? No, definitely not. Was I having a mid-life crisis? Doubtful, as who knew when I'd reach middle age? Could be hundreds of years yet, or I might die tomorrow.

I swear Wand smirked from inside my pocket.

"Ha, gotcha."

"Idiot."

"You are."

"Shut up."

With the inanimate wood in my pocket put firmly in its place, I got on with the business of why we'd come. With Vicky in tow, we eventually made it across the crowded dance floor and to the bar. It was rammed, and I hated it. I never liked crowded places, despised being jostled and barged, as I wanted to blast anyone who touched me without permission.

People from eighteen to eighty knocked my elbow, shouldered me in the back, spilled drinks on my boots, and generally acted like they deserved some Hat punishment, but I held back as I didn't want to cause a scene.

Men chatted to Vicky but she dismissed them. I scowled at anyone who tried to talk to me as I wasn't in the mood and couldn't hear a bloody thing anyway. Maybe I was showing my age, maybe it was just that places like this were crap and everyone else was pretending to enjoy themselves, although it didn't look like it.

Everyone had made an effort, dressed up in their most outlandish, freaky clothes. There was a strong overriding theme of PVC though, much of it little more than a few scraps wrapped around flesh to hide the most important bits. Piercings were de rigor, as was wild, colorful hair, and jewelery was very much in evidence. At least they'd made the effort.

Finally, I made it to the bar.

"Coffee, and a martini," I said to the barman who looked like he should have been delivering newspapers, not working somewhere where I was sure you still had to be eighteen.

The dude just stared at me, nonplussed.

"I don't expect anything fancy. You put instant in a mug, and for a martini you—"

"I know what they are. Spirits or beer," he said, pointing to the shelves and fridges full of bottles. They didn't even have draught.

"Two beers. No, make that one beer, one vodka with lemonade."

I got served, punched the barman in the face for trying to rob me blind, that or pay him an exorbitant amount of cash for two crap drinks, I forget which actually happened, then turned and squeezed my way between sweaty flesh with the drinks held above my head and found Vicky slapping some dude across the top of his bald bonce.

I angled my head over to the left where the rest of the room was separated from the dance floor and there were intimate booths with tables and comfortable looking bench seats covered with plum plastic.

We pushed through the throng and checked for space. There was none.

Vicky went to lean against a pillar but I shook my head. I led her over to a booth and put my drinks down on the table. The two young guys looked up and were about to protest that the table was taken, but I guess my demeanor gave them pause.

I leaned forward, lip curled as I stared each one hard in the eye until they averted their gaze. Then I placed some cash on the table, got up close and said, "Drinks are on me," and pointed a thumb towards the bar.

They gave each other a glance, then got up and left without any fuss. Taking the cash, obviously.

"Arthur, that was mean."

"Tough, my feet are killing me. And anyway, they didn't mind."

Vicky sipped her drink then pulled a face. She asked, "What now?"

"Now, we wait. Maybe plot?"

"Ooh, I love plotting."

"I know you do."

Why Do I Bother?

While we sat and stared at the people, I wondered again why I'd agreed to come. After telling Vicky about the mysterious woman with pink hair, she threw a wobbly. Not because this witch had tricked us and stressed her out, or because she'd impersonated Ivan and George, caused us no end of trouble, but because I'd told her to bugger off.

We were mid argument when Ivan made an appearance at Vicky's, both of us having forgotten all about his evening visit. The girls were as excited as always to see their uncle, and after he promised to come and play with them in five minutes, we quickly explained to him what had happened.

"I can't say I'm amused by such actions. She had no right to impersonate me, and I feel uneasy with her knowing so much about my business, about all of us."

"She's young, wants excitement," said Vicky, for some reason having decided it was her place to defend this woman.

"She could have just asked if we'd take the job, whatever it is."

"And you would have said no," said Vicky.

"Probably," I grumbled.

"Did you really say those things to her?" asked Ivan. "That you would never work for the vampires again, for me?"

"Yeah, you got a problem with that? I already told you."

"But I was tricked, Arthur, same as you. Mikalus used me, used us all."

"Tough. We're quits. You lot are trouble and I want nothing to do with any of you."

"As you wish." Ivan looked genuinely disappointed, but I wouldn't change my mind. All my dealings with the neck munchers ended in trouble of the worst kind. Last time it had meant bombs being dropped on my old house, almost being eaten by the original vampire, and getting on the very wrong side of Cerberus. Lesson learned.

"So we meet her tonight and find out what this is all about," said Vicky, a faraway look in her eyes.

"Oh no you don't," I warned. "We are not chasing after some alternative witch who likes being dramatic and is obviously nothing but trouble."

"But we have to," whined Vicky. "It's Inferno. Apparently it's a great club and I haven't been for a night out in a long time. Years."

"So get a date. Get Steve to take you. I hate clubs, you know that. Ugh, full of sweaty bodies and everyone stinking of booze. It's gross. And it's loud."

"You are such an old man."

"Am not."

"I can babysit," said Ivan, looking excited at the prospect.

I glared at him. "What's your game? Since when do you babysit?"

"Just trying to help."

"That's settled then," said Vicky. "You owe me, Arthur, after all this. It's your fault, and I was very scared." Vicky's eyes began to well with tears. I was sure she was playing me, but tears are my downfall, always have been.

"Fine," I muttered. "But if anyone spills a drink on me I won't be held responsible for my actions."

"Yes!" Vicky punched the air and did her terrible mom dance.

"If you do that when we're out, I'm leaving," I warned.

Vicky poked her tongue out and I glared at Ivan.

He just smiled and shrugged, the bastard.

I sighed as I came back to the present and tried not get too angry with myself for agreeing to this nonsense. I didn't go chasing down potential clients, I gave them the runaround then usually said no anyway. Things were pretty good at the moment, why ruin it? Sasha was safe and back visiting regularly after the incident in the summer, George was spending a lot of time with her, but was also being extra nice to me. Vicky was semi-stable, thanks to Steve and the fading memories of her marriage to the Slug, which now seemed like another life.

I was getting over all the crap I'd gone through, much of it because of the vampires, and I'd finally forgiven myself for the terrible things I'd done. The only bad stuff was the threat of Cerberus. Since Carmichael had shown his true colors, I'd expected them to go all out on me, but so far it hadn't happened. Maybe it wouldn't. Whatever, things were going well, and I was, dare I say it, content with life. Sure, I wouldn't mind someone to share my bed, even some of my life with, but I'd learned a hard lesson with Candy and was in no hurry to dive into anything just yet.

So here I was, sitting in a bloody nightclub, feeling about three hundred and fifty, and the worst thing of all, I was almost enjoying myself. After all, Vicky was dressed in tight PVC, the music was good, and I was actually out in the evening doing something that didn't involve getting smashed in the face. Yet.

I was also intrigued by Mrs. Pink. What was her game? Who was she? And what did she want?

"Scoot over," said she of the epic hair as she nudged against me with her ample hip and I slid across the bench. She shuffled into place, sat down, and smiled at us both.

"Hey."

"Hi, I'm Vicky."

"You know who I am," I grumbled.

"I'm Stan."

Vicky and I both stared at her for the longest time, our minds whirling. Was she in drag? Was she a transsexual? Had she had an operation? Had I misheard? Did she just have a crap name for a girl?

"Haha, just screwing with you guys. You can call me—"

"Let me guess. Mrs. Pink?" I said with a sinking feeling.

"How'd you guess?" she asked brightly, beaming at us. "So nice to meet you, Vicky. And you again, Arthur. Hopefully you guys will be up for this. It's going to be so awesome."

It was then I knew this was definitely a bad idea. Awesome? What was this, a Famous Five adventure?

"We should go," I said, as I tried to stand but was trapped by the table and "Mrs. Pink." I mean, who the hell goes by a stupid name like that? Bit obvious, don't you think? Nowhere near as cool as "The Hat."

"Arthur, don't be so rude," warned Vicky, poking me in the stomach and making me cough.

"Look, I get it," said Mrs. Pink. "I screwed up big time. I thought you guys would be impressed with what I did, and you'd let me help sort out the money and then you'd do this job for me. Guess I blew it. Well, I'm here to put things right and offer you the best job you've ever had."

"No."

"You haven't even heard what it is yet."

"I've heard enough. I told you, you don't mess with me or mine like that. What's wrong with you? You stressed Vicky out, I could have whacked Ivan thinking he'd done this on purpose, and then you impersonate George. How'd you know where I live or that I'd be there? Are you watching me?"

"Aha, secrets of the trade."

"Let's go," I told Vicky.

"Wait, please. You have to help, I don't know what else to do."

And then the worst thing possible happened. Mrs. Pink began to cry. Vicky sneered like it was all my fault, and I, reacting on instinct, patted Mrs. Pink's head and said, "There, there."

I was stuck, literally and figuratively.

Dirty Streets

We couldn't talk in the club, so it was with great relief that Vicky got Mrs. Pink to her feet, hugged her, then followed me outside. Once well away from the stench of bodies and the crowds of overly excited people, Mrs. Pink got herself together and apologized.

"Sorry for that. I had all this cool stuff in my head, thinking you'd jump at the chance to work with me, and I blew it. I'm sorry."

"That's okay," said Vicky, putting her arm back around her.

"No, it isn't. What is this crap?" I sped up, walked fast down the deserted streets of the city, kicking at takeaway cartons and wondering when so many of the stores had either closed or installed shutters over the windows. This used to be a nice area, one of the more stable ones in an ever-shifting city, but now it was a mess just like so many others. Houses were showing signs of needing repair, there was graffiti everywhere, trash littered the streets, and everything looked weary.

It was happening more and more. As new apartment blocks rose up, as more out-of-town department stores were built and independent traders couldn't compete, the city was being split in half. The haves and the have-nots. Local communities became decimated when nearby stores closed and homes were repossessed. Nobody was to blame, and yet everybody was. Everyone wanted the best price and the best deal, so they abandoned the local places and headed in droves to the superstores. Then they complained that the butcher was closing down, there was no post office, the doctor's surgery never had enough staff, and the area they'd grown up in was getting dangerous.

Everything was interlinked, everything affected everything else, and as jobs became scarce whilst property prices in already affluent areas soared, so whole streets were abandoned. It made no sense. Why would the city allow more high rises to be built when there were thousands of empty houses? The price we pay for a shiny city. Leave the unsavory areas to rot away, along with the people.

"Arthur!"

I turned at Vicky's shouting, getting the feeling she'd been talking to me for a while. Had I slept lately? Kind of. Not enough.

"What?" I snapped, depressed after thinking about these streets I'd walked a thousand times, back when they were full of people nodding to each other, stopping to chat. Now everyone drove in their cars and the place was like a ghost town. Even the pubs had closed down, and you know things are bad when that happens.

"I said we need to go somewhere and talk. Where are you off to?"

I hadn't thought about it, just wanted to get away from the club. Then I had an idea. "I have just the place," I said, a wicked grin on my face.

Vicky gave me the evil eye, Mrs. Pink brightened at the thought of getting to explain herself properly, and I figured it was the perfect way to get rid of her once and for all.

It didn't quite work out that way.

Getting to Know You

We wandered through the real parts of the city. Not the places where everything was sanitized and people lived in gated communities, not even the rundown terraced streets where communities were falling apart, but the true city. Where everyone had accepted that there was no hope, no way to continue as things had in the past, and that change was needed. That the time had already come and gone for out-of-control consumerism and chasing dreams of new cars and bigger houses.

This was HiLo.

As the population increased and the jobs became scarcer, as the gleaming office blocks and the overpriced apartments sprouted from the ground like polished cancers, huge swathes of the old city were abandoned or became so ruinous they were demolished, waiting for more tiny boxes to be built where people hid away from the world. Some people refused to accept this way of life, found new places to try something different.

The old train station was one such place. Abandoned almost thirty years ago, it was replaced with a gleaming new station at the heart of the city. Local route closures and new rail links making it redundant and too costly to renovate.

For years the local council had debated what to do with it, had looked into various offers, one year announcing it would be turned into something for the community, the next that it would be sold to developers. It never came to anything, and slowly it became a place where the homeless made a life as best they could. Then the idealists moved in, anarchists and the like, then artists who realized they could have space to get on with their work without costly studio fees. Even some local businesses moved to HiLo, at first to serve the few people who squatted there, and because they couldn't keep up with the rent on their own premises. Soon, some chose to set up business here as the crime was no worse than anywhere else, in fact it was lower than many parts of the city, and everything was done with cash.

Others followed. Those too poor to buy a house or afford rent, those who refused to live a conventional life, even some shifters had made it their home. It became a kind of zoned squat, sectioned off into groups of like-minded people, communities within a community, everyone leading alternative lives and trying to find a different way through life. Most failed in one way or another, and HiLo became a very transient place.

One thing you could always count on though, was a seat somewhere quiet and to be left alone if you wanted. Plus, the coffee was nice, and nobody spilled beer on you unless you went to one of the many unlicensed bars that specialized in one particular drink.

We went to a fairly small room where you could get coffee. Nothing fancy, nothing unpronounceable, just filtered coffee, milk and sugar if you wanted it.

Vicky was her usual chatty self, asking about the place and its history, keeping close to me as people passed, sometimes nodding, mostly keeping to themselves at this late hour.

Mrs. Pink, and damn but I hated that name, was the opposite of how I'd expected her to be. She was relaxed, confident, smiled at people, even said hello by name a few times. I'd expected her to feel out of her depth, that her attitude and looks were mostly for show, and she lived a life if not that of a citizen, then still mostly conventional, even if she was a witch.

But she was at home here, knew the people, and I wondered how come we'd never crossed paths before.

So I asked as we sat at an old table on mismatched chairs, the place to ourselves apart from the owner, a skinny guy of sixty who refused to wear anything but a pair of shorts no matter the weather.

"How come we've never met before? You know this place, you know the people, so why don't I know you?"

"Dunno. There's lot of people like me. Dropouts, people searching for a different way to live."

"I know that! I've been where they are, I know them, I know where they go. But I've never seen you."

"Guess you haven't been looking hard enough." Mrs. Pink sipped her coffee, sighed, and smiled. "So, you wanna hear about it? It's right up your guys' alley. You'll love it."

"Doubt that," I moaned, feeling knackered now we were sitting down, the tiredness creeping over me like a warm blanket, making everything feel fuzzy.

"I want to hear about it," said Vicky. "And I think it's great you showing so much determination to get to talk with us. That's clever, isn't it, Arthur?"

"No, it's bloody stupid. Are you forgetting how stressed you were yesterday? That we were up all night trying to sort this mess out. That this girl screwed us over and impersonated our family?"

"She's young, she doesn't know any better."

"I am not young, I'm twenty-three," said Mrs. Pink, pouting. "And I'm not a girl, I'm a woman." She tried to glare at me but she just looked like she had something in her eye.

"Right, that's it. What's your bloody name? And if you give me any more of this Mrs. Pink business I'm leaving." I slammed my coffee down on the table, spilling it. I glanced over at the owner then took a napkin and mopped up the mess. "See what you made me do?"

"Selma, my name's Selma," she mumbled, looking embarrassed.

"That's a nice name," said Vicky, smiling.

"Better than Mrs. Pink, that's for sure."

"I don't like to use it, don't want anyone knowing. I use loads of different names, so I can stay under the radar. Tell no one."

"Who the fuck would we tell?" I was fed up with all this crypto-bullshit.

"I don't know! Anyone." Selma glared at me, angry. I'd clearly hit a nerve here.

"Okay, promise not to tell. Now, can we please get on with this? I need to go home and punch the shit out of my pillow."

"I want you to steal Mabel's Cauldron."

"No fucking way. Come on, Vicky, we're going." I stood up, pushed back my chair, then began marching off.

"Arthur, wait!"

I ignored her, kept walking. I heard a scuffle behind me, and as I exited the room I sped up and marched past various businesses, everyone gone now. Sleeping.

"Arthur, what are you doing?" asked Vicky as she caught up with me.

"Going home."

"What's Mabel's Cauldron? Sounds silly. Mabel? Is she a witch?"

"No, Vicky, she is The Witch. You might think her name is funny, old fashioned, but that's because she is old, very old, and I won't steal from her. I've talked about her before. You never listen."

"I do too. But why not? Why won't you steal from her?"

"Why not? Because," I turned to face Selma who was right behind us, "I know who Selma is, don't I?"

"I guess," said Selma, hunching her shoulders.

"Who is she then?" asked Vicky.

"She's Mabel's bloody granddaughter, or great, great granddaughter, whatever. I'm not getting involved with witches, no fucking way. And certainly not Mabel. This could be a setup, it's how they operate."

"You want to steal from your own gran?" asked Vicky, shocked.

"You don't know what she did. What her cauldron can do. We have to get it before it's too late."

"Too late for what?" I snapped.

"Too late for everyone. Don't you know what she's planning? Can't you feel it?"

"No I bloody can't. What?" I was too tired for guessing games.

"She's going to destroy the vampires. Kill them. You have to help me. I can't stop the Queen on my own."

"Oh, for fuck's sake."

Idiot Sidekicks

We exited HiLo, and I was deflated by the whole experience. It hadn't gone as planned at all. I nodded to the two guys on guard duty at the main entrance, they nodded back then watched as we wandered off, nobody saying a word.

"Please, you have to," whined Selma once we were well away and walking the streets once more.

"No, I don't."

"Why not? It's right up your street. I can pay,"

"I'm sure you can, with the money you stole from some poor sap. The answer is still no. If she's out for the vampires, the last thing I want to do is get involved in any of that bullshit. I've done enough for them, they can deal with Mabel themselves. Have you told them?"

"I figured I'd come see you guys and we could deal with it together."

"What's your interest in this?" I asked.

Selma went to speak, but I held up a hand to stop her. The moon was out, casting a silvery glow over the streets, the wet roads shining like they were paved with silver. I glanced up, a knot in my stomach, then checked on Vicky. She was looking green, and squirming about as she shifted her head from side to side. Her jaw was moving in a weird way.

"You cannot be serious. Really, today? Now?"

"I can't help it," she whined, before coughing and spluttering and bending over double, moaning.

"Of course you can bloody help it. You're a..." I glanced at Selma then said nothing more.

"It's okay, I know."

"Know what?" I asked.

"That Vicky's a lycanthrope. That she shifts, just like Ivan. And he's a vampire. I know that, you know I know that."

"I didn't know you knew about the werewolf crap. I still don't know how you know they're related. Nobody else does."

"Well I do. I'm quite powerful you know, and in the loop."

"Yeah, because of Grandma."

"She's not my grandma, she's my great, great, great, great... Um, hang on, that's not right."

"Oh, just shut up. Come on, you, let's go." I grabbed Vicky by her coat collar and marched down the street until I saw a likely looking vehicle. We wouldn't need it for long, just to get back to my own car closer to the club.

"I don't know what your problem is, Vicky, but I thought you had this under control now?"

"I do, almost," she croaked as she ran to keep up with me, not that she had any choice as I was still half dragging her.

"Is she gonna turn?" Selma seemed a little too keen for Vicky to morph into a monstrous feral beast that could bite your head off, so when we got to the car, I stopped and stared her down.

"What's your problem? I said no, yet here you still are. And why do you want to see Vicky turn? You get off on it?"

"Of course not. It's just, you know, interesting. I've never seen a shift before."

"And you aren't going to now," said Vicky. "I've got this under control, I think. I've been practicing. Ivan helped me, but sometimes it's hard to resist."

"I thought werewolves had to turn when it was a full moon?"

"Oh, bloody hell, that's why you did all this now, isn't it?" I accused. "So you could see it. What is wrong with you?"

"Told you, I'm interested."

"Nothing to do with you assuming we would have said yes yesterday and you had it all planned to go down tonight so Vicky could do your dirty work?" She was so obvious.

"Maybe." Selma had the good grace to look guilty as accused.

"Can we please go?" asked Vicky, slapping a hand to an ear that looked decidedly hairy and pointy.

I pulled Wand from my pocket and asked silently, "You ready?"

"Sure. But we should listen to Selma. You should do the job, or at least hear her out properly, then tell Ivan."

"Why? You just want to blast stuff and hang around with young girls."

"Do not. Hmm, maybe a little, but I know about Mabel, I know all about her."

"How?"

"Because I'm magical, that's why. Plus, I know most things about most things."

"Then maybe you could start sharing that information with me a little more often."

"Will do. So listen to the kid, this is important."

"Fine," I said with a sigh as I put Wand to the lock and a tiny spark of silver magic did the necessary and unlocked the very boring looking car.

"You'll do it?" yelped Selma.

"No, I'll listen to you blather on then tell you no. But you get to make your case. First, we get Vicky hidden."

"We going to the semi?" asked Vicky, crawling into the car as her PVC outfit grew tighter than I'd believed possible and odd lumps appeared to wriggle under the surface.

"Not with her here."

"Why not?" asked Selma. "I know where it is." Then she rattled off the address.

"Goddamn, is nothing private any more?" I got in the car and Wand started it up. I may have pulled off a little too fast, and I may have smiled as both women in the back rolled around.

It's the small things in life that keep a wizard amused. And sane.

Hearing the Tale

With it being pointless trying to hide the location, but with it still rankling, I drove to the semi in the city. I bundled Vicky out and kept her covered with her coat as she half crouched, half hopped to the front door. Selma followed behind.

Once inside, I took Vicky into the living room and removed her coat even though she was protesting.

"Jesus!" Vicky looked a mess. I'd seen her shift several times, seen her change then change back too, but never when she was trying to fight it like she was now. The PVC was ruined, stretched out of shape in places, the material split where her body had tried to morph in too extreme a way for her to handle.

"It's not as bad as it looks," moaned Vicky as she collapsed onto the sofa. "Give me ten and I'll be okay."

"You sure?"

"Yes, but please get this bloody outfit off me. I feel like I'm gonna burst my skin and I can't focus properly."

I glanced to Selma who shrugged. "I can do it if you want."

"Please. I'll get some spare clothes from upstairs."

Selma's eyebrow rose like it meant Vicky and I were an item, but I didn't bother to correct her. Vicky kept clothes here because often after a job they were ruined, nothing more to it than that.

I left and gathered up new stuff then averted my gaze as I dropped the clothes on the sofa. "Tell me when you're decent." I waited outside the door while Vicky grunted and Selma helped her dress. I'd seen Vicky naked before, but that didn't mean I wanted to get another look. Okay, it did, and that's why I didn't look. It was the damn tight outfit, it was messing with my head, and something else.

"You can come in now," Vicky called, so I peeked cautiously around the door then entered once I was sure it was safe to do so.

"You are such a prude, Arthur," said Vicky.

"Just being a gentleman. Now, can you handle this?" I asked. "Is it better to just shift and be done with it?"

"No, the more I fight it, the better I am at doing it only when I want to. I need to be in charge of this, not the other way around."

"Fair enough. Brave girl."

Vicky poked her tongue out at me then winced as her arm went bumpy and lengthened. She gasped, closed her eyes, and it returned to normal.

Selma watched, fascinated. I'm not sure why, as she must change too. After all, she had the ability to impersonate others accurately. This girl knew her magic, I had to keep reminding myself of that. Was this how she even looked really?

I made coffee then returned to the living room and settled down in a chair. Vicky and Selma remained on the sofa.

"You are such a dummy," I told Vicky.

"Am not. I thought I'd be fine."

"I can't believe you came out tonight of all nights. And wearing that outfit, too."

"Don't say you didn't enjoy the view. I saw you looking."

"Only at how much like a pencil wrapped in a bin bag you looked."

Vicky was about to moan but she cramped up and doubled over. I hated seeing her like this, and it came as a shock. I'd believed she could control it now under Ivan's guidance; guess it was tougher than I'd imagined.

For several minutes we said nothing of note, but Vicky eventually got things under control and so I reluctantly turned to Selma and said, "Okay, spill it. But first, how can you appear like other people so convincingly?"

"Fooled you, didn't I?" She was proud of her ability, but I wasn't impressed.

Most competent witches could do such things, just one reason amongst many why wizards hated them. That, and a lot of other stuff that meant we never mixed, hardly ever got on. The hostility went back as far as anyone could remember, and the Council didn't help. Ours was full of wizards often blaming the witches for trouble in the magical community even though nine times out of ten it was a wizard up to no good or pushing the boundaries.

"Yeah, and I don't like it. So, you can look like other people, or do you use a spell to just make people think you look like them?"

"Same thing, isn't it?" asked Vicky.

"No," we both said at the same time. I filled Vicky in. "Not at all. For a start, you don't mess with people's heads, it isn't allowed, so if she's using magic to make people think they see something that isn't there, then she's walking a very fine line."

"I don't do that kind of thing," snapped Selma. "I use my abilities to take on another form. I look like whoever I want to."

"This all sounds like the same thing to me," said Vicky again.

"It's not," we both shouted at her.

"Okay, what do you want?"

"Told you. I want you to steal Mabel's Cauldron."

"And I said no. But why? What's going on?"

"If I tell you, you have to promise not to tell anyone else."

"Absolutely not. If I feel I need to tell Ivan, and I'm guessing I do, then I will."

"He is my brother," said Vicky.

"But you won't have to, because if we steal the cauldron then we can stop Mabel before she goes to war. Well, er, not war exactly, just..." Selma trailed off, looking worried.

"Come on, spit it out. No point being shy now. You're the one who wants us to help. You knew you'd have to tell us the reason."

"Okay, but you won't like it."

"I never do," I muttered as I sipped my coffee.

Off We Go

"It's best if I show you." Selma drained her mug then stood, as if we were all ready to go on a mystery tour. I didn't want to go anywhere, apart from home, but it didn't look like that was about to happen.

"Show us what?" I asked.

"Just come with me, please. If you say no after tonight, then I won't bother you again, but I don't think you will."

Selma had a glint in her eye, and I didn't like it. It was worrying in the extreme, as I'd seen it plenty of times before over the years. It was the look of someone who knew something you didn't, and who couldn't wait to get you embroiled in their nonsense. Trouble, that's what the look signified. Pure, uncontrollable trouble.

"Let's go," said Vicky as she pushed off with her hands and stood on shaky legs.

"You don't look in any fit state to go anywhere but to bed," I noted.

"I'm fine, all under control." Vicky tried to hide a wince as something went on in her body, but I knew the signs. It was her choice though, and I guess she had to learn how to control this thing.

"Promise not to bother me again if I say no after you show me whatever it is you want to show me?"

"Promise," said Selma, and saluted. Damn, that was something Vicky did. In many ways she was like a younger Vicky. Annoying, and too small.

Selma gave directions as I drove through the city, weaving through the silent streets, disturbing the cats who watched as we passed then went about their skulking. Foxes ran fast down roads, more than I'd ever seen, and rats scurried in the dark places. It was like the city was being overrun, the animals outnumbering the humans. Maybe that was for the best. Would there be bears and wolves next? That would be cool.

I drove for fifteen minutes until we left the city and headed into the countryside. Selma told me to take a turn and I read the sign for one of those holiday parks, basically a large field of static homes, trailers I guess, where people came to spend time in the country and get some fresh air. They're often in the most unusual of places, but this one looked nice. There were hills and woods nearby, a river for fishing, and it all seemed very relaxing.

I parked, and Selma led us to one of the cabins. She checked around us, mumbled something under her breath, and then the pressure of her wards eased up. They were good, very strong, and it was another hint as to her strength. I followed Selma inside cautiously, wary of a trap, but everything was fine. Vicky followed behind. Selma turned on the lights and we stood in her tiny place, jostling for space. There was a small kitchen crammed in before you got to the seating area with two bench seats either side of a small table where a large cloth was draped over something.

"You live here?" I asked.

"Nah, this is just somewhere I rented, in anticipation of what was to come."

"Good, because it sucks. It's so small. But then, I guess for tiny people like you and Vicky it's plenty big enough."

"Hey, I'm not small," protested Selma, standing on tip-toe like I wouldn't notice.

"Not for a gnome, no."

"Where's all your tech stuff?" asked Vicky, looking around for the gadgets that would allow Selma to hack into our accounts and do all the damage she'd done.

"Ah, about that," she said sheepishly.

"Yeah?" I had a bad feeling. The last several days had been mostly made up of nothing but bad feelings.

"I, er, well... Now, don't get cross."

"I bloody knew it," I said, stomping over to the small eating area and squeezing in between the table and seat. "You didn't do it, did you? Okay what the hell is going on here?"

"I paid a guy."

"You paid a guy?"

"Yeah."

"Liar," said Vicky. "You did it, I can tell."

"No, I really didn't. I haven't got the first clue about computers. I paid this guy, and it cost a fortune, and then I tried to get you to help me."

"I don't believe you," said Vicky as she slid in opposite me.

"Neither do I. In fact, I don't believe anything you say. This has been one massive waste of my time. Time I could have spent staring at my ceiling."

"Fine, I did do it. But my equipment isn't here, it's somewhere else. Somewhere private. I'm not showing you guys all that, it's too important."

"Oh, excuse us for wanting the truth. I don't give a shit about your computers, I wouldn't even know how to turn them on."

"No, but Vicky would."

"Can we please just get on with this?" I was despairing now. Why do these things always happen to me?

I banged a fist down on the table and the item under the cloth rattled. It sounded like metal, almost like a handle banging against the sides of something round.

Something like a...

I grabbed the black cloth and yanked it off.

"Mabel's Cauldron," I said with a sigh, not really surprised as so far this girl had proved herself to be entirely untrustworthy.

Vicky stared at it, I stared at Selma.

"Care to explain how I'm supposed to steal it when you clearly already have?"

"That's the point. I need you to steal it before she finds out."

"You must be the most stupid person I have ever met. When did you take it?"

"The other day. I'm family, so I have access to everything. I need you to go pretend to nick it, do whatever you do to make it look like it was stolen. Otherwise, I'm in big trouble."

"What are you talking about?" My brain wasn't keeping up with this.

"I'm no thief, I don't know what a robbery of magical artifacts looks like. I need you to go in and pretend to steal this so Grandma will think she's been robbed. Otherwise she'll start asking questions and I'll get into trouble."

"How old did you say you were again?"

"Twenty-three, why?"

"Because you're acting like a twelve-year-old. You want us to pretend to steal from the boss witch so it will look like she's been robbed by an outsider? Want us to make it look like a professional job, but you've already stolen it?"

"Yeah. What's wrong with that? I took the opportunity, just in case you said no, and wouldn't steal it, but I still need you to do the job."

"To make it look like a pro did it?"

"Yeah, I just said."

"But you already have it?"

"Yes!"

"Let me tell you something, Selma. Women like Mabel know who the players are, know who the best thieves are, the ones capable of stealing from her. You think she won't come looking for the top guys? You think she won't come looking for me?"

"That's stupid. She won't know who it was. She'll just see the signs of a professional robbery and we'll be in the clear. How would she know it was you?"

"She won't, because I'm not doing it. This is the worst plan I've ever heard."

"Look, you don't even have to go and get anything. Just disable all the security, make it look like you were there, and that's it."

"What for? You already have it. You had to do all that to get it, right?"

"No, it's different for the witches the Queen trusts, but there aren't many of us. We can come and go as we please from where the artifacts are stored. We can take things, just sign them in and out. People come and go all the time, so it was easy. It's pretty lax actually."

"So why would it need to look like a professional did it? This isn't making any sense." I couldn't even begin to contemplate what was going on in this young woman's mind. Her story so far was so convoluted and nonsensical I wondered if even she could keep the story straight.

Then it hit me.

"Goddamn!" I grabbed Vicky and pulled her to her feet.

"Sorry," said Selma, looking genuinely sad for what she'd done. "I blathered, couldn't think what else to say. I'm sorry, you seem like nice people."

"What's happening? I don't understand."

I felt it coming, felt the magic surge and Wand stir in my pocket.

It was too late.

The door burst open, the room went dark, and something smacked me so hard across the head that I was slammed sideways into the wall so hard it gave way.

I vaguely remember laying out on the grass with a handful of female faces peering down at me without expression.

I bloody hate witches.

Dumb and Dumber

I'd never believed I was this stupid. Sure, I knew I had my moments of daftness, that occasionally I was less cautious than I should be, but this really rankled.

It also hurt like hell.

Vicky's screaming didn't help matters. When she started growling and then baying, I began to worry.

Why? Because we were locked in a room together, lit by a bare bulb that cast a sickly yellow glow around the spartan but large space. I was strapped to a large chair bolted to the floor, secured by leather straps infused with some of the best spells in the business. The Hat wasn't going anywhere apart from maybe down Vicky's throat.

Eek!

"Um, Vicky, you aren't going to eat me, are you?" I asked politely, hoping the answer would be no. All I got was a low growl as the wolf-woman glared at me with sharp focus and craned her neck forward to sniff the air, taking in my scent. She was confused, as I was showing no fear, not outright terror anyway, but it was worrying all the same.

Vicky had turned the minute I'd been secured, still woozy and in no state to fight back. She'd done it quickly, no holding back, and as usual it was no pleasant experience. If I remained calm then she'd probably turn back, if not I'd have to wait until the morning. Assuming she didn't get peckish in the meantime.

I sat, I waited, I got bored, and I guess I nodded off. This was a strange habit I had. If I was alone in my bed then I couldn't sleep, if I was driving away from a job then I could sleep behind the wheel. If I was locked in a room by mad witches with a werewolf that could eat me at any moment, then no problem, welcome to the mini-death.

Peace, surrender. Leaving my fate in the hands of the gods.

Funny how the human mind works. I'm sure it was a stress-reaction, that I shut down rather than deal with things, but it could have just been because I was knackered. Either way, I wasn't complaining.

I did that annoying thing where your head snaps up and you get a shooting pain in your neck, but I couldn't rub the stiffness away as I was still strapped down tight and whatever spells were in the leather held fast.

Vicky was in the corner, curled up under a blanket, thankfully back to her usual form.

Light from a small high window indicated it was morning time, and judging by the shape of the ceiling we were locked in an attic room. It was empty, nothing to see here, just the chair I sat on and no other furniture. Guess they weren't taking any chances.

Vicky continued to snore as the door opened. Three women in their forties, or maybe their hundreds as it's hard to tell with witches, entered quietly, glanced at Vicky, then ignored her and focused on me.

They were stone-faced and confident. Not the confidence of youngsters like Selma where much of it is for show, but true, deep-seated confidence born of years of experience and practice in the magical arts.

Without warning, one of them smashed a fist into my face and squealed as her knuckles connected with my cheek. Poor thing hurt her hand.

I shook it off and stared at them all, maybe glared is a better description. Maybe tried to burn them alive with the power of my mind is the most accurate way of putting it.

Then the next one punched me, much harder this time, and my nose broke yet again. Blood streamed but I remained quiet, and so did they. Seemed like none of us wanted to wake Vicky and disturb her beauty sleep.

The third took a turn, and boy did it smart. I saw stars and couldn't get my thoughts straight, just knew I had to stay focused as one way or another I was getting out of here.

This was all a trap, a set-up from the get-go to capture me.

Why go to such extremes though? Because they had to get me away from my house, from George, from anywhere I could get help. Selma's ruse with the hacking hadn't worked, I hadn't just gone with the fake Ivan, so that had failed.

The meeting at the club was a way to lead me to the holiday park, and I guess Selma had panicked once I was there and her sisters hadn't shown up immediately, so had conjured up a fake cauldron and then lost the plot a little as she couldn't keep up with her own plan. Guess she was new to all this and was winging it but couldn't quite think of how to stall. Stupid, should have seen it coming a mile off.

Why talk about the cauldron and all that nonsense though? Why bring that into it? Was it the truth? Had the cauldron been real and she wanted me to pretend to steal it? Or did she just panic and as she'd already mentioned it, probably to pique my interest as I did like to steal stuff I shouldn't, then got carried away with her own convoluted plan? This is the problem with youngsters, they make no sense to me even though I know from experience that in your own head everything is going swimmingly.

Or was I barking up the wrong tree entirely and this was all just a misunderstanding and I'd be released any moment now?

I got smacked in the eye socket and figured no, they knew exactly who I was.

The door opened and Selma gasped when she saw me.

"What are you doing?" she hissed.

"Making him do what we want," said one of the women, matter-of-factly.

"That won't work. What's the matter with you?"

"Everyone agreed that he's our only hope, that if he won't do this then we're all going to pay. He has to do it."

"I know that. But this is The Hat, he won't help if you beat him to a pulp."

"Your idea didn't work, did it? What were you thinking with that cauldron on the table nonsense?"

"I thought it was worth a shot. He was going to say no, so I figured if he had to pretend to steal it he'd think it was an easier job and might go for it."

"Idiot child. You should have just told him how much money we were willing to pay."

"I got flustered, okay. One of you should have done it, I told you that."

"He only came this far because a beautiful girl was involved. If one of us approached him he would have refused outright."

I was somewhat affronted by this, but there may have been a grain of truth to it.

"Let him go. This isn't what we agreed. Now you've got us all in trouble." Selma stared at the three much older women, and they all seemed to come to the same decision so backed off.

"Arthur, I'm so sorry about them, about me being so silly too. This wasn't what I had in mind, not at all."

Selma stepped forward and muttered something. I felt the magic lift from the straps and as it did I touched Wand through my combats. He burned through instantly, was held tight in my grip. Sigils flared, the belts snapped, and I was up and blasting before anyone could say "Shiiiiiiiiiiiiiiiiiiiiiit."

A Wizard's Wrath

"No, Arthur, wait!" shouted Selma, but I was having none of it.

I didn't care what these women thought they were doing, whose side they were on, what their end goal was, any of it. All I knew was they'd played Vicky and I for fools, duped us over and over, got Selma to do their dirty work, then forced Vicky to change against her will. They'd also tied me up then beat the shit out of me.

Normally I am a gentleman when it comes to women. I open doors, doff my hat, and I never fight them if I can avoid it as it feels wrong somehow. But I wasn't feeling like a gentleman today, I was feeling right royally pissed off.

"Make it quick but make it final," I told Wand as the pressure built along the shaft and I had a hard time containing myself.

"You got it, boss. Damn, this is gonna be great. And a first. I get to kill witches."

"Yeah, big whoop-de-doo," I groaned, uneasy with his excitement and the fact he clearly had zero morals.

My sluggish will shunted down into Wand, combining effortlessly with his own innate magic and the power infused in him by the sigils I'd carved and the numerous spells forced into the very fabric of the rare faery wood he was crafted from.

Selma shouted, "No," as I lifted Wand, but she was pushed aside by the three women who stood their ground, stoic and snarling.

"Told you he'd need convincing. We'll show him who's boss and then he'll do exactly as we say. Won't you? If not, your ginger girl will be next."

"When will you people ever learn? You're supposed to ask nicely, not play games and try to trick me. Now you've blown it. Oh, and it's auburn, or red, she hates people calling her ginger. Show some fucking respect. You dare threaten my daughter?"

They'd blown it, big time.

With Wand in my hand, I experienced something for the very first time. It was as though I had eyes all over my head and I could see in every direction at once. It wasn't disorienting, it felt entirely natural, like I'd always been able to see this way. Wand was sharing his own sight with me, and it was awesome.

But that wasn't all. With this three-sixty vision came something else, the ability to take in more information, see every shift in movement, anticipate every action, almost know what would happen next.

Usually this worked on a subconscious level, not something I was actually aware of. My body reacting to stimuli and me acting before I could think to do it. Now it was as if time had slowed and I could plan ahead, think about things before I let loose. It made things rather one-sided for the women who I was sure were powerful witches when up against anyone but a pissed off Hat.

"Why haven't you done this before?" I gasped, getting some weird looks from the women, but our conversation playing out so fast I was watching their eyes close slowly as they blinked.

"Didn't know we could do it. Guess you live and learn."

"I like it."

"Me too. Let's rock."

I grinned my most evilest wizardly smile and Wand went nuts, with my blessing, and under my control. No blaming him for this, I knew exactly what I was doing.

As the women finished their blinking and their mouths slowly opened to gape, and Selma's hand rose at a snail's pace to try to stop everyone going bananas, Wand and I were already deep into it.

I spun in a circle—don't ask me why but it felt like the right thing to do—and as my jacket whipped around my thighs and my hair blew like I was in a gale, I arced Wand across the bodies of the three women who had battered my face, with every intention of chopping them into bits.

Wand spat fiery fury as if he'd exploded. Silver death crackled and popped as he shot his vitriol and my pissed-offness right at them. Their clothes burst into flames instantly and they screamed as reality returned to normal and my vision snapped back to human, which was boring in comparison.

As their heads were engulfed and their long, witchy hair burned and they batted at their bodies, I let rip with another slash. This time the magic shone bright blue against the dull room, lighting it up like a fireworks display.

I hadn't realized quite how annoyed I was by this whole charade until I lowered my arm and watched as the fire burned out on their skulls, leaving them bald, blistered, and screaming in agony. I said a silent spell, one from another time, learned in a place far from here, and their eyes brimmed with fear as their screams were cut off.

Everything was silent, everything was still, and I snarled at them as they gaped, not moving a muscle.

"What... What did you do?" squeaked Selma, aghast.

"Watch," I ordered.

One by one, the women collapsed to their knees. Selma moved forward.

"I said watch. It isn't over yet."

Selma stood still, her eyes widening as the aftereffects of the blue slash through the ether was manifest. The heads dislodged where they'd been severed from their bodies.

One head, two heads, three heads all counted for dropped to the floorboards with a dull, sickly thud.

Selma screamed, the bodies slumped forward, and Vicky stirred from the corner. She popped her head above the blankets, and asked, "What's happening?"

"We're going home, that's what's happening."
I put a hand to my nose. It really hurt.

Calming Down

"Are they dead?" asked Vicky, bleary eyed as she stood up then hastily wrapped the blanket around herself when she realized she was utterly naked.

"No, they've just got bad headaches so they're chilling," I snapped. I dashed forward and slammed the door shut as Selma tried to make her escape. "Where the fuck do you think you're going? This isn't over yet."

"I'm sorry, I'm sorry. Please don't hurt me. I screwed up, but this wasn't part of the plan. I never knew they were going to beat you, I swear. Oh my God, you killed them. You chopped their heads off!"

"What did you expect? I'm a bloody wizard, the goddamn Hat. You think this is a game? This is real life, little girl, and people get hurt. Especially those that threaten my family. People that screw with me. This is what you got yourself involved in, so suck it up and deal with it."

Looking back on it, I may have overreacted. But threatening my daughter? What did they expect?

Selma stared at me, eyes as wide as an anime character's, then they were drawn once more to the bodies. She lunged for the door again but I slapped my hand onto it and blocked her way. Wand wriggled in my pocket but he'd had enough excitement for one day.

I may have been a little harsh on her. After all, she was young, and this kind of thing isn't your everyday occurrence. By her reaction, this was the first time she'd seen a dead body, certainly any meeting their end in such a violent manner. I had to remind myself she was only a few years older than George, and that although George had seen more terrible things than this, sights like this were something I did my utmost to avoid her witnessing, especially if it was her dad doing the murdering.

"Look," I said, putting my arm around her shoulder, but she stepped away, terrified, "I don't take kindly to people beating the shit out of me, okay? I wouldn't have killed them for it though. But they said they'd hurt George. I can't have that. They got what was coming to them, and if they were your friends then you made some poor choices."

"They were desperate and didn't know what else to do. They thought they could make you help us."

"That's not how this works. Understand? You ask. You say your piece and try to convince me, not force the issue. Why make an enemy when you can make a friend? All this deceit, this impersonating people, this crap with the hacking, the cauldron, the manipulation, where has it got you? Nowhere but pissing me off and three of your friends dead, that's where. So, why don't we start again and you tell me what you want and what's going on, okay?"

Vicky nodded her approval at my change of heart. I nodded back to her, grim-faced, unsure whether this was a good idea or a very bad one. Selma visibly relaxed, a little hope returning. "Let me get you some clothes, then we can talk," she said, and glanced at the door.

"No funny business. Vicky, you go with her. And Selma?" Selma turned at the doorway. "Do not try to screw with me again. Otherwise, you'll be next. Do I make myself clear?"

"Yes."

"Watch her," I told Vicky as they disappeared from the room.

Alone, unless you count three geriatric corpses, I sat back down and put my head in my hands. Here we go again. Death, deceit, people letting you down, showing their bad side. The irony of it all was that once again I'd shown myself to be no better than anyone else, had overreacted and taken three lives because I got a bit of a beating.

I should have just hurt them, not killed them. But what if they'd got the better of me? I'd be back to square one and maybe they'd go too far and kill me, or Vicky. After all, they'd forced Vicky to turn then locked me up with her. Maybe they didn't think she'd kill me, but they certainly risked it.

No, as extreme as my actions were, I'd made the right call. It was harsh, some might say psychotic, but I was who I was. I was The Hat. A dangerous man. Such truths are hard to accept, but I'd made peace with it a long time ago. I walked in circles far removed from citizens, and the people I dealt with were often as dangerous, if not more so, than me, so I had to act accordingly if I wanted to continue leading the life I led.

And, may all the gods forgive me, I wanted to continue down this rocky road, live a life full of edginess, violence, and excitement. The alternative? Now that was something to be truly scared of.

I shuddered at the thought. Then I smiled, because I'd already made my mind up. If Selma was genuine, and bless her she seemed like she was, then I would help her. After all, it had been a while since my last adventure, and this one was already well and truly underway.

I glanced at my watch; it was almost time for the girls to be waking up. And I hadn't had breakfast with George the last few days. I grabbed my coat from the corner of the room and found my phone then called her, told her everything was okay and I'd probably be late but we would have dinner together. She said she'd be home.

Whatever happened, however bad the day or the night was, I always tried to have dinner with George. Breakfast too if possible. It was our thing, what kept us close. A little normality as we rode the waves of madness on a sinking ship that one day, inevitably, would succumb to its volatile environment.

Vicky and Selma returned a few minutes later while I remained seated, gathering my thoughts and energy.

"This place is massive," said Vicky looking altogether better now she was dressed. She had on a pair of jeans that were a little baggy, and a black cardigan over a black vest. No prizes for guessing whose clothes they were.

"Don't forget it's nearly time to take the girls to school. You wanna go or you want to call Ivan while we listen to what Selma has to say? Without any bullshit," I added as I gave Selma my best glare.

"I'll make the call," said Vicky, excited. She turned to Selma too and said, "See, I told you he was a big softy really."

All three of us stared at the corpses. "Yeah, that's me, a big softy."

Vicky called Ivan who said he'd get the girls to school, his assistant would do it as she'd come over to help babysit, and Vicky said she'd catch up with him later in the day but we were busy at the moment. Ivan was used to it. He was as much, if not more, part of the game than us.

With our morning cleared, I got to my feet and said, "Now, why don't you make coffee then get talking."

Selma glanced at the bodies once more, then squared her shoulders and said, "Follow me."

Time for answers, and I hoped for her sake she tried nothing stupid.

My Worst Nightmare

"I think there are other people in the house," whispered Vicky as we left the attic.

"No shit, Sherlock."

"Arthur, don't be so mean."

"Oh, I'm terribly sorry. It's just I've been locked in an attic with a wolf all night and three women just beat me to a pulp. Plus, I've had no coffee. Can we please just get this over with? I've promised to hear her out, that's what you want, isn't it?"

"Yes, of course. You're very good. What happened with those women?"

"Later."

We followed Selma down a narrow staircase then emerged onto a large landing. There were at least ten closed doors and the smell of witch was everywhere. I did not feel relaxed but I refused to show it.

Selma glanced back to check we were following then led us down the stairs. I took the opportunity to get a better feel for the place. It was quite spartan but with random items dotted around, a few pot plants, several pictures, and a lot of crap. They'd moved in hastily, hadn't been here long, and were definitely up to no good. The whole house had a certain smell to it that only emanated from witches.

Partially the smell of dirty washing left in a heap, partly incense as they loved a bit of that, and an overriding smell of mysterious chemicals and a lot of lavender. They couldn't get enough of it for some reason.

As we stepped down into the hall, I relaxed a little as I could see the front door. It was large, with stained glass in the main panel and sides. The floor was tiled, intricate abstract patterns popular in the Victorian era, and the decorative cornicing and skirting boards told you all about the property if you knew how to read the signs. Large but not impossibly so, well-designed but not too lavish. The rooms would be generous, with big sash windows, and no doubt the kitchen would have once been small but as with most large Victorian properties it would probably have been expanded either with an extension or by knocking through into other rooms.

It would have also cost a fortune to buy. Large townhouses like this went for crazy money. They simply didn't build them like this any more.

"Arthur, pay attention," said Vicky as she jabbed me in the ribs.

"Ow, that hurt."

Vicky rolled her eyes and indicated with her head that I should look. I snapped out of my architectural appreciation and realized we'd walked into the kitchen while I was still staring at the coving. I was right about the kitchen. It had been knocked through into the dining room, making for a large if very outdated space.

The cupboards were from the sixties, probably worth a lot of money on the retro market now, the oven was one of those freestanding things with the grill on the top, the fridge was one of the first to be made, and most of the room was taken up by a huge table that could easily seat twenty.

And, oh woe is me, take me now Death and never let me return, sat at the table, nursing mugs of strange brews that smelled like flowers stuck in hot water, were nine witches. Another was putting milk away in the fridge.

My worst nightmare had come true, and I panicked inside but forced myself to stare at them without showing signs of weakness. Witches were stressful, always banging on about herbs and the power of little rocks and crystals. Obsessed with trinkets, ruthless when it came to the dangers of eating anything but beans and organic produce, and obsessed with the many and varied uses for hemp, when the only thing I'd ever found it good for was getting off my tits.

And they were all staring at me, aghast.

"It's the hat, isn't it? You like it, don't you?"

Mugs were dropped, hands went to mouths, and the woman who was now by the kettle swore as she got a nasty burn.

"Can I have a coffee, please? I don't think chamomile will do it after the night I've had."

"Everyone," said Selma nervously, "this is Arthur. The Hat. And, um, this is Vicky, his partner."

"Dimwitted sidekick," I muttered.

"Arthur! Pleased to meet you everyone. Um, can I have coffee too please?" Vicky toyed with her ponytail, I just rubbed my beard. Funny how sometimes only the fondling of your own body hair can calm you down.

"Um, there's been a bit of an incident," said Selma quietly. "Sharon, Cece, and Angel are all dead. Arthur, er, chopped their heads off."

Ten witches gasped. Ten witches muttered dangerous spells under their breath. Ten witches reached for their pouches of pot-pourri, or whatever it was they liked to sprinkle when they said their spells.

One wizard gulped and wondered when the coffee would be ready.

"It was an accident," I explained, holding my hands up. Which, looking back on it, probably wasn't the best of ideas. I didn't even remember pulling Wand out of my pocket, but I guess it was easy for them to get the wrong idea.

The Best Coffee

"Whoa! Easy, ladies, just a mistake. See, I'm putting him away."

"What, and make me miss all the fun?" moaned Wand.

"Shut up, or you'll get us into trouble," I may or may not have said out loud.

"I think we're already in trouble, dude. Man, these are some pasty, wrinkly looking bints. It's like an old age pensioner slumber party. They look like hippies steeped in prune juice. All wrinkly and like their clothes are on acid. Are they tripping? They look like they're tripping. Their eyes are all googly looking."

"I said shut up," I ordered through gritted teeth.

One woman, three hundred if she was a day, or maybe she'd just had a hard life and was bad for late fifties, pushed back her chair, adjusted her voluminous skirt that swept the floor as she walked, the chaos of pastel colors making my eyes hurt, and walked right up to me. Surprisingly, she ignored me, and instead stared at Wand.

"I can hear you, you stupid stick," she hissed.

"Oh."

There was an uncomfortable silence, then one of the other women asked, "What did he say?"

"Don't you tell them," said Wand, panicked. "I was just messing about. You all look lovely. Nice dress, goes perfectly with the orange vest. Makes your long, lank, greasy hair shine like a cloud on a shit day."

The witch flicked Wand's tip with her blunt finger.

"Ouch. No need for that. I was paying you a compliment."

"You'll have to excuse my twat of a friend, he doesn't get out much, and he won't be getting out again for a while." I pocketed Wand and he had the good grace to sulk in silence.

"You should teach him some manners," said the woman as she peered up at me. Was it just me or did so many of the most annoying women in my life seem to be short? Or had I grown? I didn't think I had, my clothes still fit.

She turned away and addressed the room. "His familiar was just being cheeky, but it's innocent enough."

"Apart from it, and him, killing three of our own," said another witch. The others murmured their agreement.

"They had it coming," I blurted. "I don't know what you ladies have going on here, but if you think tying people to chairs and beating the crap out of them is okay, then getting your head chopped off is also okay."

"You decapitated them? Our sisters?" asked the witch still worryingly close.

"Yeah. You got a problem with that?"

She turned to Selma and asked, "What happened? I thought you were still out trying to convince him."

"It didn't work, and the others decided to just grab him, bring him back. They said they'd talk to him. It all got out of hand. I said some stupid things, got flustered, and it all went wrong." Selma began to cry. The women gathered around her, telling her it was okay, muttering about her being too young to be sent on such an important task, me and Vicky forgotten.

While they stank the place up with lavender and what I was sure was patchouli, and what a blast from the past that was, I took the opportunity to go make a cuppa.

I flipped the kettle back on, rummaged around in the cupboards, found two mugs, obviously in the shape of fruit and whatnot as why have a boring old mug when you can have something that looks "interesting" and spooned something that looked and smelled a little like coffee into them.

I was aware that the room had gone silent. I turned from my most important task and found twelve women staring at me in horror.

"What? Oh, sorry, anyone else want a cuppa?"

The silence and the staring continued.

"Is he funny in the head?" asked one witch.

"No, he's just not very good with manners," said Vicky, shaking her head in dismay.

"What have I done?" I asked.

"You chopped the heads off three of our sisters," screamed a very tall witch with hair longer and grayer than the rest.

"Oh, that. Yes, I did. And if any of you have a problem with that then now is the time to speak up." The kettle switched off and I glanced at it then back at the women. "Actually, hold that thought. I need a drink first. So, anyone else want a drink or not? And you better all want it the same way. I'm not dicking about making thirteen drinks where everyone wants something different and some take sugar, others don't."

"He is definitely funny in the head," said another witch.

"A screw loose," said another.

"You sure this is him? The Hat?" asked the one with the long dress, although, actually, that didn't narrow it down to any less than excluding me, Vicky, and Selma.

"It's him," said Selma. "And I blew it. He didn't fall for the hacking ruse, he agreed to listen at the cabin, but I got nervous and pretended I'd already stolen the cauldron, then the others knocked him out and made Vicky turn wolf and locked them upstairs in the attic and put a ward up so none of you would know. I'm sorry."

More hugs, more grumbles and commiserations.

I made coffee for me and Vicky then took them over to the table and sat down.

This could go on all day and I'd had enough of it.

I took a sip. "Mmm, nice brew. Your loss."

Twelve perplexed women turned to stare at me. Witches! Don't know what their problem is.

Too Many Cooks

After staring at me some more, the witches all took turns hugging Selma as she went over and over the story of the last several days. I reminded myself of something I'd known for many years. Witches were scatty as hell.

Talk about disorganized. Most had no idea what day it was, had no clue when Selma had been let loose on us, let alone when she'd done the hack then impersonated Ivan. Their days were more blurry than mine, and their sense of time was akin to the fae's. They knew they had a plan, that Selma had been tasked with accomplishing it, aided, and abetted, by the three dead women upstairs, but it seemed that none of them had kept close tabs on progress beyond being told which parts had failed and that Selma was onto the next attempt to win me over by any means necessary.

I couldn't understand it, couldn't figure out how they could be so disorganized. As they babbled, I ran through the course of events just so I knew where I was up to. It had started the day before yesterday. The hack was done early morning, I went to Vicky's, then it took all that night to get it fixed. I'd gone home, met Selma impersonating George, then returned to Vicky's that evening and we'd gone to the club. Then we'd been led to the cabin and I woke up in the attic this morning. Simple enough, even for me in my current state.

These lot kept getting it all mixed up like this had spanned weeks, and I could tell that even Selma, unfortunately seemingly one of the smartest and most on-the-ball of the bunch, was getting muddled as they jabbered in her face and seemed hellbent on confusing the poor girl.

Yes, that's right, after seeing what she was involved in I felt sorry for her. She was young, inexperienced, and although clearly very powerful with magic she had little real world experience. And it's all very well being able to transform yourself to appear to be someone else, but if you don't know how to fight or get out of a sticky situation, then you'll get into a lot of hot water in short order.

Vicky squeezed through the throng of women and sat beside me with a sigh. She rolled her eyes then gave up and drank her coffee. Comes to something when Vicky finds the company a little too dippy, as in my dictionary at the time if I looked up babbling fool there was one word. Vicky.

"Like to talk, don't they?" I commented.

"Yeah, but it's like they don't know what's happening in their own lives. They're so unorganized. How can they function like this?"

"It's all the herbs. Their brains are mush. I blame the hemp, or maybe the lavender. Who knows what a lifetime of sniffing their potions has done to them?"

"Do they really make potions? I know next to nothing about witches."

"Some of them, especially the old-timers. And I'm guessing most of this lot are seriously old. They grew up in different times, when witches all wore long cloaks and pointy hats and carried around big bags of dried leaves. Most lived in the woods and cackled a lot as they chucked worrying things into cauldrons and stirred them with big spoons."

"Arthur, don't be so silly."

"I'm actually not. You've got to remember that until recently anyone seen as different was persecuted or ostracized. Magic users had to be very careful. Wizards and witches were outcasts of sorts, only survived because of the magic they could harness. You either had to be a seer or a fortune teller, or something like that so people wouldn't come jab you with the closest pitchfork. Different times. So most witches chose to live away from their local communities, sometimes in groups, often alone, and they spent their time making potions for their serious magic and mixing up innocent concoctions on the side to appease the locals. Where do you think most medicine comes from?"

"Dunno, never thought about it."

"From the knowledge passed down by the witches. They are in tune with nature like most wizards aren't, and they figured out a lot of stuff. What plant mixes with what element to help cure stomach ache, cures for warts, mild potions to ease sickness, all that stuff came from them."

We turned to stare at the chattering women, now deep into an argument about what to do next, seemingly having decided we were harmless even though I'd just killed three of them.

It was hard to believe most modern medicine came from such minds.

"What now?" asked Vicky.

"Guess we hear them out. I promised Selma, but if they don't get a move on then we'll just leave. I don't think they'd even notice."

Vicky and I continued to drink our coffee. In a bizarre twist of events, we remained silent. Vicky knew when she was outclassed in the "banging on and on about stuff without ever getting to the point" department.

Finally, the room quietened down, and the women all turned and made their way as a group the whole three steps over to the table.

"We've made a decision," said the one with the most voluminous of skirts.

"We have," another agreed.

"We're going to let you help us," said a third.

"I thought we agreed I was going to do the talking?" said Big Skirt, scowling at her fellow witch.

"I was just sayin'. No need to snap."

"I wasn't snapping, I was merely pointing out that I am the—"

"Can you please just get on with it. You're giving me a headache here. In case you've forgotten, we've been locked up all night, we haven't been home, Vicky misses her kids, and I miss my kitchen. And my bed."

Selma stepped forward, and I was glad she did. Seemed like she was the only one with any sense amongst the lot of them.

"Will you please help us?"

"Depends. Tell me what you want and why you want it, and then we'll see. No promises, but I'll hear you out."

"Great," said one witch.

"He's going to listen."

"Tell him then, go on."

"Whoa! I said I'll listen, but to Selma. If you lie, or if any of you butt in and start jabbering, then we're out of here. Understand?"

The women nodded silently.

This was going to be hell.

Aargh

Fifteen minutes later, and with witches crowded close, peering at me, leaning over my shoulder, breathing heavily, interrupting continually, bickering, waving pouches of herbs about, and jostling for position, I'd had enough.

"Okay, everyone apart from Selma, out. I can't stand it. If you want my help then I at least need to know what the problem really is. You're all driving me nuts!"

They argued, they complained, they sulked, but Selma finally got them to agree to leave us alone while we talked. It was with a great sense of relief that the room emptied and the witches went off to perform their morning ablutions. I could only imagine how that would go with ten women all trying to use the bathroom. Maybe they all had en-suites in this place, wherever it was.

"Now, can you please explain all of this? And don't tell me any lies. Just the truth."

"I will. Promise."

"How do you handle them?" I couldn't resist asking; Selma seemed so different to the others.

"They're sweet really. Most of them, anyway. Some of them are just old, from a different time, and well, I guess I like it. They taught me everything I know, them and some of the others. And Grandma, of course. You probably don't know much about us, do you?"

"No, not a lot," I admitted. "Witches and wizards don't really mix, and there aren't that many of you anyway. You keep to yourselves, more secretive than wizards. It is what it is. For the best. There'd be no end of hassle if we got involved in each other's business."

"That's what Grandma always said, that it was for the best. Things have been changing lately though. She's changed. We aren't like we used to be. We've moved with the times. I know it doesn't look like it, but the witches are different now."

"The hacking, you mean?" asked Vicky. "That was very clever. Did you really hire someone?"

"No, er, it was me. But it isn't what you think. I didn't do it like you. You're awesome, Vicky. I learned all about you before I tried to get you guys to work for us. You're a legend."

Vicky blushed and beamed as she puffed out her chest. "You think so?"

"Sure. I hear the talk. I hear about your hacking, your work, and I hear how the shifters talk about you. You're ace!"

Vicky smiled so broadly she looked like her teeth were about to fall out.

"So, you did the hack?"

"Yeah, kinda. I used magic to do it, got so far, but I'm not like Vicky, so I used a spell to get into your computers. It's hard to describe, but I made it look like a hack although it wasn't. Your money never went anywhere and it would have all gone back to normal on its own, but Vicky beat me to it. She beat my magic."

"That explains it, I guess," I said, unconvinced but not wanting to push the matter. "So what's been going on? Why all this?"

"Grandma has been losing the plot. She's gone power hungry, wants us to have more control."

"Of what?"

"Of everything."

"Oh."

"We keep a low profile, but we're part of the underground too. We just don't let on. We're very good at getting what we want. We do jobs too, not like you, not artifacts, but other stuff. The community is involved in things you would never guess. But Grandma wants more. She's been sending the women on more jobs, causing more trouble, and it's getting worse. Some refused to do it anymore, said it wasn't the witch way, and she got angry. She threw them out and me too after I wouldn't do something I didn't want to do."

"What?"

"It doesn't matter, just a job. She wanted me to get involved in fae business. Something about a woman wanting help to get revenge for something in the past. Grandma never told me the details because as soon as she mentioned fae I said no. She threw a wobbly, which she does a lot, and told me to leave."

I wondered if what she was talking about was the trouble Sasha had, but decided to keep quiet as it was personal business. Had Carmichael approached them, or had it been Sasha's nemesis? Guess I'd never know now.

"So you're all here as you got thrown out of your homes? Or you all lived with Mabel?"

"We were all together in a house. The Residence. You know it?"

I nodded. I knew it, a massive place on the edge of the city where the witches mostly lived together. Not many, and they kept to themselves, never bothered anyone. They were a lot closer than wizards, but we outnumbered them vastly.

"So you got thrown out?"

"Yes, but not before she'd told me what she wanted us to do. Grandma has always confided in me. I think she saw me as her successor, or maybe just her dogsbody. She wants to take over, and she wants to destroy Ivan. She wanted us to all go and eliminate him after Mikalus got killed. Said this was our chance, to take over, be the rulers, that's how she put it."

"So you all said no and she went mental. Why are you talking to me though? Why haven't you gone to Ivan and told him?"

"Because then he'll want revenge and he'll kill my sisters. I don't want anyone to die, I just want Mabel stopped."

"You think if you told Ivan he'd just kill you all?"

"He would, wouldn't he? I'm sorry, Vicky, I know he's your brother, but am I right?"

Vicky frowned, and stuck out her tongue, meaning she was in deep thought. "I don't know. Maybe. He's kind, and he loves us, but he's dangerous. A vampire but also a gangster. He's had a hard life, and violence is all he knows. If he thinks you're trying to kill him he'll act quickly and do whatever it takes."

I nodded in agreement. "He has that right. If Mabel is trying to take him out then he'll destroy her and anyone he thinks would seek revenge. Makes sense. It's what I'd do."

"Exactly, and I don't want that. Mabel's twisted and she's twisting the others. You've seen what they're like." Selma leaned forward and after checking nobody was listening she whispered, "You might have noticed, they're a little scatterbrained."

"Really? Shock, horror."

"Okay, but that doesn't mean they're bad. They can be easily led. Many of the women are quite naive, have spent most of their lives being nothing but witches. They don't know much about the modern world. Nearly all of them only mix with their sisters, never go out alone, and don't understand this world. In some ways, the Residence is like a convent. The women have their duties, they perfect their magic, do as Mabel asks, and don't mix with citizens. They're innocents."

"Not all. Like those upstairs that locked us up."

"You don't know them," Selma snapped. "Sorry, but you have to understand. They were desperate, thinking of the greater good. And like I said, they can be a bit dippy. They were watching all night, and wouldn't have let anything happen. Nothing too serious."

"Okay, so Mabel's got a screw loose, she wants to take over the vampires' business and eliminate Ivan, what's this got to do with Mabel's Cauldron?"

"Everything. It's got everything to do with it. She's going to use it to do something so wild that it will change everything. You're a wizard, you know how powerful magic is. But you don't know what we're capable of, what we can do when we put our minds to it."

"Come on, it's just a cauldron. Okay, a magical cauldron, which they all are, and I know it's old, named after her, but it's still just for making potions."

"You wizards," said Selma with a sigh. "You think you know it all, think you're the best. You underestimate us, all of us. You've seen what I can do, and I'm just getting started. I'm young, have so much to learn. What do you think the older women can do? I know you think they're all daft and weak, but any one of the women in this house could turn you to mush in an instant. They talk a lot and act daft, but that's the witch way. We hide our true strength. It's so much a part of us we don't know any other way. But trust me, every woman here apart from me has killed, done extreme things for our sisters and our future, so don't underestimate us."

"Okay, I won't. Jeez, I was only asking. If you're all such hotshots why don't you destroy the Queen?"

"She's my Grandma. My great, great, whatever Grandma. I don't want her hurt, I want her stopped.

Want the cauldron taken away so she can't do what she's planning to do. Once that's gone, she won't be able to act, at least for a while, as for some reason she's hellbent on using her cauldron, and hopefully she'll see sense. If not, then we'll think of something. And as a last resort, she'll have to die."

"You know if I tell Ivan this he'll kill her. You're taking a big risk telling us."

"I know. But there's no other choice. You have to do it. You're the best, and this affects you. You're perfect for the job."

"You mean because of George, right?"

"Exactly. At the moment she's in the early years of her training, but soon she'll be introduced to the others, to Mabel, and you don't want her caught up in any of this madness. You want her kept safe, so this has to be settled. Things must return to normal before George becomes a part of this. It's why we chose you."

"Why the hell didn't you just say all this to start with?"

"Because we figured you'd just agree to it after the hack. That way we wouldn't have to go into detail and risk you telling Ivan."

"But now you have."

"Now we have," agreed Selma.

"Let me think about it."

Selma nodded then left.

I honestly wasn't sure what to do. This was serious, and big scale. Involving matters that went way beyond my usual line of work. I'd also vowed never to help the vampires again.

Vicky looked at me with her best puppy dog eyes.
What a decision to have to make.

Decisions

"What should we do?" I asked Vicky.

Vicky was taken aback. "You're asking me?"

"Yeah, I am. What should we do? Should I agree to this, or not? Sounds flaky, stealing a cauldron to stop the wicked witch trying to be the top gangster in the country. Sounds far-fetched as hell too. There's something else going on, that's for sure. Things Selma isn't telling us. But she's a good girl, I'm sure of that. She's trying to stop Mabel risking everything, risking the lives of the others, and leading them into a life most don't want. So, I'll ask you again, what should I do? What should we do? This involves both of us."

"You never ask my opinion."

"But this time I am. He's your brother, Vicky. Is it right to keep quiet, not warn him? He's looking after your kids as we speak. Okay, they're in school, but you know what I mean. He's nuts, and dangerous, and has got me into a lot of trouble, but he's also a good guy. We know where we stand with him, kind of. These witches, I don't know them. At all. Should we take their word and do as they ask to maybe protect Ivan, or do we tell him and let him deal with the matter? He's family, these are strangers."

It wasn't an easy decision to make, and I understood that. I was also thinking of what Selma had said about George. She had enough crap to deal with without the witches dragging her into any nonsense. What was best for her? If Ivan went wild and killed most witches, where would that leave George? She needed like-minded people to mix with as she grew older, but she also didn't want a father who betrayed the top vampire.

If we got involved in this, it had to go perfectly otherwise the shit really would hit the fan. Ivan would be apoplectic if he knew we'd had the chance to save him by telling him and had failed to do so. Secrets between family are never a good idea, especially when they are gangster vampire family.

Vicky had a tough decision to make. So did I.

"Well?"

"I'm still thinking," said Vicky.

"I'm not. I know exactly how to play this. You gonna back me up?"

Vicky smiled with relief at the decision being taken out of her hands. "You betcha, boss."

"Blimey, that's a first."

"What?

"You agreeing with me, and calling me boss. You really love him, huh?"

"He's family."

"Yeah, family. You either kill them or keep them safe, what other choice is there?" Vicky stared at me funny. That was one tale I wasn't ready to tell her. Maybe I never would be.

"Call Selma back in. Actually," I said, dread creeping up my spine at the thought, "tell them all to come in. I have a plan."

"A cunning one?" asked Vicky with a grin.

"You betcha. I'm The Hat, all my plans are cunning."

Apart from the ones that go spectacularly wrong, of course.

Deep Breath

The women filed back into the kitchen. Or should I say, they babbled and argued and shoved as they all tried to get in first, seemingly so they could all stand around and try to vibe me and Vicky into doing what they wanted. It was unsettling. They had stares better than Vicky, and hers were Olympic standard.

"Is he going to do it?"

"What's he waiting for?"

"Why is the tiny woman glaring at us like that? I don't like it."

"Ooh, she's good. Is she a witch?"

"Does he always look like that? Why is he so wrinkled? How old is he?"

"Quiet!" Man, it was enough to make you do a runner. I would have too, if they weren't all blocking the way. "Look, can you all settle down? We've come to a decision, and we will help. If," I warned, "you agree to let me do this my way. No interfering." Even as I said it, I sighed inwardly, knowing there wasn't a hope in hell of these mad bints staying out of this. I could try, that's all I could do.

They grumbled and muttered and I began to reconsider. Why didn't I just go tell Ivan and let him have at Mabel? He'd send his people and that would be that. Except it wouldn't. If he attacked first it would be an all-out war between the witches and the vampires. And then the wizards would get involved. However much they steered clear of the women who liked essential oils way too much, and were masters of the evil eye, for obvious reasons as nobody likes being glared at quite so intently, if the vampires began to attack whole sections of the magical community there was no way the wizards would just sit back and watch. They hated witches, but they hated vampires more. Mainly because nobody knew enough about them, and they'd returned to their secretive ways.

"Is he all right?"

"What's he doing?"

"Does he need his tablets?"

"Arthur, get on with it," said Vicky as she cast a worried glance at me and I came back to the present.

"Sorry. Feeling tired. For some reason," I gave them a glare as it had become very one-sided, "I didn't get much sleep last night."

"We said we were sorry," said Selma.

"Yeah, whatever. We'll do it, but you have to stay out of this. Ivan will go mental on all of you if he thinks the Queen is up to anything, and I'm still tempted to just tell him. But we'll give this one shot, see if you all behave, and if you do then we'll try to keep the vampires out of this. Agreed?"

"Agreed," they chorused, looking both relieved and apprehensive.

"What I don't want, and this isn't up for debate, is any more of your stupid games. I don't know what's wrong with you all. Why didn't you just ask me rather than all this pretend hacking business and Selma impersonating everyone?"

"We thought it was a good plan," muttered Huge Skirt.

"It wasn't. Damn, I heard witches liked to complicate things, but this is nuts."

"We needed a plan. We spent ages on it," said Selma.

"Yeah, well it was crap. This why you wanted me involved, as you couldn't figure out how to get the cauldron without getting caught?"

"Mabel will know straight away if we take it. She'll come and ask and you can't lie to her. Nobody can. She isn't a bad person, just fed up with us getting no respect. She wants Ivan gone and then we will get some attention."

"You'd get that, with bells on. From every gangster in the country. From every vampire too. It would be a bloodbath." And it would. Even if they took down Ivan, his council would be all over the witches in a heartbeat. Witches may be adept, but vampires are vampires. They can sneak up on you, looking like the everyman, utterly normal, impossible to recall, entirely forgettable until it's too late and they're sucking the life force out of you, leaving you a husk.

They didn't do it often, hardly ever took a life, but they were more than capable when provoked. I'd learned that much the hard way. Mabel was on very shaky ground. What the hell was wrong with her?

"So, I need some information from you all before we proceed. I need details, and I need some time. How long do we have?"

Before anyone could speak, I felt a familiar tingling just before the room lost its sense of permanence.

I sighed. Here we go again.

Not Again

Sasha appeared in the middle of the room between us and the witches. She looked divine as always, and faery dust drifted down to the tiles languidly as she tucked a perfect golden lock behind her entirely lickable ear.

I sighed, but accepted it, as what else could I do?

Sasha beamed at me and Vicky then turned her head a fraction and squinted ever so slightly at the witches. It was still a beautiful expression, and brief, but it conveyed so much that the women gasped. Partly in awe at seeing a faery such as Sasha, partly out of bone-trembling fear. For Sasha was not to be messed with, and I guess everyone in the magical community had heard at least a little of what had gone down previously about a certain insane woman, her son, and the Hangman.

People talked, and you couldn't stop them, so the rumors had spread and although nobody knew the whole story they were more than happy to make up the parts they were clueless about. It all added to the legend of The Hat, Vicky too, and Sasha had been spoken of in hushed voices, her exploits exaggerated as everyone loved to gossip about the faery that deemed humans worthy of attention.

Me, I was just annoyed and trying not to show it.

Sasha wore a green dress so tight it was like a second skin. It clung to curves so perfect it made your eyes bleed, and several witches did actually have to wipe away the blood, others tears of joy and fear. It shed faery dust that sparkled and danced around her feet, her high heels making her calf muscles taut and as perfect as the rest of her legs, the dress so short most of her thighs were in evidence. I had to look away, as daydreams of those thighs wrapped around my back as I... You get the picture.

"It's you again. Hi, Sasha."

"Hello, Arthur," Sasha said with a beautiful smile then an extra glare at the witches. "I'm here to protect you. Are these women giving you any trouble? Should I send them to a terrible place within the Nolands to spend an eternity in the presence of one of the terrible beasts that reside there?"

"Um, no, it's okay. I'm good."

"Are you sure, my sweet?" Sasha raised an eyebrow and my blood pressure shot through the roof. Goddamn, but she got lovelier by the day. I shook away the mesmerizing effects of her trans-dimensional beauty and focused.

"You don't need to be here, honestly."

"Hello, Sasha," said Vicky, practically fawning.

"How are you, dear Vicky?"

"Great. We're just dealing with these ladies."

"Yes, I can see. I don't like the look of them." Sasha turned, whirling fast, faery dust flinging away from her. The witches gasped, awed and terrified in equal measure.

"It's fine." I tried to remain calm, to not be cross, but it was getting difficult. "Sasha, I'm fine, Vicky's fine, everyone's fine. You don't need to keep doing this."

"Doing what?"

I kept my voice low and moved closer, Vicky tagging along like we were about to share secrets. "You don't need to keep popping up to check on me. I told you already, I can handle myself."

"But you've needed my assistance in the past, and without the lives I bestowed on you you would be dead many times over."

I glanced up only to see a room full of women craning their necks forward to catch our conversation. They stepped back and suddenly their fingernails become inordinately interesting.

"I know that," I whispered. "But this is getting out of control. Please stop turning up all the time. I'm a big boy."

"But it's my job to protect you. I have been remiss in the past, but no longer. I'm here for you, Arthur, my sweet, and I always will be. We made a promise to each other, and I intend to keep it."

I groaned inwardly, not showing her my annoyance, but this had to stop. Ever since I'd helped save her from a woman intent on her destruction, Sasha had been turning up on an increasingly regular basis.

She'd pop up, bash some heads, or not, as sometimes she said she couldn't interfere, other times she'd be right at it, but most of the time she either came too early or too late.

She was becoming a liability, and no way could I tell her that. It was enough having Vicky to deal with; last thing I needed was an over zealous faery godmother thinking she owed me and doing her utmost to protect me. She'd get me killed with all her sudden appearances. It was off-putting.

"I have this handled. We have this handled," I corrected as Vicky jabbed me in the ribs and glared. Damn, way too much glaring for one morning.

"If you're sure?" Sasha eyed the women again just for good measure.

"I'm sure. I do appreciate it though, you looking out for me."

"It's my pleasure. We made a deal, the contract."

"Yeah, you're a real friend. And I... Hang on, you've never mentioned a contract before. Death said something about that, when he tried to pretend I'd had a heart attack but just wanted company."

"You've met Death?" asked a witch.

I turned and scowled. "Stop listening to a private conversation."

"Be gone," said Sasha as she waved a hand at the awestruck witches. They shrieked as they were shunted backwards out of the room and the door slammed shut behind them. "Ah, that's better." Sasha turned back to me with a sweet smile. Who could stay angry with such a divine creature?

Sasha was definitely losing the plot. Her attempts to make up for her absence before the events of the summer had got out of hand and now she was interfering with my business.

"You have to stop this," I said gently.

"Stop what?"

"Turning up so often. I was talking to them. They're a bit batty, did some stupid stuff, but I handled it. If you were going to show up then it would have been better if you did it last night when Vicky was a wolf and I was tied to a chair in the attic."

"Oh, no. I've failed you again. I'm such a bad faery godmother."

Ugh. Not this. Faery tears are the worst, make you feel so sad and miserable you want to rip your ears off and stuff them up your nose. Don't ask me why, it's just the effect they have.

"No, no, you're doing great," I said hurriedly. "It's just that I don't want you to keep going to all this trouble. And look, what's this about a contract? I never saw a contract."

"Nothing to worry about, just standard procedure. I have to go. And sorry." With that, Sasha was gone.

"She's up to something," I told Vicky.

"She's a faery. It's Sasha," said Vicky, like that was meant to allay my fears.

"Exactly. And fae are always up to something. Can you have a word with her? Tell her to stop appearing all the time. It's gonna get us into trouble."

"No chance. She's Sasha, you don't tell her what to do."

"Fair enough. It was worth a shot."

There was a knock at the kitchen door. "Can we come in now?" asked Selma.

"Yeah, come in," I grumbled. Guess it was time to get this over with.

Give Me Strength

"Was that really a faery?" came a voice.

"Of course it was. Didn't you see the faery dust?"

"She was so lovely."

"I can't believe she pushed us out of our own kitchen!"

"Where does she buy her clothes?"

"Was that Sasha?"

"Is that the woman who destroyed the Hangman?" That smarted. Seemed she was getting the credit.

"Is she the one that Arthur saved from the Hangman?" That was more like it.

"No, he saved her from her evil twin."

"No, that's not right. It was her sister."

"I heard it was another faery that didn't like her being a faery godmother."

"Well I heard Arthur saved her from her sister because she killed her son."

"Will you lot shut up! Don't you ever stop talking?"

This was doing my head in. We had to get out of here, and fast.

The room was silent, all eyes on The Hat.

"Thank you. Now, is there anything I need to know?"

Of all the dumb questions I have ever asked, and I once asked an elf if he thought it was a good idea to have short hair because it made his ears look big and that did not go down well, this was undoubtedly the most idiotic by a huge margin.

Three hours later, with my stomach swishing with coffee, my head all mushy from being talked to by a coven of excited witches, plus Vicky who kept butting in to ask for clarification and seemed to enjoy the company of these mad women, I said goodbye once more to the women standing at the threshold then sighed as the door closed and we walked down a short front garden onto a quiet suburban street close to the city center.

"That was the worst morning of my entire life."

"Even worse than the time you fell over in the mud as I shifted back. Do you remember? You got your nose stuck right up my—"

"Yeah, I remember. And this was worse. Just."

"I thought they were nice."

"What are you so bloody chirpy about? You forgot what they did to us? How stressed out you were? That they just held us captive and now we've somehow agreed to help them even after what they did? They've got one over on us." I felt well and truly played. I wasn't sure how they'd done it, or even exactly when, but I got the feeling this was all an elaborate set-up they'd planned in minute detail right from the get-go.

If I didn't know better, and honestly I didn't, I could swear that every single thing that had happened had been orchestrated. They knew what they were doing, all right. This was how they operated. They were masters of manipulation, and I was well and truly outclassed. That, or they were as daft as they seemed.

"And you're only just realizing that?" asked Vicky, squinting up at me.

"What do you mean?"

"It's obvious. They had it all planned. I bet those women you killed were ones they didn't trust so they used them as part of the plan. Bet they wanted them dead and so got them to kidnap us and then they could all be shocked and we'd feel bad and then they'd explain and act all daft and lost and we'd agree to help."

"You think?" I scratched at my beard; I needed a shave and a big sleep in a deep hole.

"You're pretty dumb for a wizard, aren't you?"

"I think you're right. Ugh, where are we? I need to get home."

"Home? But we have to go get the cauldron."

"Vicky, my simple, size-challenged dimwit sidekick, there is much to do before we try to steal the prize possession of the most powerful witch in the whole country. We have to plan, we have to pack equipment, and we have to ready ourselves for what's to come."

Vicky stood on tiptoe and stared hard into my eyes. "You just want to go home and sit on your arse, don't you?"

"No, I want to lie down in a very dark room where there are no women. Unless said women are naked and have big boobs."

"I told you, and we agreed, we aren't suited for each other. Sorry."

"Not you, you muppet. And I said big boobs, not pancakes with tiny cherries on top."

"Arthur, that is so mean. They aren't that small." Vicky grabbed a breast in each hand and squeezed.

I gulped, despite myself. Ugh, I hated being a fickle man at times.

"They aren't, are they? What's wrong with them?"

"Nothing. They're ah, lovely. Perfect." They were too, even tasted nice.

"You think so?" Vicky gave them an extra squeeze and then a wiggle from side to side for good measure. Memories of us naked and her bouncing around on top rushed to my mind. I coughed then said, "Let's go. And yes, they are truly lovely boobs."

Vicky grinned and finally released what has been many a man's downfall. I glanced around, saw the curtains twitch at the witches' house, and sulked. They must think we're utterly mad.

I marched down the street with Vicky jogging to catch up. I needed to hang around with more men. How was I supposed to focus with images of bouncing boobies pushing away my sinister plotting?

Some Down Time

We returned to Vicky's home, an oasis of calm after the chaos of a witch-infested den. The girls were in school, Ivan and his aide were nowhere to be seen, a note on the kitchen counter stating he'd pick them up and bring them home unless he heard otherwise, so it was just me and Vicky.

"Shower?" she asked.

"Okay, but only because there will be soap," I agreed with a wink.

"Not together, you muppet. I meant do you want one? I feel so gross."

"Yeah, thanks."

Vicky studied me with scary intensity, and she was on tip-toe so I knew it was serious. I felt like a butterfly pinned to a board, not that I let her know.

"Would you?" she asked.

"Would I what?"

"You know, have a shower with me?" Vicky's cheeks blushed a little but she held my gaze and things got sweat-inducingly uncomfortable.

"You remember what happened last time?"

"I do. It was nice and all, but it felt wrong too."

"Exactly."

"But you didn't answer my question."

I tried to think about it, but visions of Vicky clutching her chest in the street, not to mention memories of us naked in her bedroom, stopped much in the way of thought. I decided to be honest, and give a truthful insight into the pathetic mind of men.

"Vicky, it could have been the worst sex in the world, which it certainly wasn't, but if you stripped naked right now and began er, doing anything at all, then I would agree to pretty much anything you wanted. If we were in the shower together, all soapy and naked, which we should be if we were in the shower, then I most certainly would not say no. But don't take it personally," I added. "If sex is offered, it's nigh on impossible to resist. It's hardwired. I could have the flu, I could be on death's door, I could be in the middle of an epic battle, hell, be having my leg amputated, but if a woman bounced her boobs or wobbled her bottom I'd go along with whatever she had in mind. It's the same for all men. It's why we're idiots sometimes, and why we're distracted most of the time."

"Men are such fools," sighed Vicky.

"Agreed."

"So, you would?"

"I would. But it would be a bad idea. Why, you want to?"

"Nope. Just asking." Vicky turned and walked, dare I say sashayed, to the kitchen doorway then wiggled her bottom, glanced coyly over her shoulder, then laughed as she went to get clean.

It's so unfair. Women shouldn't have this power over us. Damn, I didn't even fancy her and yet I was left there in the kitchen feeling so frustrated I could have... Trust me, you don't want to know what I could have done.

With Vicky gone, I settled down with a coffee at the kitchen table and thought a little about what had happened. I was still in two minds about whether this was a good idea or not. Ivan was family, Vicky's anyway, and had looked after her children all night, ensured they got to school, and would get them picked up if need be. He had a business to run, was an important, powerful man, yet would drop it all to look after family.

Shouldn't we just tell him and be done with this whole sorry affair?

It went further than that though. Even taking the fact this was family out of the picture, letting him loose on the witches wasn't a good move. It would cause utter carnage and the repercussions would be felt for years. The vamps would be out of hiding as the battles raged, magic would fly, death would descend, and all would be chaos.

That wasn't good. It would make a mess of everything. Who knew what the vampires would end up doing if they had to act in unison to defeat the witches, and then the wizards? Which they surely would as word would spread and there would be no going back.

If I didn't intervene in any way? Kept quiet, didn't act, let Mabel try to defeat Ivan? If she succeeded, the vamps would go nuts anyway, wizards too, as no way would they stand for witches taking over most criminal activity. And if this so-called Queen failed, Ivan would destroy most witches for their association with her, and that would lead to its own set of problems.

No, there were two choices. Either tell Ivan or steal the cauldron and somehow ensure Mabel didn't still try to destroy Ivan. And we'd agreed to the latter. I was a man of my word, so that's what I'd do. I'd go steal a bloody cauldron of all things, and somehow find a way to stop Mabel's madness infecting the whole magical community and causing decades of misery for all of us.

What I couldn't understand was why Mabel thought she could get away with this, and what madness had possessed her. This wasn't normal behavior, but maybe the witches had felt oppressed for so long that her, and her closest followers, had simply finally had enough. Stranger, much stranger, things had certainly happened.

When Vicky returned, I went and had a shower then dressed in spare clothes I kept for such emergencies, emerging feeling clearer of head, and cleaner of body. Downstairs, I smiled at Vicky as she prepared lunch. This was such a picture of marital bliss that I panicked for a moment, thinking of her earlier offer, but then remembered it wasn't an offer, it was her sounding me out, making sure there was nothing more between us. Part of me wished there was, that we had a connection on a physical level, but it wasn't to be.

And I surprised myself, because it made me sad. For all our ups and downs, the fact she drove me nuts and talked incessantly, I loved Vicky. If we were together, we would be happy. We knew more about each other than anyone else, were best friends, already almost family. She had two children I adored, she loved George and George loved her, and we spent a lot of time together as it was.

Then it clicked. Maybe I already had more than I deserved. A true friend, a partner, kids, family dinners, playing on weekends, comfortable and relaxed in each other's company.

That's what many people search for their whole lives, and here I was already living it. I just hadn't noticed. Somehow, life had crept up on me, the sneaky sod. So as I stood in the kitchen watching Vicky make sandwiches, I understood that I was already a family man, just a rather unconventional one.

Life sure is funny.

"What you staring at, you weirdo?" asked Vicky, waving a knife around to get my attention.

"Just realized I'm a lucky man," I said gruffly.

"I could have told you that a long time ago. Get the butter."

"Yes, boss."

Time to Plan

Lunch over, and with me insisting on tidying the kitchen, as Vicky's idea of a clean kitchen is to make everything in sight clean and sparkly but hide most of the dirty stuff out of sight just to aggravate my OCD, plus she always leaves crumbs and coffee spills, claiming she doesn't see them, we got down to work.

I told Vicky all I knew of the witches' residence, or the Residence as they liked to call it, thinking it made them sound important, like an official home of the Queen or something. It was a large house on the outskirts of the city, ancient, some would say crumbling, about as witch-like as you could possibly imagine by all accounts.

As far as I knew, and I'd never been inside, only stood outside and been shouted at many times by old crones, it was all a bit backward.

Sure, some of them had taken to technology, but they were mostly interested in magic same as wizards, and anything technical was used out of necessity rather than for fun. Young ones like Selma were changing things, just like George, and she was a part of this community whether she liked it or not. Come to think of it, she'd been there several times, had even been offered a place, which came as a surprise to us all as they knew who her father was.

She'd refused, but she'd be a mine of information.

"We should call her then, see if she's around."

"Good idea." I made the call. George was on her way home after a lesson with her local teacher, so the timing couldn't have been better. It meant we could have dinner together, although Vicky would return to get the children. She called Ivan to say thanks and that she'd pick the girls up, and then we headed off.

Vicky drove so she'd have a car, and I also couldn't quite remember where mine was. Turns out it was right on the street where my city semi was!

Through the Gate of Bakaudif, into the barn, a drive home, and there we were. Back in the comfort and safety of my own home, where my kitchen sparkled, only ruined by the massacre resulting from George fixing herself lunch.

We filled George in on all that had happened, the club, Selma, the kidnapping, the mad witches, the dead ones, the cauldron, all of it.

As usual, she took it all in her stride. It wasn't as weird as other stuff we'd been through, and she knew we'd made our minds up anyway.

"But we need your intel," I said.

"That's quite an ask. What if I don't agree? What if I think you should stay out of this and let Ivan handle it? Or what if I don't want to betray the most powerful witch in the country and possibly risk my entire future?"

"Oh. Yeah, course."

George punched me playfully on the arm—her faery strength meant it really hurt—and laughed. "Just messing. What do you want to know? That Mabel character is really odd, so this doesn't surprise me. And there's been lots of talk lately, how she's losing the plot, doing wild and dangerous things. A lot of witches aren't happy, not that they'd dare do anything to show it. Mabel's powerful, and she frightens them. Even my teacher, all this way from the city, is scared of her. Good riddance. But," George held up a finger, "you better watch out. She's got serious clout, and if you kill her there will be hell to pay."

"I know. That's the problem."

"Just be warned. She can kick your ass, Dad, and I mean it."

"Warning taken and understood. So, tell us all you know about the Residence."

The Nitty Gritty

I was mostly right about my impressions of the Residence, and George filled us in on the rest.

The place was all low beamed ceilings, tiny poky rooms, ancient flagstone floors, and no place for a wizard of even average height. They were fond of brass things nailed to walls and everywhere you went were bunches of drying herbs, lots and lots of cats, and more thick curtains and misshapen cushions than was good for your sanity. Plus loads of witches, of course.

They had rooms each, or shared with a few of their friends, there was a massive communal kitchen where pots bubbled permanently and they vied for space to boil up one potion or another. But many spent more time in the various outbuildings, old sheds, prefabs, and large barns housing a cornucopia of esoteric or mundane equipment. From gardening tools to a full forge, smelting works, to stills for booze and potions, several Quiet Rooms, and boy did they need them, and who knew what else.

The place was disorganized, stuff everywhere, the grounds always looked wild and overgrown, but apparently were a "cottage style" perfect for growing their numerous plants. Sounded like an excuse to not mow the lawn, but whatever.

Basically, imagine how they used to live, same as wizards, in mud huts with open fires, bubbling cauldrons, lots of herbs, cats, wands, and staffs, and all that cackling, then scale it up so there are loads of them in a building that was at its peak in the seventeen hundreds. That about summed it up.

There was one exception; they weren't as backward with their tech as I'd assumed. George said there were many young witches now, more than there had ever been, and so the house had wi-fi, even hotspots out in the gardens, and they used technology openly inside the house. They had a modern kitchen along with old stoves and even open fires for the older women, but the youngsters spent a lot of time online and had updated most antiquated systems.

There was lighting that worked off sensors throughout the house, as witches were prone to being absentminded, same as wizards, so never switched off anything they turned on. They had cable TV, everyone had an app to control the temperature in their room, although most never used it, and there were a lot of TVs. They also had a state-of-the-art security system, covering the entire property, the outbuildings that held important stuff, and the artifact room.

George had never been inside the important rooms, only invited into the house to take a look around and see if she wanted to continue her training there, and then a few more times on witch business and to pick things up for her teacher. Seems Mabel was generous to a fault with lending out artifacts to whoever wanted them, and the fully trained witches, those she knew and trusted, were allowed to come and go as they pleased from the artifact room, taking whatever they wished as long as everything was logged in and out properly.

George had been told all about the room containing artifacts, and it sounded awesome, just as I knew it would be. Witches have been around as long as wizards, and imagine if we'd had a central hoard for all the various artifacts, one person that oversaw it all. It would be amazing, but very frustrating too. Wizards had no such organization, wouldn't dream of living in such a way, but witches were different, more community minded, and had suffered more injustice over the years so preferred to keep most valuable items secured under their watchful eye.

Nobody had ever stolen from them. Now and then things went missing, but it was always one of their own who took it. Nobody would dream of actually breaking in. Apart from The Hat. Tee-hee.

For a moment, I contemplated giving George the Teleron and asking her to jump right to the door to the room and see if she could get in, but dismissed it immediately as too dangerous for her. No, I had to do this, and I had to know exactly what I was letting myself in for.

How much time did we have? Not long according to Selma and her gaggle of mad old bints. However, this could not be rushed. One mistake and it would all be over. Mabel would know we were on to her, and then the war would be upon us all.

With a big thank you to George, I said I was going for a lie down, and, for the first time ever, Vicky asked if she could come too.

"What, for a lie down? Course, there's plenty of spare rooms."

"No, with you," she mumbled, blushing sweetly as she glanced at George who smiled and went to clean up her mess. Meaning, smear butter about the counter and brush crumbs onto the tiles.

"We talked about this. I told you what I'd do given half the chance, even though I know it isn't a good idea. And you don't want this either."

"I don't mean S E X, I mean—"

"I can spell, you know," said George, grinning like an idiot.

"Fine, I may as well say it. I just want a cuddle. There, happy now?" Vicky crossed her arms over her chest and sulked.

George and I exchanged a glance. I shrugged, but then realized what an idiot I was.

I held out my hand, said, "Come on," and led Vicky up to my bedroom.

It wasn't a repeat of the last time we were in a room with a bed, this was something different and altogether more intimate.

"I'm sorry," I said, as I sat on the bed and patted it.

"What for?" Vicky sat beside me.

"For not thinking about how upsetting it can be sometimes. For not thinking about how stressful it is, and that you're very worried for your brother and aren't sure what the right thing to do is."

"It's not just that, Arthur."

"I know, honey. I know exactly what it is. It's everything, right?" Vicky nodded.

I scooted up to the pillows and Vicky joined me. We got under the covers, clothes still on, then wriggled up close.

Vicky turned her back to me and I cuddled her tight while her tiny body shook as she cried into my pillow.

Sometimes this life is fucking cruel, and the only thing that makes it better is a cuddle. It's not one particular thing that can send you over the edge, it's the little things that pile up until it seems like life is just too damn hard to deal with.

So I cuddled Vicky, and never said a word about needing a cuddle of my own, because, let's face it, I wasn't handling life well and sometimes I felt so sad and overwhelmed I wanted to die.

But she needed me, so I kept quiet, and did the only thing I could to make it all better.

Back and Forth

We awoke when my Mickey Mouse alarm clock struck quarter to three. I sat bolt upright, panicking, then sank back down and sighed with a rare feeling of blissful happiness. Such is the wonder of a mini-death, that most blessed and rare of things, an afternoon snooze rather than an afternoon lie-awake-in-bed-and-get-annoyed.

Vicky and I smiled coyly at each other, then snapped out of it and bickered about who should plump up the pillows and make the bed. Not arguing that we each wanted the other to do it, mind you. I wanted it to look neat and nice so no way was Vicky allowed to "tidy it up a bit."

Back on the usual track, me getting annoyed by her, her knowing I was right and awed by my stupendousness, we went downstairs.

George was in the kitchen, seemingly unable to fill her stomach. Where did she put it all? She had a figure any woman would be proud of. Must have hollow legs.

"Before you start," she said, "I don't want to hear anything about it."

"About what?" I asked.

"About you two getting it on upstairs. So gross. You're too old for that kind of thing."

"You're never too old," I assured her. "Never. And it wasn't like that. We cuddled."

George rolled her eyes. "Is that what the oldies call it? Ugh." George shook.

"Arthur was very sweet. He—"

"Lalalalala." George covered her ears and sang. Didn't blame her.

Vicky and I exchanged a smile then we told George what the plan for the day was and she said she'd be here.

So, I took Vicky to the barn, saw her through to the city, then returned and did chores. No point trying to formulate a proper plan until this evening. I needed Vicky's expertise to ensure I knew what I was getting myself involved in.

Hours later, with the kitchen properly clean, the floor mopped, the carpets vacuumed, the chickens and pigs cleaned out, even my boots had a polish, I set about making dinner as I waited for the home invasion to begin.

Neither of us had realized it was Friday, so Vicky was bringing the girls for the weekend so George could look after them and they could hang with her while she ran her business. The weekends were always a busy time, with her clients coming to ride the horses she stabled or to have lessons. The twins often hung around for the weekend these days, helping George, playing, riding, and devising cunning plans to disrupt my home and destroy what little sanity I foolishly clung to.

I guess I enjoyed it, but I am a glutton for punishment.

At five o'clock, I once again returned to the city, walked them through the gate, reminding them yet again how important it was to keep holding hands or they'd all be torn to bits and stay that way, the twins rolling their eyes at something that had long ago lost its fascination, magical portals now seemingly about as interesting as homework. And then I drove everyone back to the house while I was regaled with tales of mean girls and how it was so unfair that boys were allowed to ride skateboards and girls weren't.

"I don't know what kind of school you go to, but if you want to ride a skateboard then ride one. Who said girls can't?"

"The boys," they chorused.

"Trust me, boys don't know anything."

Vicky punched me on the arm. "Ow!"

"I don't want them riding skateboards," she hissed.

"It's the principle. They can do it if they want."

"You don't have to buy them, teach them how to ride, then take them to the hospital when they hurt themselves."

"That's why I said it was a good idea."

Vicky punched me again.

Home Invasion

Dinner was nice, mainly because I cooked it. I loved George more than my hat, and she excelled at many things, but cooking was not one of them. She could burn a boiled egg and once set fire to a pan of boiling water—even wizards have a hard job doing that and no, she didn't use magic, just ineptitude. I made lasagna, and I had the weirdest feeling while I was trying to peel open the foil covering the garlic bread and repeatedly burning my fingers.

As the girls chattered non-stop, all four of them, and I dished up, I got a peculiar sense of deja-vu, but not the one where it feels like you've done the exact same thing in the past, but the one where you feel like you are reliving something yet to happen. I'm sure there's a word for it, but I don't know what it is. As though you're performing a variation on a task you'll repeat in the future in a slightly different way, maybe for different people, maybe even a different place, but with the same feeling inside.

It's hard to explain, and unless you've experienced it I guess it's impossible to understand. All I knew was that I hoped I was right. I had a calmness inside, a feeling of everything being just right. Happiness, I think that's what it might have been. Although don't hold me to that, as it's not the easiest of emotions for me to be sure of. Contentment maybe. At home, doing what I loved doing, with people I loved being with. Almost like normal, like citizens ready to eat and talk about their day.

Except I couldn't just talk openly about my day, as there were young children present, and I had killed three women that morning as if it was nothing, and for no other reason than they'd hurt my pride more than my face. What kind of sick, twisted person was I?

I scalded my hand on the insanely volatile bread as I tried to rip it into pieces. Served me right.

With my mood darkened—and I had to have a serious word with my head as why did I keep doing this to myself?—I let thoughts of death drift away before I sank any deeper, and focused on the present.

We ate quickly, everyone ravenous. The adults from the stresses of this magical life, the youngsters from the much greater stresses of finding a place in the world and trying to understand how the many disparate pieces fit together. They had one hell of a journey ahead of them, one that would never end.

The talk was loud, the words often meaningless, as children seem to have a language all of their own, but it was fun, and I was even allowed to clean up the kitchen in peace as everyone went to snuggle up on the sofa in the den once the girls had got their nighties on and brushed their teeth.

I pottered about, enjoying the silence, the chance to perform mundane tasks to the very best of my ability. It centered me, calmed me, allowed me to put this thing called life into perspective.

Soon enough the girls were off to bed, giving Uncle Arthur a nice kiss before they headed off wiping their faces and moaning about my kisses being all bristly.

George came in behind me in the kitchen and wafted a cigarette in front of my face.

"You forgot," she said with a smile.

"I didn't forget, I just couldn't bear for the girls to moan about how my breath smelled if I smoked before giving them a kiss." I snatched the rollie and nodded thanks.

"You big softy." George kissed me on the cheek then yawned. "Damn, I'm shattered."

"Me too."

"I'm going up to my room to chill out. You okay, Dad?"

"Yes, honey, I'm fine."

"Don't get into any trouble," she warned.

"As if." I winked at George then watched her leave. I don't know what I did to deserve her, but damn I was one lucky man.

Outside, I lit up then inhaled deeply, blowing smoke into the frosty night air. There was a clear sky, billions of stars shining, and I stared for the longest time at this universe I had a tiny place in, so insignificant as to be meaningless yet at the same time knowing I'd created this entire universe, this world I inhabited, as no two are alike. We each see things differently, understand things in a unique way, and there are as many worlds as people, reality nothing more than a manifestation of our own existence.

We are as naught yet we are everything, and every time a person dies a whole world dies with them. It can depress you if you let it. I smoked until I could smoke no more, the filter burning my already blistered fingers, then returned to the kitchen to find Vicky sitting at the table with two cups of coffee.

"So?" she asked, eyes sparkling.

"So, now we plan."

"With some dastardly plotting thrown in?"

"You betcha."

Time to get busy.

Popping Round to Ivan's

Vicky and I bickered for half an hour while she set up her laptop and we went over what we needed to find out. Once she'd listened, and promised to do as I asked, she told me to bugger off as she had a lot of work to do. It would take her several hours and she wanted no interruptions. This was how she usually worked when deep into black hat territory in the digital world I knew nothing about. Her hacking skills were top tier, but she needed quiet and focus, and I knew I'd only be in the way. I decided to take a little trip to ease my mind and ensure we were going about this madness in the right way.

I hadn't been to Ivan's new place yet, as he'd moved yet again, trying to find somewhere he felt comfortable with.

As I pulled up outside his very posh, very expensive Georgian townhouse, I knew he'd made the right decision this time. He lived on a row of identical houses, each with freshly painted wrought iron fencing and gates, the facades so white they gleamed even with only the light of the streetlights. Original windows and brightly painted front doors complete with gleaming brass door furniture told you that you were in a street where everyone had money. And if the three-story townhouses weren't enough, the array of mind-blowingly expensive cars parked on the street confirmed that these cats had cash.

I knocked on Ivan's door and ten seconds later a woman I'd seen several times but not yet spoken to answered. His new aide. A decision I found odd but understandable if you thought about it logically. I just didn't see Ivan having someone running around after him, but then, he wasn't the man he once was, and times change.

"Hi, is Ivan at home?" I asked.

"He is. Please, come in. Is he expecting you?" asked the woman whose name I'd forgotten. She had a very thin frame, angular features, pale skin, and a short blond bob that made her look like a tomboy but attractive with it. She wore a finely tailored suit with a simple white blouse, her wide, swimmer's shoulders making it hang stylishly.

"Nope."

"Please, wait in here." She indicated an informal room with sofas, bookcases, and a nice roaring fire. It even had a drinks area.

Ivan had made the place classy; I was impressed. Thick rugs, dark walls, several old landscape paintings, and even the odd nick-nack made it homely yet rather grand without being ostentatious. I liked it. I sank into a wingback chair and sighed. What a nice place to live.

Ivan appeared soon after, looking smart in his usual dark suit, his hair limp and wet like he'd not long showered. He was alert, a little too alert, and his eyes were deep and focused, sparkling orange as they caught the light of the fire that filled the room with the pungent smell of aged oak.

"Damn, sorry. I forgot. You planning on letting loose this evening?"

"No, not this month. And don't mention it, Arthur, you're always welcome. I'm glad you've come. We don't spend much time together any more."

"You know how it is. So, you're not changing tonight?"

"No. What about Vicky, did she change yesterday?"

"You could say that. But don't worry about it." I'd completely forgotten about the moon, that Vicky had shifted last night and this time of the month was important for Ivan too. But he could control it at will, had the option to change for several days either side of the full moon. The vampire nature had hardened his resolve, made him stronger and increased his will, so he often forewent the change.

"To what do I owe the pleasure? Is this about the strangeness the other day? What was that all about?"

"Oh, you know how these things go. All sorted now. Thanks for looking after the girls. Vicky really appreciates it, you know."

"I know. It was my pleasure. Were you doing anything important?"

"Let's not talk too much business. I wanted to see how you were doing, how life's treating you with your new role, all this responsibility."

"And you said you didn't want to talk business. Something's happening, isn't it?"

Ivan was a smart man, knew something was up, as why else would Vicky be getting him to watch the girls, so I had to be careful or he'd be spying on us and we didn't need the hassle.

"No, just the usual. Maniacs playing games, Vicky doing some hacking. Normal insanity I can do in my sleep. Um, if I could get any."

"I see."

"So, what's it like being in charge? Still no trouble?"

"No, none to speak of. It's gone smoothly. I told you all this last year after Mikalus..."

"Yeah, after that. Just wondered how it was now everyone's had time to settle in to it, get used to you being in charge. And the council, how's that working out?"

"Very well. It keeps everyone happy, allows things to run smoothly so I can focus on what I know. They do the vampire business, keep track of everyone, ensure nobody steps out of line and everyone knows the rules, and I do the same for the less than savory side of things."

I knew all about the unsavory side. Ivan was a mass of contradictions. He'd inherited, after killing his old boss, the role as head of crime in the city and surrounding areas and had quickly consolidated it, changed many things, and taken over most of the criminal activity in the country. He ruled with an iron fist, but was fair, and citizens were kept out of the business.

Ivan would not stand for innocents getting hurt, so there were no shakedowns, no slave labor, no human trafficking of any sort. It had made a difference. Crime figures were at an all time low, but he also oversaw most of the drug traffic, including heroin, and it didn't sit well with me. Sure, if he wasn't doing it, and doing it well and as safely as you can when dealing with a drug that undoubtedly ruined countless lives, someone less savory would take control, but still, it rankled. I knew he hated it too, but was a pragmatist, yet it was there, a real concern. He babysat for the girls, yet he was a drug dealing vampire boss of the criminal underworld.

"So?" Ivan raised an eyebrow.

"Nothing, just a visit to say hi. I know I've been angry with you, a little aloof, but that's all in the past, right?"

"Sure. I had hoped you would work for me, but I understand."

"Good. And Ivan?"

"Hmm?"

"You're a good uncle, and the girls love you."

"You too. Thank you for saying so, it means a lot."

"They're great kids, aren't they?"

"The best."

There was a knock at the door and an entirely average voice said, "Excuse me."

"Come in. What is it?"

"A call you should take," said the ordinary looking man as he stepped into the room. I remembered him, just, although it was hard to be sure. But with my new knowledge of vampires and the fact I was on a similar wavelength to them now when in their presence, I could recall him. This was the Second, the true Second from my first encounter way back when I'd handed over Mikalus' ashes and set all this insanity in motion.

"Hi," I said with a smile.

The Second nodded and waited for Ivan.

Damn, he was so bland, so normal in every way it was almost impossible to recall him the moment you looked away. I had to remind myself this was how all the vampires appeared to citizens and magic users alike. They were faceless nobodies, impossible to recall, easy to forget, able to hide in plain sight. The perfect camouflage.

Dangerous, that's what they were. If they wanted they could destroy us. You'd never remember them, never be able to identify them, they could do what they wanted and get away with it. Yet they remained in the shadows, kept a low profile so they could conduct their business and not be interfered with.

One day I knew I'd discover what their true intentions were. No way were they going to just stay quiet and remain so aloof forever. They were up to something, I was sure, but I had no idea what.

"Arthur?"

"Sorry, miles away."

"If you'll excuse me?"

"Sure, see me out, this was just a quick visit to say hi."

Ivan looked confused but nodded.

We said our goodbyes at the door and the Second closed it behind him. I'd already forgotten what he looked like.

A Fear of Hairy Balls

I got in the car and drove through the settling city, keeping my mind blank, empty of emotion or thought. I wanted to wait to think about all this, feel relaxed and clear-headed, plus, I had already formulated a partial plan of how I could possibly pull this off, and if I thought about it too much, I was sure to change my mind.

With the roads deserted, only the workaholics, the alcoholics, the homeless, or the students now out and about, I drove to somewhere that was a sanctuary for the weary wizard. A place where you were always welcome, if you had a membership, and there was always a grunt to greet you.

Satan's Breath.

As I pulled up outside, I sat with the engine ticking as it cooled in the frigid evening air, neither waiting for anything or to muster energy, just sitting.

The car park was almost empty, just several battered old vehicles and a bicycle belonging to my fellow wizards. There were no street lights in this part of the city, the factories and industrial buildings now mostly abandoned, left to rot and be reclaimed by the city that seemed to be winning the battle against man's progress. From the exterior, Satan's Breath was uninspiring, a boxy building with little in the way of redeeming features apart from the strange, oversized entrance.

I stepped out into the freezing night, wrapped my coat tight, and exhaled my frustration and indecision.

Pushing through the doors, I was greeted with an inferno of heat and steam, and this was just the lobby. Between a counter that was new a mere year ago but now looked ready to rot, and shelves lined with rolled up towels looking equally as dubious, stood the Turk. His mustache had grown, something I thought impossible, and it sat thick and limp on the Turk's fat, blotchy face like a well-fed caterpillar that had found a peculiar home but had decided to make do and not cause a fuss.

His vest, once white, now as gray as the towels, was stained. Sweat marks could be seen running from his armpits before joining those caused by his huge belly pushing tight against the cheap cotton. He never seemed to sleep, was always at his station, but that was his business.

"Evening," I whispered, although I don't know why. Maybe it was because this place was almost holy. Shame it offered no redemption.

"Arthur. Been a while." The Turk scratched at his belly; flesh rippled beneath the vest.

"Yeah, been busy. How're things?"

"The usual. Idiots keep bringing lobsters with them, think I won't mind."

"You have to admit, it is pretty hot."

"If I made it cooler you lot would complain. Do you know how much it costs me to heat the water to that degree? Believe me, if I could have it cold, I would."

"Wouldn't be much of a sauna and steam room if it was cold."

"Exactly. So I told them, no bloody lobsters."

"Fair enough. I have no lobsters about my person. You wanna check?"

The Turk eyed me suspiciously then grinned, a worrying expression on his sweaty face. He grunted, "Sign in."

I did as I was told then took the towel offered and headed into the changing room.

I checked my wards were intact and performing properly, cast a suspicious glance around but the place was deserted, then opened up my private locker and stashed my clothes. There were several items inside that I needed for the job, but that could wait until after.

With the familiar trepidation, I wrapped the towel around my waist and headed for the main room where the pool was. I pictured wizards dropping their lobsters into the water and waiting for them to boil. It wouldn't take long.

Grace circulated cool air so my head didn't melt and slide down my shoulders, but I was already sweating by the time I walked through one of the many arches. One wizard was in the water, bright red and grinning worryingly, two others lounged on recliners, seemingly asleep.

I sat on the edge and slowly put my feet in the water, watching with interest as the skin turned puce and my body fought not to go into shock. Over the next ten minutes I lowered myself into the boiling water until only my head was above the water line, and it was there I stayed for fifteen minutes, letting the aches and pains ease, the magical healing properties of the water dissolve bruises, cuts, and scrapes. When I got up the nerve, I splashed my face, easing the pain in my nose and the strange ache I had in my ears. What was that all about?

Finally, I could stand it no more, so jumped out and went for a freezing cold shower before returning and relaxing on a recliner. I lay there for the longest time, letting idle thoughts float on by, allowing my mind to assimilate the information I'd received over the last few days, to weigh things up, form opinions unfettered by others, and for inspiration to hit.

Nothing came to mind, so all was as well as it would get. There were no deep revelations, everything seemed exactly as it had been presented. The trip to Ivan's had been worthwhile, just to see him. It had confirmed that we were making the right decision, that he was certainly full of faults but didn't deserve what Mabel had in mind. More than that. Nobody did, as her actions would be a major headache for all of us, could change our way of life for good. Bad as things sometimes were, life was stable in an odd way, and I didn't want that messed with.

I knew Vicky would be getting antsy now, as however much she insisted she wanted to be left alone to work, she went rabid if she didn't have someone to talk to for more than an hour. Maybe she'd finished doing what she needed to do.

I got up, dripping like I'd just had a shower, making a note to get some salt in me when I got home, then returned to the locker room to dry off as best I could and retrieve several very important items.

No Time Like the Present

Drive. Gates. Barn. Another car. Home.

Sometimes my life felt like one big merry-go-round, one I could get off if I wasn't so damn paranoid because everyone was out to get me. Never mind, I was here now, safe in the comfort of my own home.

"Where the hell have you been?" screeched Vicky as I stepped into my kitchen, no longer an oasis of tranquility.

"What have you done to my kitchen?" I screeched back, aghast at the carnage. Spilled coffee, knives left out, containers coated in sticky substances, tea towels were off center where they hung over the counter, and there was even a drawer partially open.

"Arthur, you have serious issues, you do know that, right?"

"I do not. You made a mess. You should clean up after yourself. I put the knife in the dishwasher, brushed away the crumbs, wiped the drip of coffee, and straightened the tea towel. Then I could think.

"Now, you were telling me off for something?" I said as I turned.

"Where were you? I finished ages ago. I thought we were going to make a plan."

"We were. We are. I've only been a few hours. What's up?"

"What's up is I worried you'd be out all night. You didn't answer your phone. I didn't know where you were or if you were okay."

"I turned it off. Took the sim out."

"Idiot."

"Am not."

It went on like that for a while until Vicky had finished with her insults and I was no longer listening.

"So, you ready then?" I asked.

"For what?"

"To go steal a cauldron from a witch."

"What, now? Tonight?"

"Yes, now. Yes, tonight," I snapped. "What's wrong with you?"

"I thought we were going to go over the plans properly. I haven't told you about the security system, how we can get in, any of it."

"Let me guess. It's all taken care of. You can disable the sensors, get me to the room no problem, and then we'll have to get creative. You think you might be able to gain access to the room, but you have a sneaking suspicion that there's something you're missing, that they've put in something else that you can't find remotely and there's no other way but to just get there and see what's what?"

"You... How...? Then why...? Arthur, you're so mean sometimes." Vicky's bottom lip wobbled and I thought fast to ward off any tears.

"I'm sure you've done an amazing job. It's what you do best. But you know what witches are like."

"No, not really."

"Neither do I, actually. Come on, let's get our stuff together and then we'll go."

"But this is so sudden."

"Vicky, my moaning minion, you know this is how I work. No point putting it off if we're going to do this. It may as well be now. You know that as soon as a job gets requested it's only a matter of time before everyone hears about it. People talk, rumors spread, the marks get nervous or suspicious, so let's do this now and be done with it."

"Fine, but I need a wee first, and to check on the girls. And how long will this take? We need to be back by morning."

"Fine. And of course we'll be back by morning, why wouldn't we be?"

Famous last words, right?

A Disturbance in the Force

Calm enveloped me as I climbed through the window, the house as silent as my slow beating heart. Everything was as it should be. Security no problem, such as it was, just sensors for when the windows or doors were opened, not that we had to worry as when Vicky went to shut it all down she realized that nobody had even bothered to set the alarm in the first place. This might be easier than I'd thought.

I was in a TV room. There were sofas everywhere, tatty things with ripped arms and way too many knitted blankets. There were cushions of all sizes and provenance, ranging from bed-sized to so small I couldn't for the life of me see what the point was. Crocheted things were draped over most surfaces, half empty mugs everywhere, and a huge TV dominated one wall.

It smelled funny too, like somebody had opened all the spice jars then sprinkled them generously on the carpet several years ago and hadn't vacuumed since.

I stopped and listened. Silence. Just the creaking of a house at rest, cooling now the central heating was off for the night.

Vicky bumped into the back of me and I refrained from smacking her about the head with the nearest cushion.

"I told you to wait outside," I scolded, not for the first time on a job. Vicky shrugged and smiled, as if saying what did I expect.

Sighing, I continued my silent, ninja-esque advance through the room, heading for the door. Vicky kept stepping on my heels, ruining my moves. I bet she touched stuff too, leaving evidence behind.

I adjusted the bag slung awkwardly over my shoulders backpack style but not really meant to be carried this way. It was heavy beyond measure, containing as it did items so numerous and varied that it was a wonder it could be lifted. I tapped Wand through my combats just to be sure he was awake.

"How you doing?" I asked silently.

"Ready to rock-n-roll. Hey, do you think the witches wander around in the buff if they need a pee? Should we check upstairs just in case we need to silence any of them?"

"No, I'm good." I shuddered. Last thing I needed was to witness any centuries-old naked witches flashing wrinkly flesh. I'd probably die before they did.

"Spoilsport."

"If you want to perv, then do it on your own time. You get plenty of time off."

"I'm a stick, I have no legs."

"There you go then. Now, be quiet, I need to focus."

I slid across the floor like Michael Jackson, poked my head around the doorway, then dashed down the hallway like a spider, blending into the shadows and absolutely not nearly knocking a lamp over that was balanced on a narrow table covered in misshapen rocks and bits of fossil.

Vicky scraped my heel with her stupid foot and I took three deep breaths in and out slowly to stop from battering her with said wobbly lamp.

Knowing the breathing wasn't enough, I crouched down low and stilled my mind, forced myself to not get annoyed. I wasn't nervous so much as excited. After all, I'd done this enough times before, but I did feel something different. The stakes were higher than usual for this one, and it wasn't just personal, just for money or kicks. I was acting to protect others, to save our community from the mad people.

But something wasn't right, and I don't mean Vicky.

Mind made up, I stood and turned to face my expectant partner in crime.

"We're leaving," I whispered, glancing around, ready to fend off whatever was coming.

"What? We can't. We're here, we almost have it."

"No, something's off. There's a weird vibe and this is not going to end well."

"Arthur, don't be silly."

"Vicky, I'm a pro, and if something doesn't feel right then you can bet your ass that I'm correct. Out. Now." I grabbed her by her jacket collar, turned her, then frogmarched her back to the window and said, "Out you go."

Vicky began to protest then saw my expression and reluctantly she exited through the window. I wiped down the sill and frame, climbed out after her, then used the cloths to pull the window closed before erasing our prints on the outside.

We sneaked away silently and it wasn't until we were back at the car that either of us spoke.

"What was that all about?" asked Vicky.

"I'm not sure, but I got a worrying feeling. We can't steal anything if we're dead, and I don't want to be dead. Better to come back again, try a different approach, not sure."

"You're acting strange." Vicky was clearly disappointed, but I was old enough to know you never ignored that inner sense that told you when something was wrong. I'd done it in the past to my peril, but I had to know what it was.

"Wait here."

"No way."

"Vicky, I'm serious. I'm going back to take a look around, quietly, and I don't want you to get hurt. This time, I want you to listen, and promise me you'll stay put. If anything goes wrong, I'll call, but don't call me. Last thing I need is my phone going off."

"Fine." Vicky was in a huff and I didn't blame her, but this was for her own good.

"I won't be long. Just need to check something out. Okay?"

"Whatever."

"This is for Ivan. I'm doing this for him as much as anyone else. You want it to go wrong?"

"No, of course not!"

"Then let me do this. I do not want this to go pear-shaped."

"Don't be long."

"I won't."

I headed back to the house, dawdling as I tried to figure out what my senses were telling me.

Glutton for Punishment

Why return?

Because something was telling me I had to. I knew there was a problem, that this would not end well. I should have driven away and remained safe, but I was certain that if this didn't happen tonight then it never would. It was crunch time, now or never. And I'd done what I needed to. Namely, keeping Vicky safe so she'd be there for the girls.

But I had to be cautious, tread carefully and do my utmost to keep this from blowing up spectacularly. What was wrong?

I couldn't put my finger on it. Was it that the alarms were disabled? Was this a trap? Had I been played from the get-go? No, Selma and her biddies were on the level, although deceptively manipulative.

Did Mabel know I was coming, and was waiting for me? It was a possibility, but a chance I was willing to take. One way or another, she had to be stopped. I knew taking the cauldron would only be the start of it, but had no other choice in the matter. I guess in my mind this was showing her that people were on to her. That she should think twice and that nowhere was safe.

What then?

Guess I'd find out.

I entered the building again, made it as far as the hallway before stopping in the same spot, waiting for inspiration to hit, some insight into the jitters that were growing by the second, spoiling my cool, calm demeanor. I was excited, looking forward to doing this and getting away, but that feeling was overridden by the knowledge that things were not how they appeared.

"Any ideas?" I asked Wand as I took him out and held him up.

"Yeah, go home."

"That's not much help."

"Oh, it's plenty of help. If you do that, we both survive. If you stay, then who knows?"

"But do you know what's wrong?"

"No, but something is. Something is very, very wrong, and if I could say that in a spooky voice then I would. That's how wrong it feels."

"Yeah, I get the same vibe. Keep an eye out. Keep all your eyes out."

"Will do."

I kept low, crept through the house, a maze of hallways and small rooms, closed doors and odd decor. There were branches and herbs, plants and strange things hanging from the ceilings, stuffed bears and countless creatures behind glass that would give a taxidermist nightmares.

Finally, I was outside the artifact room. I stopped, the dread creeping.

I spun away from facing the door, knowing I wouldn't like what I saw.

Standing before me in a large semi-circle were at least fifteen witches, all in night attire, all looking pissed off, all holding wands or staffs, some with cats rubbing up against their legs, several with ravens perched on their shoulders.

"Got a plan?" I asked Wand.

"I would say run, but I think it's too late for that."

"Yeah, me too."

So That's Why

I glanced nervously up and down the hall, the thought of running still the main focus. I wouldn't make it a step before they were on me. So, I waited.

They glared, they squinted, they vibed. They scared the hell out of me.

Even in their nighties or ancient pajamas they looked formidable. Old, wrinkly, sinewy arms clutched tight to wands or leaned on staffs that had clearly seen plenty of action.

These were not harmless old ladies who liked to play with herbs and spices, these were adepts. And there were loads of them.

Cats purred, others hissed, and tartan slippers plus a few pink ones with big pom-poms shifted as the women moved as one.

They edged away on one side, leaving me with an opening to go deeper into the house. Looked like I didn't have a choice, so I obliged, and walked backwards down the hall as they stared after me then followed.

As I moved, the tingling at my neck indicating something being very wrong increased until it was practically screaming at me. Every fiber of my being was telling me to run. To run fast and never look back. That nothing I saw or did here would be for the good, and all I'd get was sorrow and pain.

But I was trapped, and the idea of blasting them all didn't enter my head because I would lose and then I would be dead. So I did as I was silently told, and went where I was led, the women so close now I could smell their night creams and whatever other ineffective emollients they smothered on their crepey skin before they went to bed.

I backed through the door into the kitchen and the temperature rose several degrees. All I could hear was their raspy breathing and the sound of things bubbling away.

Something else too.

Fear. I could hear, and smell, fear. The deep, shallow breaths of people who were very afraid.

"My sisters, I apologize for waking you, but we have traitors in our midst and they have employed this man to steal from us."

The witches murmured and grumbled as they stared behind me at the person who had spoken. No prizes for guessing who.

"I have been informed of their treachery by one of our own, someone loyal, and now they must be punished. What do we do with traitors?"

"We kill them," said the women, speaking in unison like zombies, no emotion in their words.

These women were odd and then some. What was with them? Normally witches were all non-stop talking and mad energy, this lot seemed out of it, like they were under a spell. Maybe they were. Or maybe they were merely Mabel's most ardent followers so did exactly as they were told. That would explain why they were all older, and why they were all clearly so powerful. Her posse, I guess.

It was like a damn cult. Which, I guess most magic cliques are.

I figured now would be a good time to turn and see what the hell I was facing, but I was hesitant. I knew that once I did, things would get real, and I was in no mood for an epic battle to the death. I'd planned on being a ninja, not getting involved in this nonsense.

Reluctantly, I turned to face the room, and my fate.

Unexpected

The kitchen was larger than expected, a truly vast space. Dated, rammed full of cupboards of all description, heavy dressers laden with plates and weird items only witches knew the use for. Several modern ovens and induction hobs seemed out of place either side of an ancient, huge Rayburn. There was a cast iron range in the fireplace, a behemoth of a thing, ancient pots bubbling away.

Running down the center of the room was a battle-worn, scrubbed oak table, easily large enough to seat thirty. Nobody was sitting at it now.

Standing the other side of it was Queen Mabel, looking angry, powerful, and utterly deranged. Her gray hair caught the overhead lights, shining almost white, washing out her features. Dark shadows under angular cheekbones on her weathered face made her look gaunt. She wore a simple brown blouse and a pair of jeans, someone you wouldn't look twice at if you saw them on the street. Her fingers were adorned with rings, and she held a vicious knife in her right hand.

Next to her, Selma was shaking with fear. And next to Selma was the witch with the flowing skirt. She had betrayed the others.

Lined up on the table like meat for the butcher, were the witches I'd met earlier. They were trussed, then secured to the table in a row, ten witches each gagged and terrified. Looking back on it, I wonder why they didn't use every ounce of magic they had to extricate themselves, but I guess however Mabel had captured them had left them certain that if they fought back they would be killed outright. Now, they were merely hoping that she'd be merciful, would punish them but not take things to their inevitable, at least in my eyes, conclusion.

As the women struggled, Big Skirt mumbled under her breath and their bindings tightened, causing the women to gasp then still.

"Our sisters have betrayed us. They have conspired to deceive, and to stop our plans. They wish to remain outcasts, would see us fail. They deserve no forgiveness, they have cheated us. And you," Mabel turned to Selma, "you are young, have much to learn, but it is only because you are my blood that you will not meet the same end as your coven of filth!"

"Guess there's no coffee then?" I asked.

Mabel ignored me, acted like I wasn't even there, then she spoke. "This man would steal from us, from me! What do we do to thieves?"

"Let me guess? Kill them?" I interrupted before the others replied.

Without warning, Mabel lifted the knife as she held my gaze, and walked, almost casually, from one end of the table to the other. As she did so, she slit the throat of every woman tied there.

Selma collapsed, her legs giving way, and she whacked her head on the table as she fell to land in a heap on the once spotless quarry tiles, now pooling with liters of blood. Mabel grabbed her and picked her up like she weighed nothing, then leaned her against the counter, Selma neither comatose nor quite conscious.

The women behind me gasped. This was too much for them, too cold and heartless. There were murmurs of disapproval, even dissent, but they were silenced with a look from Mabel.

"Be gone, all of you. Let this be a reminder that I will not be stopped, that we will have our time and we do not turn our backs on one another."

The women retreated without a word; I doubted they'd get much sleep for the rest of the night.

It was then that the wall in the hall exploded.

Accidents Will Happen

It was eerily quiet for a moment as I ran back into the hall, then my ears began ringing. Women were screaming, but not many. Lying in broken heaps, covered in brick and bits of wall, were what remained of the witches. Most were dead, heads caved in, bodies broken beyond repair, several still clutching at life, but not for long.

Through the dust, I saw a familiar shape, but I must have been wrong, it couldn't be. I ran forward over the piles of flesh and brick, into the artifact room, what was left of it. The wall was almost entirely down, the door little but strips of curled steel, and there stood Vicky, staring numbly at her hands, and what she held.

"I just picked it up and it shot a... a ball of fire." She stared at the staff, an object so beautiful, so perfect in every way yet at the same time merely a long shaft of wood, that I understood.

Some artifacts are benign, and you have to know a lot about them, and be powerful, to ever activate them. Others are almost sentient, close to Wand's ability, a few are even more awake than him, activated by touch, even by thought. This was one of those items. Touch it without knowing what you're doing and it will try to destroy you and anything conscious around it. Vicky was lucky to be alive, but it wouldn't last long.

"Drop it, right now," I ordered.

She stared down at her hands as she strained, the knuckles white and the tendons proud as she tried to open her fingers. But the staff had other ideas, was waking up, and it needed touch to recover to true life.

"I'm trying, but it won't let me."

"What are you doing here? How did you get in? Why did you?"

"I didn't want to miss out, and I thought you were in here. Then I heard people coming so I panicked and broke the code on the door."

"I told you to wait at the car. Won't you ever learn?"

Vicky's eyes widened as she stared past me at the carnage of the dead bodies in the hall. "Oh my God, did I do that?"

"No, the staff did. Now drop it."

Vicky's jaw clenched as she struggled to release her fingers, and as she did she stumbled backward, banging into a large table with many artifacts laid out carefully. As she fell against the table, the staff snapped up and fired a pulse of red light that morphed into a fiery cannonball. It shot straight at the wall with the kitchen the other side.

Brick exploded, the room filled with dust, and as I reached out to grab Vicky the damn staff continued its upward trajectory and the shaft smacked with incredible force right into Vicky's forehead.

She dropped like a stone; the staff came loose as her body went limp.

"Maybe next time you'll do as I say," I muttered, although I doubted it.

I kicked the staff away and it fired once more then rolled into a dark space under a set of shelves. There was a scream from the kitchen. Hopefully Mabel was dying.

I checked on Vicky but it was hard to see with all the dust, and the only thing I knew for certain was that she had a pulse. Goddammit, why wouldn't she ever do as she was told?

"Sasha, that interfering you keep doing? Now would be a great time to do it again," I whispered into the air, holding my breath, hoping for faery dust to fall.

Nothing, just more of the brick and plaster variety.

The screams died down from the next room, so I edged carefully toward the kitchen, not needing to use the hall as the hole in the wall was massive and getting bigger as bricks dislodged.

I saw Selma on the floor, her arm at an obscene angle, bricks all around her, a massive cut on the side of her face, blood flowing freely.

And beside her, looking unfortunately very much alive, was Mabel.

I think she was annoyed with me now.

The Beginning of the End

I reached for Wand, but it was as though I was moving through molasses, everything slow and heavy, the air, and seemingly time itself, fighting me.

Mabel cackled.

I forged on, knowing I had to get Wand and get him quick if I was to leave this place alive, never mind save my fool of a sidekick.

"You don't know who you're messing with, little man. You don't know what this room contains, what treasures you have disturbed. This is the home of the witches, the Residence, did you genuinely believe you could come in here and steal from us? From me?"

"I was gonna give it a go, only to keep the peace," I said, the words coming out slow and slurred. Even my tongue felt like it was weighed down.

"Enough of your foolishness. You will never leave here, and I will have my place in the world of magic." Mabel stared at something in the room, without once physically moving towards me, and then she twisted her head sharply until her gaze returned to lock on mine.

What was that about?

I soon found out as a sharp pain stabbed into my side and I jumped back as another pain hit me on the leg, then the arm, then seemingly everywhere at once. My bag, still secured on my back, felt like thousands of the dislodged bricks had been rammed inside, and I struggled to keep on my feet.

Strange tendrils were piercing my clothes and flesh, silver strands that pulsed as a white, milky light spasmed through them, leading away from my body to a large ball on a small table.

"Yes, I have it, and many other artifacts you have only dreamed of. Your magic will be devoured, and then you will be nothing."

Mabel chortled as I struggled to get this thing off me. I felt myself weaken, felt life force and magic being drained, sapped of my power as a wizard, the same for Wand.

I didn't know what this artifact was, but I'd seen weirder, only knew that I had to extricate myself or I was done for. I thrashed, I stumbled, I crashed into tables. I smashed against walls, I picked up rubble and attacked the tendrils as thin as a finger but as one was broken off or retreated so another shot out to take its place.

I knocked over countless artifacts, something I hit flaring into life, exploding up and destroying the ceiling. Plaster, dust, and wood rained down, making it impossible to see, but I knew where I was so grabbed hold of something cold and hard. As I fumbled with the bag and stuffed the item inside, Wand vibrated in my pocket.

"It's now or never, buddy. You want me to, or try to save it for later?" Wand asked.

"If you don't do this now, there will be no later," I grunted, then hoisted the bag onto my back again and readied for the nightmare I knew was to come.

"Your funeral," said Wand, with a symbolic shrug.

"Yours too, if it comes to that."

Wand flared through my pocket, then magic engulfed us, spasming out and impossibly bright, causing more destruction to the room, burning up delicate artifacts, sending others screaming for the corners, the whole room erupting in disarray as objects large and small scattered in all directions.

The tendril attack vanished in an instant, the artifact either destroyed or damaged enough to keep its distance, but at a severe cost.

I felt my energy drain like a large plug had been pulled, leaving me a husk of a man, empty of the good stuff. Wand was still.

An intense tiredness enveloped me, so extreme I had to struggle to remain upright as all I wanted to do was to sleep and never, ever wake up. But I had to. This woman had to be stopped. I had to fight on and I had to beat her, but how?

The dust cleared, there were no more screams as everyone else was either dead or unconscious, and I staggered forward.

I fell immediately, devoid of energy, exposed, alone, and not in the best of positions for the epic battle that was yet to even begin.

Better Than Magic

I clambered awkwardly to my feet, clutching the side of the destroyed wall for assistance. Brick crumbled to dust under my touch, the wall collapsing and me along with it. As I toppled sideways and got a mouthful of mortar, I cursed out loud, then my body trembled as more bricks tumbled from the other side of the opening, pummeling my body like rain sent down by angry gods to destroy what little was left of The Hat.

Refusing to give in, even as my body protested and my clothes tore, my flesh was ripped, and my bones were dented yet somehow not breaking, I stood, tearing away the Velcro on my side pocket.

Wand was deep in slumber, the lucky sod, and yet I had to wake him if I was to survive this. We were too closely connected, he a manifestation of me and my energy, me a reflection of him, our combined magic inseparable. I shook him desperately even as the woman I'd severely underestimated stepped around the table and sneered. Wand was comatose, he wasn't going to wake up any time soon.

My magic was non-existent, I was truly running on fumes, but I did all I could and put up as strong a defensive barrier as I could muster under the circumstances. Those being, I was utterly exhausted, weak beyond anything I'd experienced for years, my shoulders sagging, my knees ready to buckle, feeling like I carried the weight of the world.

I felt the familiar tingle of magic encompassing my body, my confidence rising as I forced my will to hold on to this sliver of protection that would save my life. I moved awkwardly over the bricks, dust billowing in my wake as I repeatedly lost my footing. How I didn't twist my ankle is a miracle but my hands were cut to ribbons as I kept falling.

Clear of the carnage, I focused on the magic, the only thing that made any sense, then panicked as Mabel smiled a knowing smile. I felt it a moment after, the stuttering like the flame on a lighter as it runs out of fuel.

My body shook, the magic drifted away, and then it died.

Wand had done all he could to help, was way beyond that now, so I pocketed him to keep my friend safe, or as safe as I could.

"You will pay for this destruction," said Mabel as she reached into a satchel on the counter beside her and pulled out something unexpected.

"A gun?"

"Why not? You wizards are so foolish. Witches have intelligence. Sometimes magic is the answer, sometimes not. Why waste a good spell when you can use a tool much easier to control?"

She had a point, but it wasn't the done thing. This simply wasn't playing by the rules.

Mabel lifted her right arm, closed one eye, took time to adjust her aim, then fired.

I died along with the magic.

A Familiar Meeting

On the pebble beach of Imaginary Figure of Death's timeless home—although I should stop calling him that as this was definitely no figment of my exhausted imagination—I glanced up at the myopic, endless sky, took in the whispering, lapping waters at the shores of whatever purgatory awaited me one day, and stared down the beach until the repetitive nature of this place began to make my head swim.

"Shit," I groaned, which I felt was apt, if a little too tame. Talk about inconvenient, and altogether unwanted.

Not only was this bad timing, but I'd been dreading my next encounter with Death as he'd been in a peculiar mood the last year or so. First he was happy, which was perturbing, then he'd been miserable, and questioning the point of existence, which was even more worrying. Death can't be the one having an existential crisis, that was reserved for those of us who were alive. Were being the operative word at the moment. I was currently dead, and that's no way to win an epic battle against an all-powerful witch. Especially when she's got a gun.

"Kevlar, I need Kevlar," I noted, wondering if they made nice shirts, or maybe jackets, in material that could stop bullets. Maybe I could get one to deflect magic too, that would be awesome. I added it to the list of things I wished I had but probably never would, and focused on the here and now. The sooner I got out of here the better, but I suppose a plan when I returned wouldn't go amiss.

I searched the shore for Death. He was usually there being dramatic, standing facing the gray waters where you sailed away on the final voyage.

He was missing.

"Huh?"

Death was always here, it was his thing. He set the tone by looking all menacing in his tattered black cloak, his infinite scythe, the Grim Reaper vibe making you want to get on with the whole sorry business and go meet your fate.

Except I was different. Sasha had bestowed seemingly endless lives upon me and I had entries spanning multiple pages in Death's ledger. Sure, they'd run out eventually, and I wasn't sure when, but surely today wasn't that day?

There was no way to find out if the big fella wasn't around.

Was this how it worked if it was your time? Did he not bother to appear and you just slunk off to your fate? No, this was his job. He had to be here; it was how it all worked.

"Hello?"

Nothing, not even an echo, just my voice being sucked away into infinity, leaving me feeling cold and desolate and a little unsure of myself.

Ten minutes later, and I was done with the desolation and uncertainty. I was merely antsy. Where the fuck was Death when you needed him? Didn't he know I had shit I needed to do? Like throw my morals away and beat the crap out of Mabel. If I could, obviously.

I should have listened more closely to what Selma had been telling me. Namely, Mabel was truly mad, and extremely dangerous. I hadn't considered the state she must have been in to believe it was a viable option for gaining power. It was kinda obvious looking back at it—she was nuts and then some. Maybe even suicidal. In fact definitely suicidal.

Where the hell was Death?

I checked behind me, just on the off chance there was something to break the monotony. How did he handle this? Everything was so damn boring, so samey. No wonder he was depressed.

The beach was the same, no surprises there. But the more I looked, the more I was certain there was a tiny dark shape way off in the distance. So, for the first time, I went for a walk in the place Death called home. I wondered what he did call it. Limbo? Maybe his own private purgatory?

The going was tough and slow. The pebbles, although small, hurt my feet, and I kept sliding down the slight incline, as though the water was calling to me, wanting to clutch me in its cold embrace and never let me surface again. It began to freak me out so I moved away from the shore and continued.

After what felt like numerous exceedingly boring lifetimes, I finally seemed to be getting somewhere. My vision was blurry—no change in scenery can do funny things to your eyes—but after several wipes with my sleeve, I got my focus back and was sure it was Death.

I crunched forward, making one hell of a racket, but the figure never moved. Maybe it wasn't him after all. But what else could it be?

As I got close there was no doubt, this was Death all right, but still he didn't move or even acknowledge me.

Slowing, I considered my options. I had none. Freaked out, but with no choice, and my usual cockiness gone under such a weird vibe, I stepped up beside Death and stared up at the towering figure of the immortal creature responsible for helping every soul transition. At least that used to be the way of things. Now I wasn't so sure. Last meeting he'd said a lot of oddball stuff, and I was doubting everything I knew about the afterlife.

Death turned fractionally and looked down at me. I stared into the absolute blackness beneath the cowl, no hint of the person or thing hidden in there somewhere.

"Hi." I smiled my most winningest of smiles, but he just kept staring.

"It's me. Arthur. Did you miss me?"

"Go away."

"That's not very nice. How are you feeling? You were a bit down in the dumps last time."

Nothing. Just more stares.

"Hey, what's up?"

"Go away."

"I would if I could."

Death shrugged his bony shoulders almost imperceptibly and lifted his head. The familiar table dropped down to land on the beach followed by the largest, heaviest book you're ever likely to see. The ledger thudded onto the desk and dust billowed. The pages snapped open, a quill darted from the sky, dipped angrily into an inkwell, then slashed across the page, presumably putting a line through my name.

Without warning, the book slammed shut, shot skyward, the table the same, and I stumbled as my head went woozy and a familiar feeling washed over me.

"Hey, I'm not ready yet. I thought we were friends?"

Too late, I was going right back to the land of the living, but I was in no position to do so. I hadn't thought this through. Encounters with Death took no time at all, meaning, I'd be standing right in front of Mabel, or lying more likely, with a fast-repairing hole somewhere nasty, and she still had a loaded gun. How many bullets did modern weaponry hold? I wasn't up on guns, it wasn't the wizardly way to shoot someone with a tiny lump of metal when you could blast them and make their head explode anyway.

I gasped for air. My hand went to my forehead where I poked around a fast healing hole.

Guess Kevlar wouldn't be much good if you got shot in the head.

"So, it's true?" asked Mabel, looking impressed.

"True?"

"About your extra lives?"

"I guess."

"Let's see how many you've got."

Mabel let loose.

Ugh

Same sky. Same beach. Same water. Same old shit.

Except things weren't the same. Nowhere near it.

Never once in the many lives I had lost due to idiocy or accident, weariness or lack of magic, had I been killed twice in strict succession like this. I'd lost count now of how many times I'd died, but I think it was maybe ten. Each time I returned, I extricated myself from the situation, but not this time.

I couldn't just go back. She'd shoot me again, wouldn't she? Maybe not. Maybe she'd do something else and I'd have a chance to escape. But how? I needed to think, to plan something, assuming this wasn't the final time.

And to be honest, I was a little miffed with Death. Why was he being so stand-offish? What gave him the right to treat me like this? Just because he was having a bad day didn't mean he could screw around with my life. Not that he really had, but I was somewhat out of sorts after being shot twice.

And so it was, with a deep sigh, and trepidation in my heart, that I turned and trudged down the beach to the remote figure once more.

"Before you do anything, can you maybe talk to me?" I asked as I stood in a repeat of last time, staring up at the towering figure.

"I said go away." Death turned from me, like that would make his request happen.

"I can't. I just got killed again. Any ideas about that? Can you help me out here?"

"Not my department. Thought you didn't like it here? Last time I wanted you to stay you were in a mad rush to get back."

"That's because you killed me, made me think I had a heart attack. I was annoyed."

"There you go then."

"What does that even mean?"

"Just go away." Death searched the sky and right on cue the table and book slammed down. This time he didn't even bother with the dust effect. He was definitely feeling down as he lived—or died—for this stuff. The pen darted down and wriggled about in the viscous ink like it was trying to stab it into submission and then the quill rose, splashing ink all over the open pages, poised to put a line through my name yet again.

"Wait! I want to ask you something. Please? I don't know how many chances I have left."

"Tough. Not my problem."

Death sliced a vague blurry outline I assumed was a finger through the air and the pen slashed harshly at the page.

I wobbled, I went all fuzzy, and then he spun his scythe right at my neck, as if to prove his point.

I gasped, sucking down air and brick dust.

As I scrambled about amid bits of wall, I poked at my forehead, my finger going surprisingly deep before it popped out as the wound healed, and I stared up at the barrel of a gun.

"That's very impressive," said Mabel. "Let's see how it goes this time."

She pressed the barrel against my forehead, the steel burning hot, making my skin sizzle. Her trigger finger twitched a moment before my head exploded.

I ducked down and clutched my head then sat on a pebble beach in what I was now sure was my afterlife.

This was it. I was already dead after the first shot and this was my purgatory. To relive over and over the final moments of my life until I was driven insane and there was nothing left of the old Hat.

Or, and I was kind of banking on this one, I was being fucked with by a deranged witch and Death was pissed off with me so wasn't being much help.

I needed a plan. And quick.

Death appeared beside me, holding the ledger in one hand, quill in another.

"You're beginning to annoy me," he said, sounding so depressed I wanted to give him a cuddle.

"And you're beginning to make it fucking hard to be your friend. What is this? Why are you doing this?"

"I'm not doing anything. You have your extra lives, so I'm letting you use them. What else am I supposed to do?"

He had a point. "Um, you could delay things a while, leave me looking dead for a few hours, then I could make my escape."

"That's not how it works."

"It works however you want it to," I shouted.

"Correct."

And with that, Death crossed out my name for the third time in as many mortal seconds.

Oh

I could still hear the crack of gunfire, and I panicked. More than that, I utterly freaked. Even as I was considering freaking out, then proceeding to do so, I lost the ability to think. I felt my brains being blown out the back of my head, sensed the loss of the old gray matter as a bullet exploded through my skull, splintering bone. I'd come back a split second too soon and was still experiencing the effects of the death I'd returned from.

Mabel stepped back, seemingly satisfied, as I gasped and felt consciousness return, and with it one hell of a pain. I felt the bone snap back into place, neurons reconfigure, and the hole in my forehead close up, slower than last time.

Mabel actually looked surprised, and I guess I did too. Who wouldn't?

"You really are the lucky one, aren't you?"

"Yeah, that's me. Mr. Lucky," I gasped, clawing at the bricks, trying to get up and away from this Groundhog Day of death.

"Oh no you don't," she said with a tut. "Stay right here. I haven't finished with you yet."

"Let me guess, you want to tell me off then send me on my way?"

"Not quite. Let's see how long this goes on for."

Mabel took careful aim then shot me again.

Getting Miffed

I hardly had time to see the quill flick ink and the ledger slam shut before Death swung at me again.

"Hello," said Mabel.

I gasped, "Hi."

Mabel pulled the trigger.

On a Loop

I opened my eyes.

The quill struck the page.

Death swung his scythe.

I gasped, then smiled at Mabel. "Guess who?"

"My, this is fun."

Mabel fired.

Ad Infinitum

The quill struck. Death swung. I gasped.

The gun fired. I died. The quill struck. Death swung.

The gun fired. I died. The quill struck. Death swung.

The gun fired. The quill. Swing.

Gun. Quill. Swing.

Dead. Dead. Dead.

On and on.

How many bullets did this woman own?

How many more chances did I have?

Gun. Quill. Swing.

Gun. Quill. Swing. Duck.

"Ha, you missed." I smiled a smug smile but it soon faded as Death just waved a hand and I returned to the land of the living.

"I knew that bloody scythe was just symbolic," I muttered.

"What's that?" asked Mabel.

"Oh, nothing. Carry on."

Mabel shrugged then fired again.

As the quill dripped ink and readied to strike, I launched forward and grabbed the mighty tome in hands so covered in brick dust they were red.

"You can't do that," said Death, surprised.

"Watch me." I clutched the book tight to my chest and did a runner down the beach.

"This is my realm, you can't run from me," said Death as he kept pace with me, seemingly without effort, while I ran as fast as I could.

"I can try. I'm fed up getting shot, and you're not being fair. Since when were we enemies? I thought we were friends."

"You made it very clear we weren't friends last time. I wanted to talk, but you couldn't get away fast enough."

"I was kind of in the middle of a crisis."

"You were smoking a cigarette."

"No, that's not exactly true. I'd finished, and was heading back inside to try to figure out how to protect my family from a raving lunatic."

"That's just an excuse." Death snatched the book from me and I came to a standstill even though my legs were still moving like I was running. I looked down only to find I was several inches off the ground.

"Guess I'll stop doing the running thing," I sighed.

So I did. And Death clicked his fingers and I was back in the world of the insane once again.

"Can we talk about this?" I asked Mabel as she raised the gun.

"Nope, I'm good."

Mabel fired.
I died.
This would end soon.
No way was anyone this lucky.
Not even The Hat.

Growing Concerned

"Hello," said Death, somehow sounding more perky.

"Um, hi?" I ventured, not sure where this was going, only knowing it wouldn't be in my favor.

"Are you bored yet?" Death cocked his head slightly.

"Getting there. More worried than anything. This can't go on forever."

"True. Nobody has infinite lives. I mean, where would the fun be in that?"

"Fair point. So, what's up?" I clambered slowly to my feet, the pebbles hurting my knees, although they should have been the least of my concerns.

"You don't want to know. You're just making conversation so you don't have to go back and lose yet another life." Death looked skyward and held out his hands. The ledger landed in his outstretched arms with a thud and the familiar dust. Guess he was feeling a little better.

"I admit, I'm a little preoccupied, but I thought we had an understanding. I know I was mad last time, but there's something up. You can tell me, maybe I can help."

"You can't, but you can." Death sounded conflicted, as though he was holding back on saying something. Why can't people, and immortal entities, just get to the point?

"If you don't want to tell me..."

"It isn't that." Death glided close and whispered in my ear, "There are rules."

A shiver ran down my spine, his words like worms wriggling into my brain and chewing away important bits. "You're fed up. It's getting boring. But you were happy before. Can you tell me anything about that?"

"Not really. There was a chance, of change, but it fell through. That's all I can say."

"Nothing else?"

"No. If you were... Ah, never mind. I can't discuss it."

"If you're sure?"

"I am." Death's shoulders sagged; he really was in a bad way. What could this possibly be about? What was affecting him so deeply? And how badly would this impact on me and my current predicament?

"Hey, don't suppose you can tell me how many entries I have left? I'm getting a little stressed that the next bullet could be the final one."

Death glanced down at the ledger, quill suddenly in hand, and struck a line through my name. "One less than before, that's all I can say. But my advice, if you want to live to a ripe old age, is to be careful about getting killed from now on. I know what you wizards are like, you always meet a gruesome end eventually, so if you want that to happen then don't keep getting shot at such a young age. You're only in your forties, you could have many centuries if you play your cards right."

"Thanks for the heads-up." I felt worse than ever. A beautiful, long, exhausting, and stressful future awaited me if I stopped getting caught up in stupid shit. I merely had to figure out a way to avoid said nonsense.

"My pleasure." Death kicked at the pebbles with feet clouded by mist, sending them sailing through the air. They landed in the water with a plonk. What was with this guy?

"Is there anything I can do to help?"

"There is, but you can't."

"Why not?"

"Because I can't tell you. The rules, remember?"

"Yeah, right. Can I guess?"

"No, because you never will. And I'm not allowed to help."

"Man, the law's tough around here, isn't it?"

Death nodded.

"So," I said, rubbing at the pebbles with my foot, not sure how best to approach this. "Um, don't suppose there's any way you can help me out here?"

"Can't interfere."

"Right. Um, what about letting me stay for a while so she thinks I'm dead and just buggers off somewhere?"

"No can do. It doesn't matter how long you stay here, at least as a mortal, when you return hardly any time will have passed. Or, hey," Death brightened, "maybe years will have passed. It's out of my control. It's all built in, works however it wants."

"Ah, right." I tried to think back to all my previous deaths; it was always a second or two I was gone at most. Guess I'd drawn the short straw when it came to being lucky in death. Apart from the extra lives, of course.

"So... Any news?" asked Death.

"You know, the usual."

"Right."

"What the fuck is wrong with you?" I spluttered. "Of course there's news. I'm facing certain death as I keep getting shot in the fucking head!" Looking back on it, I may have overreacted. I certainly misjudged how much of a downer Death was currently on.

"I knew you were mean!" Death clicked his fingers and I was gasping for breath once more.

I put my fingers to my eyes as I couldn't seem to see out of the left one. Hardly surprising, as when I poked around all I felt was a gaping hole.

"Ugh, so gross," said Mabel with a frown.

"Then stop fucking shooting me in the face," I screamed, losing my cool entirely, panic settling in and making itself at home for the foreseeable future.

"When you stop returning to life, I'll stop shooting." Mabel slammed a cartridge into the underside of the gun with a loud snick, then took aim once more.

"So you haven't run out of bullets and decided I'm too much of a danger to you and you're gonna do a runner and give up all plans to dominate the underworld?"

"No, but I do have a nice surprise for you."

"And what's that?" I may have squealed a little at this point as my eyeball popped back into existence and the result was me with a finger stuck fast in newly formed gelatinous liquid. I pulled it out with a sickening squelch and moments later the eyesight cleared and all was right in the world. Not.

"You can have a choice this time." Mabel reached behind her and pulled out what looked suspiciously like a short sword. It shone bright even in the gloom and through the still falling brick dust. Looked as sharp as Death's.

"I'll stick to the gun if you don't mind."

"Thought you'd say that. Blade it is then," she chirruped happily.

And with that, quick as a flash, Mabel pounced on me. The last thing I saw, and felt, was the sword arcing before it hacked right into the side of my neck.

Decapitation by witch, who wudda thunk it?

A New One

"That's it," I mumbled. "You have to do something."

Death looked down at me for the longest time, then, ever so slowly, he began to vibrate. As I stared, the vibrations got faster until his whole body was shaking so much I thought he'd rattle himself to pieces.

"What? Are you laughing? What's so funny?"

"You look so silly," he chortled once he got himself together, which was more than could be said for me. "Your head is under your arm."

"I know that! She chopped the bloody thing off. But this is on you. There's no reason why I shouldn't have my head where it belongs when I'm here. It's degrading."

"Sorry, thought it would make it a little more interesting. I assumed you'd like it."

"Like it? Like it! Of course I don't bloody like it. I'm dead and my head's been chopped off. What's there to like?"

"Keeps things fresh." Death shrugged.

I put a hand to the space above my shoulders, pleased to find my head was there. No hat though. She'd knocked my bloody hat off. This was going too far.

"I'll give you fresh," I snapped.

"What does that mean?"

"Um, not sure," I said, deflated. I think at this point I was becoming somewhat depressed.

Here came the ledger. Here came the quill. Here came another strike through.

"Just send me back. I'm not in the mood for this."

"As you wish."

Death readied to swing his scythe at my neck.

"Seriously? Don't you think that's in rather bad taste?"

"Oops. My bad." Death chuckled, then clicked his fingers. Guess he'd at least cheered up.

This time I was ready.

I had a cunning plan. That, or it would all go tits up and I'd be back before Death stopped laughing.

Make or Break

"Death wasn't amused by that," I said, making sure to stare Mabel right in the eye as I put Grace back where she belonged.

"I thought it was rather entertaining," she said, smiling wryly as she stepped away after hacking my head off.

I couldn't help wonder how it looked to her, seeing my head pop back into place and all the grisly regrowth that went along with it.

"He didn't. I mentioned you, you know. Told him who was doing this, who was causing him all this trouble." As I spoke, I winced as I angled sideways on my uncomfortable bed of bricks as if I was trying to ease my obvious pain. As the Velcro ripped, I coughed to cover the noise. Not that she was worried about me reaching for Wand anyway. She knew as well as I did that he was useless at the moment, but I didn't want to push my luck, not yet.

"I'm not the one causing trouble," snapped Mabel.

"That's not how he sees it. He's pissed off. He's got other clients, doesn't want to keep seeing my ugly mug."

"So hurry up and die. I'm busy too. You think I want to keep killing you?"

"You could always stop."

"I will, when you die for good."

"Haha," I exclaimed as I pulled Wand out and waved him about.

"Oh, please. He's useless, we both know that. You're spent, so is he. I know how wands work. I am a witch. A witch who has bettered you, I might add." Mabel couldn't resist smiling smugly at the thought of having finally bested a powerful wizard. Guess she had confidence issues.

"Then at least allow me to hold him while you administer my medicine," I said meekly. "I don't want to go out alone."

"So be it. You are a foolish man for believing you could better me. I am more powerful than you, can harness more magic, and look at you, lying down, accepting your fate like the weakling you are." Mabel was full of scorn, and damn haughty with it. Nobody likes a show-off.

She was right about one thing though, she was more powerful than me, had more control over magic, and was much older with plenty more experience. Not that she'd done anything but shoot me so far, but I'd heard the stories, knew what I was up against.

But I had one thing on my side.

Conviction.

And Wand, and Mabel, were about to witness just how far I would go in order to win.

I hate losing, I also hate smug. And haughty. It's so condescending it makes my blood boil. Nobody is better than anyone else just because they have more skill or ability. It doesn't make you a better person, and without humility to go along with it, it makes you a much lesser person than the one you're standing on and lording it over.

I lifted Wand, currently nothing more than a nice comfortable stick to hold, then made up my mind. No going back.

As Mabel raised the gun, with a smug smile, ready to play her game of let's see how long it takes Arthur to die for real, I gripped Wand with both hands, turned him horizontal, bent my legs, and pulled him down toward a knobbly knee with every intention of snapping him in two.

Hard Wood

Mabel's eyes widened as Wand came at my knee with enough force to break him clean in two.

You didn't do this, not ever. It would be like a witch breaking the neck of a cat familiar, or strangling her raven. Familiars, sentient objects, wands, staffs, even cloaks—although who in their right mind would want to wear sentient clothing?—were never destroyed by owners as the bond was too great. It was like murdering a part of yourself. No, they passed on when the owner died, a little piece of them along with it.

But I would do this, I would see it through. My magical will may have been all dried up, same as Wand's, but my will as a man, to do what I said I would, was still intact and I would not be stopped.

Mabel's arm was still rising and I saw the panic in her eyes. She wanted Wand for herself, knew what potential lay within the faery wood as he aged and matured.

Wand hit my knee as Mabel fired, the splintering louder than the crack of the gun as the bullet was ejected from the barrel at an ungodly speed.

Exploding Wood

The conversation went something like this, all done and dusted in basically zero time. Less a conversation than a rapid exchange of emotions that flowed like words but I knew was much deeper, comprised of feelings, understanding, and acceptance.

"Hey, what the hell?" said Wand, waking from his slumber as the certainty of my choice of action slammed into his sleeping mind like a shockwave.

"Sorry, no choice."

"No way, buster."

"Up to you," I said, nonchalantly.

"You wouldn't, would you?"

"I have to."

"But I know you won't."

"I already am. I'm breaking you in two, then you'll be no more. Dead."

"But I am you, you are me. I can read your mind, can see that you're doing this so I will save the day. That you're banking on this risk of annihilation to wake me up and force me to draw on magic from somewhere to save us both."

"That's right. So you're aware I'm doing this, right now, and will go through with it if you don't do something? And anyway, what if I'd been killed for real?"

"Course I'm aware. I'm a bloody smart stick. The smartest."

"Then get to it, because you've got about a millisecond before you're broken clean in two. I already heard the splintering of your physical being, so if you don't stop it right now you're a goner, mate."

"Damn, but you're mean."

"Hey, it's this or I get killed and you spend the rest of your days hanging around with Mabel. How's that sound?"

"She has boobs," said Wand, clearly considering a lifetime spent maybe tucked down her bra or something equally unlikely and certainly less than arousing.

Wand clearly made up his mind, as pain flared in my hands until I was certain he was melting them and leaving me with the new nickname, Mr. Stumpy.

Time returned to something approaching normal in a sudden whoosh of violent eruptions.

As the gun went off, Wand stiffened, the result being that it felt like I was trying to break an iron bar over my knee as he hardened himself, repairing the damage already done as the sigils flared.

"Where's my fucking finger?" I screamed.

"Had to get the magic from somewhere, smartass," said Wand, sounding smug.

Have I mentioned I hate smug? And that I also enjoy my fingers? I use them for pointing, and other stuff.

Nobody Listens

Have you ever watched with magic-infused sight as a bullet speeds towards your face?

Neither have I, as they move really fucking fast. I imagined it though, pictured the bullet coming right at me, and it wasn't fun.

As Wand erupted into life, the sigils flaring, the power thrumming through my hand, the air alive with unknowable forces, I willed something, anything, to protect me from getting punctured yet again. My luck was definitely running out, some would say it already had, but no way was I going out for the final time like this.

What felt like a train smashing into my skull—a bullet train, haha—sent me reeling backward, cracking my head on a pillow of bricks. As my vision cleared and the pain engulfed me, I understood that I hadn't died, but wasn't so sure it was worth the cost. My vision was clouded, but returned to clarity as the shield protecting my face faded along with Wand's help.

It was enough though, and Mabel would pay for her cockiness. I leaned forward and grabbed for the gun, getting a hand on the barrel. It burned my flesh so badly that I could smell myself cooking, and my grip was less than it should have been thanks to the missing fingertip. But I yanked, and Mabel's trigger finger broke with a satisfying crunch as I twisted the gun.

She screamed and I wasted no time. Hell, she hadn't even used magic yet and she'd already bested me multiple times.

I crawled over the brick, my body protesting as wounds tore wider, new ones were added to my already ravaged knees, and I even scraped my shins, which always seems to hurt the worst. My finger throbbed, and my head pounded like the worst hangover I'd ever had. I scrambled faster as Mabel backed away, muttering under her breath, the air taking on a strange hue as magic gathered. Searching frantically, I cursed myself for being an idiot and grabbed a brick with my left hand. Without hesitation, I slammed it into her gun hand, breaking the rest of her fingers, stopping her forming her spell with one fell swoop. She screamed again and I swung wildly, but with all the force I could muster, and smashed the brick into her temple.

It split in two and fell. Mabel fell right along with it, out cold.

My world was one of pain and noise as I became aware of my surroundings. Women were moaning and screaming, so the witches obviously hadn't all died. I scooted manically, failing miserably to avoid the witches' blood that dripped slowly now, a slick sea of thick dark tar across the floor. Selma was sitting in the middle of it, slumped against the cupboards, still out cold. I checked her for a pulse. She was alive, so I shook her until she woke up.

"You okay?" I asked, knowing it was a stupid question.

"I'm so sorry. What have I done?"

"It's not your fault. But I told you this was a bad idea."

"I'm sorry." Selma moved, wincing with the pain, but she didn't cry out, didn't complain. Her face was a mess. A massive gaping cut ran from her eye down to her lip, a huge bruise on her head the size of an egg looked ready to pop.

"These things happen," I grunted, and cried out as I got to my feet using the table for support. Guess she was braver than me.

"I have to check on Vicky."

Selma nodded and I moved away.

Getting back into the artifact room was a lesson in pain, but I endured, even though every nerve was alight. Vicky was stirring, but she was a mess too. Battered, bruised, lumpy in all the wrong places, groggy, and not really with it at all.

"I told you to wait in the car," I said softly.

"I don't like missing out," she said with a weak smile before her eyes rolled up and she lost consciousness.

"Idiot," I whispered, before I scooped her up and carried her through the hole in the wall into the hallway, leaving the hurt women there to manage themselves, my priority Vicky.

Outside, I sat her against the wall and dropped the bag from my shoulders, fumbled about inside, and pulled out the wrong item repeatedly until I found what I wanted.

"Take this," I ordered.

Vicky took it without even looking, then her eyes widened as she realized what I'd given her.

"Yes, it's the Teleron, so be bloody careful. Think about home, very carefully, and absolutely nowhere the children could possibly be, or you might end up fused to them and that won't be pretty. Then turn this." I showed her what to do then nodded.

"But I can't leave you here," she protested.

"You can, and you will. You have to get home, sort the girls out in the morning, and get yourself fixed. I'll be back later in the day, but this mess needs to be cleaned up. Somehow. Got it?"

"No, Arthur, I can't."

"Vicky, you will do as you are told for once. Look at this place, the mess we're in. We should never have agreed to help. This is our fault, and now we have to get on with life. So go home, and do not," I warned, "let the girls see the Teleron or know about it. Understand?"

"I understand."

"Good, now go."

Vicky hesitated. I could tell she wasn't going to use it.

"If you don't use that thing right this second, I will never, ever, take you on a job with me again. If I can't rely on you to do as I ask when it's life or death then that's it. We're done."

She knew I meant it.

She mouthed a silent, "Sorry," then closed her eyes, stuck out her tongue to the side as she concentrated, then twisted the dial and was gone.

Right, now I just needed to figure out what to do.

I walked back to the house, knowing there was no good resolution to this.

Busy Boy

At the front door, I changed my mind and made a detour, heading over to the extensive workshops and sheds. Inside a large tool shed, the place musty and dark, full of spiders and other nasties, I hunted about until I found what I wanted.

Heavy pick in hand, spade slung over my shoulder, I wandered around to the back and found a suitable spot in a clearing where the grass was short but it was nice and sheltered from the wind and I had light from the windows.

I began to dig.

The first contact with the earth felt like the last, the ground so hard and heavy I regretted my decision instantly, but I ignored my screaming muscles, the pain in my knees, the bleeding gashes and the utter agony of my already torn hands as they gripped the cold wooden handle of the pick.

Over and over, I used as much force as I could muster to dig, the going easier the deeper I dug and the further away I got from the frozen topsoil. I'm no gardener, but it was nice to see the worms going about their business, oblivious to the goings-on of the idiot humans above ground. They were content with their lot, lived a life without care or concern, merely knew what they had to do and got on with it without complaint.

Like an automated scarecrow, I swung, ripping through tufts of grass, tearing at the earth then scooping it out with the shovel. My back was on fire, the muscles straining against such unusual activity. I'd be bloody sore after this, but it wouldn't matter. I had so many injuries that tired muscles were the least of my concerns. So I continued, digging throughout the night, never stopping, forcing my body to keep working, calling on mental and physical reserves I by rights shouldn't have.

So much death, why was there always so much death? And how could I stop it? I couldn't. I was as much a part of the problem as everyone else. This was the way we were, how we acted, our solution to all our woes.

I paused to wipe the sweat from my brow and rested on the handle of the pick.

Faery dust fell into the holes and my faery godmother stood beside me looking resplendent in a bright red, and very tight, sparkly dress.

"I'm here. Sorry about the delay," said Sasha as she searched for enemies to destroy.

"You're too late, it's over," I said, not believing it for one minute, but wishing with all my remaining energy that it was.

"Sorry, my love. I mistimed my assistance. But you are alive, and well?"

"I'm alive, but not well. Have you ever dug a large hole?"

Sasha arched a perfect eyebrow as she held out her hands and showed me her delicate fingers and perfect nails. "I am a faery, I do not dig in the dirt."

"Didn't think so. You should try it some time, it's good for the soul."

"My soul is perfectly fine, thank you very much."

"Just a suggestion. Hey, let me ask you something."

"Anything. And please, call me if you need me, I will come to your aid."

"I did call you, and you didn't come. I'm not blaming you, I don't expect you to get me out of the trouble I cause, but yeah, I called."

"Please forgive me, Arthur, I am not myself at the moment. I can't seem to get things to flow properly. It's always a problem for the fae when they come to the human realm."

"I know. Don't sweat it. Now, this question. How well do you know Death?"

Sasha shifted almost imperceptibly, but I noted the change in her body language. "Not very well. We have met, have spoken on occasion. He is a strange fellow."

"And he's okay with this extra life thing?"

"He accepts it. It's not how it usually works, as you know, but he makes exceptions." Sasha shifted her gaze from me to stare at the house.

"And what's this about a contract?"

"Oh, nothing for you to concern yourself with. A mere detail."

"Death said I had one, that there was a contract. Who made it? I never signed any contract."

"Such things don't always require a physical signature. A verbal agreement is enough. The quill will sign on your behalf if you are in agreement."

"In agreement for what?"

"Now, are you sure you don't need my help here? I am very busy." Sasha was already halfway to leaving. The faery dust gathered, her dress shimmered, her body vibrated, and my head was dizzy with her loveliness.

"Er, no, I'm good."

"Goodbye, Arthur."

It wasn't until later that I realized she hadn't answered my question.

I returned to my work, fought through the pain barrier only to come up hard against another, then another. But I didn't stop, I kept on swinging that pick and digging with the spade until I was empty inside.

Empty of the hurt, empty of the sadness, empty of the cruelty I harbored. Empty of everything.

I was the pick, and the pick was me. A machine built for one purpose only. To dig.

At some point I must have become aware that night had turned to day, and that there were others standing on the crisp grass watching me. I didn't even acknowledge their presence for I was so far down the rabbit hole now, no longer a man, just a pick with a fleshy attachment.

Through the dawn then the early morning, I continued, until finally my work was done.

I crawled out of a hole, surprised I even could, and without glancing at my audience I returned to the kitchen and untied the women still secured to the table.

One by one, I dragged them out into the open air and dropped them into their final resting place. By body three I was struggling hard, and I think maybe I began to cry. A whole life lived and this was what it came down to. Some guy dragging you across the grass and dumping you in a grave he'd dug to try to bring about his own selfish salvation.

I slipped and fell and I don't think I could have got up on my own. Arms reached out and helped me to my feet, and then we pulled the bodies together, all three of us. Nobody said a word.

Back we went for the next, this time carrying the body, the going easier with help. Then the next, and the next, and so it went until all the witches that had wanted to do something, anything, to keep the peace were buried.

They deserved this at least. For wanting no more death, for trying to find a way to solve a problem way beyond their means, for standing up for what they thought was right. They deserved more but this was all I could give them.

I picked up the shovel and I buried them, shoveled the dirt over their faces, watched the worms fall on the open wounds at their necks, watched lumps of soil block the gaping holes where their life had bled out.

I buried them all, and then I was done.

Standing there, panting, sweating, exhausted, I didn't say a prayer, didn't give them any last words. They were dead, already gone. What would be the point?

"Why is there one hole left?" asked Mabel, studying me with steely resolve.

"Because I assumed one of us would be going in it soon enough," I said as I turned to face her. Unafraid, not even concerned if I'm truthful, part of me wishing for the cold embrace of a final death, a way out of all of this, to be forever apart from the madness.

"But this is over now, isn't it?" asked Selma, looking truly terrible, unsteady on her feet, face ashen, ready to collapse.

"Ask her," I said, turning back to Mabel.

"Oh, it's far from over." Mabel sneered at me, and I honestly didn't care.

In fact, I cared so little, was so empty, that I lost consciousness and fell.

A Well-Deserved Rest

There is something immensely satisfying about waking up six feet down in a hole you dug with your own ravaged hands. As I lay in a freezing pit, watching the sun traveling low and lazy across a crisp, clear sky, I thanked it for the generosity of the warmth I felt as it devoured the shadows in my resting place and flooded the narrow space with light.

It was doubtful I would ever walk on the surface of the earth again, and that sense of finality gave its own kind of happiness. My body ached, not only from magical shenanigans, but from true, honest labor. I had dug ten burial plots and then given the witches the peace they undoubtedly deserved. The ones who had sided with Mabel would have to make their own arrangements, and they weren't all dead anyway. I wondered absentmindedly what had happened to the witch who had betrayed Selma and her buddies, she of the flowing skirt, but she was probably somewhere amid the rubble, not my concern.

My arms were locked, not only stuck behind my head because of the narrow hole I had fallen into, but because my muscles had seized up. My back so tired, my shoulders and arms so spent that they were locked solid with a cramp that had passed from being pure pain to a dull and distant ache I paid no mind to.

"What you doing?" asked Vicky as she peered down at me, blocking the sun.

"Just having a rest," I said, somehow not surprised to see her.

"You want to get out, or are you staying put?"

I had to think about that one. It was an important question and one I had no ready answer to. Should I stay, wait for the worms to eat me? Where were Mabel and Selma? Why hadn't she finished me off? I'd been uncertain what she would do, unsure if she'd kill me and keep at it until I was truly dead, maybe bury me alive and get the same result, or just dismiss me and let me be on my way. Which seemed doubtful as I was there to stop her. Whatever had happened, I was still alive, and Vicky was here, which rather annoyingly returned me to the present and the concerns we all have about the immediate future.

"Help me out," I said, mind made up.

"Wait here." Vicky disappeared and the sun shone down on me once more. It was nice.

Several minutes later I was disturbed from my slumber by the rattling of a small metal ladder being lowered. I reluctantly got to my feet, both surprised and pleased to find my bag still on my back, and once my arms began to work, I made the short climb feeling like it would last a lifetime. Vicky helped me off the ladder and I somehow remained standing.

"What happened?" she asked, indicating the graves and then looking me up and down.

"You were here, remember? Everything went to shit, you blew up the wall, Mabel killed Selma's buddies, I got beaten and killed repeatedly, then you left and I dug graves."

"Where's Mabel? Is Selma alive?"

"I don't know the answer to either of those questions. How did you know where I was?"

"I didn't. I used the Teleron and jumped to the front, then ran around to the back so nobody would see me. I haven't been inside. Do you think we can still get the cauldron?"

"Don't worry about that now. We need to find Mabel and Selma, see what the score is."

"What do you mean? She's insane."

"That's what I thought, but maybe not. This life gets twisted, so do the people living it. Mabel killed people she'd trusted, probably for decades. She thought they were traitors, that they wanted her killed, so she acted first. I'm not defending her, far from it, she is clearly off her rocker, but insane? No. Just determined, or she was. Now I'm not so sure."

"What then?"

"We go back in and finish this."

"Arthur, you're a walking corpse. You were in a grave. And if you dug all these then you must be exhausted."

"I am. And I'm out of magic, Wand is just a stick at the moment, and Mabel already beat me."

"So, let's go. Let's get out of here and think before you do anything rash."

"Did you bring me some clothes?"

"What do you think I am, an amateur?" Vicky grinned as she pulled out a small vacuum-packed bag from her backpack. We had many such packs in many places; such is the life of a wizard and his tiny helper.

I took the packet from Vicky and broke the seal to let the air in and allow the contents to expand. Then, not caring who saw, I shucked off the backpack and stripped until I was naked. I fumbled for the wet wipes, the super-sized ones for extra nasty clean-ups, and cursed as I tried to get the pack open.

"Let me." Vicky took the pack from me, opened it, then pulled out a fistful of wipes.

"Hey, I can do that," I said, groaning as I reached out.

"Don't be stupid. Stand still. What happened to your finger?"

"Wand stole it." Vicky raised an eyebrow. "Take it up with him." Even as we spoke, it tried to grow back. A tiny pink nub emerged, then retreated, like a newborn taking a peek at the world of madness that awaited and deciding, fuck that.

And so it was, that I stood naked in the freezing cold, body shivering, teeth chattering, beside the graves of nine witches as Vicky wiped me clean of blood, dirt, and dust. She cleaned up the many and varied wounds that had dented, scratched, torn, and snagged my already ravaged body.

I was a mess of bruises and damaged flesh, cuts and scrapes and strips of loose flesh where it had been half torn off. My shins were bloodied and scabbed, my knees looked like someone had attacked them with a meat tenderizer, and the rest of me hadn't fared much better.

I said nothing as Vicky tended me professionally, and she didn't say a word either. She finished by wiping my face, and as she did we stared at each other, held our gaze as she removed blood, dirt, and tears. She was a good woman; better than I deserved. Or maybe I did deserve her, as she sure was trouble sometimes.

"Finished." Vicky bagged the filthy wipes, no need to litter, and then stepped back to survey my naked awesomeness.

"Feeling cold?" she asked with a smirk as her eyes locked on something small.

"Yeah, and you know how the saying goes. If you don't use it, you lose it. Well, I'm definitely losing it." Modesty truly returned under her disapproving gaze, I dressed in clothes vacuum fresh and boy did it feel awesome. I felt almost human again as I pulled on fresh underwear, clean combats, put Wand in his pocket, and dragged a nice, and uber fresh smelling brown shirt across my lumpy muscles.

With Grace back on my head, my backpack secured, and a tap of my pocket, the stars aligned.

"Now, let's get this over with."

"No, Arthur, we can't. You aren't ready."

"We have no choice. What about Selma?"

"Mabel didn't kill her, she's family. Just wait, okay? We came, we lost, we got beaten. Let's go."

"The Hat is never beaten," I muttered, but nonetheless, we walked around to the front of the house where my car was.

Mabel and Selma were waiting for us.

What Next?

"You were in that grave for a long time," said Mabel, with about as much emotion as a wrinkled cabbage leaf, which was what she reminded me of.

"I had a lot to think about, and I was tired."

"You know I could have killed you." Mabel studied me carefully as if weighing my worth. I don't think I'd impressed her greatly, probably because she'd kicked my ass so easily.

"Maybe, maybe not. I'm not easy to kill. And besides, you haven't met me at my best."

"I do hope not. But that's in the past. What matters is that you conspired against me, and you ruined my home, the Residence." Mabel glared at Vicky, and to be fair, it was mostly her fault. For once, Vicky kept quiet.

"I'm sure you can fix it. And let's face it, I was attacked by that weird tentacle thing. It took all my strength, so it wasn't a fair fight between you and me."

"You wizards, you seem to think life should be fair."

"Oh, I know for a fact it isn't."

"But you wish to fight when your opponent is as strong as you?" she asked, genuinely interested.

"Um, no, I want to be stronger so I can kick their ass."

"There you go then." Mabel appeared almost amused, and very different to the woman I'd been beaten by. She seemed almost nice, and reasonable.

"Look," I said with a sigh, "what do you really want?"

"Want? Don't you mean deserve? I want equal footing with the wizards. I want to be in control, for my kind to get the respect they deserve."

"Wizards don't run things. We stick to our business, you stick to yours. This isn't a discussion about equal pay in the workplace, this is you wanting to overthrow the vampires and take what isn't yours."

"Why should they have all the power? Why should Ivan be in charge?"

"You've got it all wrong," I said, frustrated because, like most others, she didn't understand. "He's not in charge. He runs the crime, he keeps people safe, the citizens, and he heads up the vampires at the moment. But that's their business, their thing. Why in all the gods' names would you want that? It's not power, it's responsibility. You think most people spare a thought as to who runs the underground? They're too busy trying to wade through life as best they can. You think Ivan enjoys it? He doesn't want it, circumstances led him to where he is now. But he does a good job, and runs his business. He doesn't control the wizards though, he doesn't control me, and he sure as shit doesn't have an enviable position."

"We are ignored."

"Lucky you. Goddamn, what is wrong with you? The witches are living in the best time in their history, wizards and all other magic users too. We have freedom like never before, you can hide in plain sight, have to answer only to yourselves and your own rules. Isn't that enough?"

"No, it isn't. I want respect for my sisters, for us to be truly powerful and acknowledged as strong."

"Well, good luck with that. What about Selma?"

Selma shifted beside Mabel, and she looked terrible, if slightly recovered. The lump on her forehead had gone down, the wound had stopped bleeding, but it had left a nasty open cut that would scar and take time to heal. Although, knowing the witches, and Selma's powers, I wouldn't be surprised if the scar faded within a day or two. She'd probably put leaves steeped in something gross on it and voila, new face.

"There has been enough killing for one day. She may do as she wishes. But this is far from over, Arthur 'The Hat' Salzman."

"If you say so. Selma, you want to leave?"

"If Grandma isn't going to kill me, then I'll stay, see if we can work this out."

"Your call. We're going."

"Not so fast," said Mabel, shifting forward.

My stomach flipped but I kept cool and calm, acted relaxed. "What?" I snapped, not in the mood for games.

"Next time, I won't be so forgiving," warned Mabel.

"And I won't be in such a good mood. Or as distracted."

I opened the car door for Vicky and closed it once she was in. Then I went around to the driver's side, trying to walk normally but so stiff I felt like a half-defrosted penguin. But I managed to get in, the car started first time, and I drove off.

Unfinished Business

We drove in silence, but then it all came out at once.

"This feels weird," said Vicky.

"Unfinished, right?"

"Yeah."

"I know what you mean. Normally after something like this, it's done, the battle fought or lost, the conclusion good or bad, but it always feels final. This is just... Dunno."

"Up in the air, no resolution, no real outcome."

"Exactly. There's something missing from all this, an event yet to happen. I can't begin to imagine what, but it's coming. I had an idea for a very cool ending, and that will still happen, hopefully, but there is something off."

"Like what though? Mabel's still alive, but we weren't meant to kill her anyway as that would cause too much trouble. She might be stopped for a bit, but she can still act, still do what she wanted even without those women that accidentally got killed when a wall somehow fell down."

I turned and looked at Vicky, who was now gazing out of the window. "Yeah, real mystery that one."

"So, what's the missing piece?"

"I don't know, but I can feel it coming."

We continued in silence until we hit the city center, not that I was consciously heading that way. I was being called, and I didn't like it. I had an awful feeling in my churning stomach and my nerves felt frayed. This was not how I felt during such situations. As bad as it had been, and it had been awful, especially the repeatedly getting killed bit, it wasn't like nothing terrible had ever happened before. There was something else, something that would make what had gone before pale into insignificance, make it seem like a nice picnic.

Calamity and terror awaited. A monumentally awful event was around the corner and I knew only one thing. I had to face it alone.

I pulled up in a side street and unbuckled my seatbelt.

"Arthur what are you doing?"

"I'm not sure, but I have to go into the shopping district and walk the streets. I can't describe it, but I need to do this."

"What are you talking about? You need to rest, go home and sleep. Recover. Mabel is still alive, she won't give up, and you're a wreck."

"I know. It doesn't matter, this is more important. I'll see you later, okay? Did you get the kids to school?"

"No, and I think you knew that. It's the weekend, but I forgot and you sent me home knowing that. I felt like a right muppet when I got them up in the morning and realized it was Sunday."

"Damn, I forgot. But it kept you safe, that's the main thing."

"Hmm."

"Use the Teleron to get home, I'll use the gates. See you at mine for Sunday dinner. I'll cook something nice."

"You'll cook? In your state?"

"Yes, that's exactly why I'll cook. I need something normal to do. Something nice. Family and friends, smiling faces. See you later."

With that, I got out and walked toward the high street. It was bustling even on a Sunday. Seemed nothing closed any more, never a day off for some down time.

Something was waiting for me, I just didn't know how truly, astoundingly terrible it would be. How could I have guessed?

Infinite Problems

I not so much ambled, or swaggered, as staggered down the high street. It wasn't as busy as a Saturday, but the city center was still doing a brisk trade. Men looked depressed as they'd obviously been charged with getting the kids out of the house so the wife could have some peace, couples wandered aimlessly, killing time, others were gung-ho, determined to spend money no matter what they bought, and a few even seemed to be enjoying themselves.

Normal life going on all around me while I tried to escape I didn't know what, and fulfill my destiny at the same time. I was being called, and I knew better than to ignore such feelings. Whatever this was, it was important, maybe the most important thing that would ever happen to me. Was it to do with Mabel and her madness? How would that end? It already felt so distant, but it wasn't done with, and I suspected the only reason I'd been allowed to walk out of there alive was because of the graves I'd dug and the respect I'd shown to the women she'd murdered.

I saw the regret she held inside, for what she'd done, but, like all people holding a certain position, when you're betrayed there is only one course of action if you want to hold on to your power. She killed them because they'd acted against her and the others, and had to pay the price. Harsh, but a fact of life in our world. Everyone knew the risks. Witches may have been scatty and odd, even by my standards, but they were just as cold and calculating, certainly as ruthless, when their backs were against the wall.

No, it wasn't over, and it wasn't just because of the fact she'd bested me, but because of what I'd done while nobody was looking. I shifted the bag-cum-uncomfortable backpack and used the magical properties it contained to flatten it out against my back like it had been for so many hours previously, the load instantly feeling lighter than a feather. Feeling better, I continued my walk, heading nowhere, and in no hurry.

I hurt so much that walking was a lesson in pain, but it didn't matter. This was more important. Suddenly, the bag, my infinite bag, seemed to change its mind about exactly where it would like to be, and the shape it was in, and I panicked. It contained a lot of stuff, and I mean an awful lot, and some of those things were big, some were even scary. If it played up now, and while it was on my back, then it wouldn't bode well for me, or my bones. I didn't even want to think what would happen if it decided to open itself.

It had happened before, and it was one hell of a clean up job, which was why I usually kept it secured in my ward-protected locker at Satan's Breath. I should never have brought it, but it had seemed like a good idea at the time. The main problem was it didn't like looking like anything but how it wanted to look. It would morph into almost any bag shape, but it had a definite preference and it was this configuration it was trying to return to as it squirmed on my shoulders like it contained a nest of snakes. Which it probably did, amongst other things—when you have an infinite bag, it's easy to forget what you have inside, let alone find said thing.

"Fine," I said, "have it your way." I shucked it off, the straps morphing as I did so, and as I set it down it expanded in all manner of weird directions, changing shape constantly as if trying to remember its true form. Suddenly, it snapped back into shape with a bounce off the floor and then there it was, a small, strange looking holdall like a doctor's medical case or a posh knitting bag.

Guess I'd be carrying it from now on. I bent and grabbed the handle, moved to lift it, but it was playing silly buggers and was impossible to budge.

"That's enough," I hissed, not in the mood. The bag shook, and I peered at it suspiciously. "Are you trying to be funny? Are you laughing? Behave, or you won't get to come out again."

The infinite bag settled down with a sulky sagging and I once again bent, this time heaved on the handle to yank it from the floor, and as I lifted it, weighing nothing at all, I reeled backward and banged into something then went flying, the bag grasped tight.

Electric shockwaves rippled through my body and I knew this was it. I was utterly terrified by what I saw.

A Meeting With Fate

I've been scared many times in my life, even terrified a few times. But I was jaded now, didn't get worked up very often. Angry, sure, even worried, sometimes a little desperate when it came to concerns about the wellbeing of my family. But terrified? No. It had been burned, clawed, scraped, yanked, torn, and mangled out of me, an emotion I no longer had any use for.

But as I stared into the eyes of a stranger, I felt terror. Pure, abject terror the likes of which I had never experienced before and hadn't even known existed.

I was so scared I worried I was having another heart attack as my heart beat so fast, it repeatedly twitched, maybe spasmed, or was merely trying to escape the inevitable.

This was no myocardial infarction though. It was much, much worse than that.

Somehow, against all the odds, and certainly the last thing I had on my mind, I had smacked right into something so terrible, so truly, astoundingly worrying and inexplicable, that I sank to my knees right there in the middle of the street and I cried.

As the woman bent to me while everyone else merely hurried past, hardly aware of us, their thoughts on what they would have for dinner, or utterly lost to the small screens most stared at, she said, "Are you all right?"

"No. I'm not," I growled. "I'm in love."

Worst Feeling in the World

"Oh, that's nice," she said, a tiny smile on her rather wide face. Her lip quivered in amusement but then turned to concern as she noticed I was crying. "It is, isn't it?"

"No, it's awful," I sighed, wiping at my face.

"Is she lovely?"

"Who?"

"The woman you're in love with?"

"I have no bloody idea. I only met her a few seconds ago." I observed this woman with utter fear, yet was unable to look away even as she frowned but didn't scarper from the obvious nutter splayed out before her. She stayed crouching there, something compelling her to. She had the loveliest lips I had ever seen, plump yet kind of stretched wide too. Her jaw muscles were thick and angular as if they got worked overtime because she smiled so much.

She had pale skin, flawed like the rest of us, an aquiline nose, faint eyebrows perched high like the world was a constant surprise to her, and then there were the eyes.

God, what eyes.

Big, but maybe that's just me as I got lost in them, hazel, with long thick lashes, and full of mirth, sadness too, at the obvious distress of a stranger. She had waves of long hair that matched her eyes, falling down her back and hanging in front as she bent down.

We stared at each other for the longest time, and somehow, in the middle of the shopping district, we were inexplicably holding hands. Hers were warm, and rough, and it felt entirely natural for our fingers to be entwined. There was no ring, and her shopping bag had split, revealing a bottle of some diet drink and a ready meal of lasagna. Single! Buster's Hat, could I avoid this awful fate?

"I can cook," I blurted, making the matter worse.

Inside I was screaming, "Run away, run away now before it's too late. This will end badly. She'll betray you, she'll hate you, she certainly won't fancy you. You'll kill her or she you. This is your downfall, Arthur, don't say I didn't warn you."

But my heart had other ideas, and as she cocked her head to the side, not understanding, I said, "I'm a good cook. I just had my kitchen renovated. And, er, you can buy reusable bags now, save the plastic ones getting ripped."

This woman glanced at the broken bag and the spilled contents and her cheeks blushed. "Yeah, and I got stung for five pence for the bag. Bloody ripoff."

"Right, it is, isn't it?" I said, both of us somehow getting to our feet while still holding hands and staring deep into each other's eyes. "I mean, it's a good idea to have a reusable, but they shouldn't charge you if you happen to forget. You do recycle, don't you?"

What was wrong with me?

"I, er, yes, of course."

"Me too," I said lamely.

"Er, that's good."

"Yeah."

"I have dinner with my daughter every evening at seven if I can possibly manage it. It's a tradition, a thing we have so we get to spend time with each other." Good God, I must have gone insane.

"Oh, that's nice. No children."

"What about no children?"

"I, er, I don't have any."

"Would you like to?" Take me now, Lord, or even the Devil, I'm not fussed.

"I would. But I can't."

"Oh, I'm sorry. But you do eat, right?" That was a lame question, even by my standards.

The woman glanced at the food on the ground to answer my question, and then we both bent to pick it up at the same time.

We smashed our heads together.

And then, oh no, talk about sealing the deal, we laughed as we bent again and retrieved her shopping.

She had the broken bag and the drink, I had the lasagna.

I don't know what I was thinking, certainly not how I had the nerve, the presumption. My body had betrayed me, my heart was already hers, and I couldn't stop myself. I walked boldly to the nearest bin and threw her lasagna in.

"Hey, you can't do that," she protested.

"I told you, I can cook. Not every day, but sometimes. And I'm not bothered about having children, not any more. I have a teenage daughter and I'm enough trouble for her as it is."

"You don't say?" She raised an eyebrow. I wanted to lick it. Is that weird? It is, isn't it?

Somehow, we were back close to each other, holding hands again, studying each other. She could have had the legs of a rhino, or no legs at all, the notice I'd taken. And it wouldn't have mattered. I was lost in her face, her warm hands. Where was her low-cal drink? I glanced down to find she'd dropped it and it was fizzing as it emptied its contents. We didn't care.

"I'm Arthur."

"I'm Penelope."

"Can I ask you something?"

"Maybe."

"Do you like Buster Keaton?"

Penelope's face lit up. "I love him."

I groaned.

This was it. Game over for The Hat. She was perfect, and I was done for.

"Oh my God, you're so normal."

"Gee, thanks."

Goddamn, she even looked sexy when she pouted and was cross. I was history. There was still a chance though, still a way to get out of this.

"Please, please tell me you have a weird-ass job. For the love of God, don't tell me you work in a shop or something."

"How did you know?" asked Penelope, her cheeks reddening as if her job was something to be embarrassed about. "It's not much, and I really should try to better myself, but I like the freedom. I change jobs every few years when I get bored and my bosses don't seem to like the fact I don't constantly bang on about how awesome it is to work in retail. Not good for the resume. I work in a local place. We sell—"

"Nope. I can't stand it. If you tell me you sell something boring like slippers then this is it."

"It, what?" she asked, her eyes twinkling, probably amused by the madman she'd just met.

"It. You know. It."

"You are a very peculiar man."

"Am not. You are."

She frowned at my words for what felt like an eternity, then we were both laughing again. She had a perfect laugh. It was normal. Just nice.

"Promise you won't laugh if I tell you where I work?"

"Nope."

"I work in Tea Toweled."

I opened my mouth, then closed it again. Then opened it and left my jaw slack.

"Actually, it's pretty cool," she said defensively, getting annoyed. "You may be surprised to know that there's a lot to tea towels. And we sell other stuff too. Loads of interesting items for the kitchen."

"I go there every week," I blurted. "It's my favorite shop. Haven't seen you there."

"I only started last week. Got lucky. I think it's my dream job. I love tea towels."

"Me too."

"Don't make fun of me."

"I'm not. I'll show you my tea towel collection any time you want." Of all the lines, of all the ways to talk to a woman, that had to be the worst one used in the history of idiot man.

"Bet you say that to all the girls," said Penelope, doing this peculiar wobble with her head, like it would help her understand the fool before her.

"Trust me, I don't. I love my kitchen though, love Tea Toweled. I've spent a fortune in there."

"So, that's me. What about you?"

Ah, this was where it would get rather awkward if I wasn't actually doing my best to find fault with this woman and an excuse to run away very fast.

"I'm a wizard."

When she stopped laughing, she said, "Fine, you don't want to tell me. Anyway, nice meeting you. I think." She stared at me quizzically, trying to suss me out, then shrugged and went to move off.

"Wait!" I shouted, kicking myself for not just letting her go and changing tea towel supplier.

"You can't go now. I have to make you dinner. And besides, I'm going to marry you."

"Are you now?" she said, her smile changing as she realized I was serious.

"Yes," I said glumly. "But I warn you, my last relationship did not end well."

"I wonder why?"

"You don't know the half of it."

Revelation After Revelation

I was amazed she'd agreed to get in the car with me. I think she was even more surprised. After all, one thing everyone knows is that you don't let strangers who throw away your crap lasagna, then tell you they're a wizard, and that they're going to marry you, drive you off somewhere. That's how you get murdered in nasty ways, or locked in a basement for years.

"Do you think saying those things is making me feel at ease?" asked Penelope.

"Damn, did I say all that out loud?"

Penelope looked at me strangely, which had already become a habit I was getting used to. "Yes, you did. And now I'm considering jumping out of a moving vehicle so I don't become a sex slave."

"Hmm, sex slave." I pondered the possibilities then came out of my reverie as Penelope screamed. I swerved to avoid a car coming from a side street then smiled an apology.

"Don't worry, I'm an expert at crashing. I sometimes fall asleep after a busy day and Vicky is always telling me off about it."

"Vicky? And you weren't really considering keeping me as a sex slave, were you? And you crash a lot? Things just keep getting better." Penelope was smiling, but there was obvious concern. She'd be wondering what the hell she'd got herself into, and unsure why on earth she'd let it go this far. There was something between us, we both knew it, and we couldn't stop it if we wanted to.

I felt awful. I knew, on this fateful day, that my life would never, could never, be the same again. It was the same feeling I got when George stood at my door and told me she was my daughter. Elation mixed with abject terror.

"Don't worry, Vicky's just my sidekick. Oh, we did have a thing, once, but it was weird, so no worries there," I blurted.

"Gee, thanks for sharing."

"And no, I won't keep you as a sex slave. Not unless you want me to?" I asked with a wink.

"Let me think about that amazing offer. Would there be handcuffs?"

"Of course. Everyone knows all slave masters have handcuffs. Whips are optional, handcuffs are de rigueur."

"Good, because I don't want to feel short-changed."

I was feeling warm, and my heart was beating fast, so I thought it best to change the subject. "You live locally?"

"Sure do. And you? Do you live close?"

"Ah, in a manner of speaking. Just wait and see." I fidgeted with my pocket, felt the hard wood stir, but knew it was a little premature for such mighty introductions.

Several minutes later we pulled up a short walk away from my city home and I turned off the engine.

"This is me. Sort of. Just around the corner. Look, um, I don't know how to explain this without sounding like a complete nutter, but I get the feeling I have to be utterly honest with you. Will you keep an open mind? What I'm about to show you has never been seen by another citizen. It's private. It's scary too, but you'll be safe with me. Trust me?"

"Arthur, you are the oddest man I have ever met. You're scaring me, yet I trust you. This is crazy." Penelope shook her head, her beautiful, ordinary head, and seemed to come to a decision. "I think you should take me home. Nobody knows where I am, who I'm with, and you are too peculiar, even for me."

"Please, give me a chance. This is just as weird for me, even more so once you see what I'm risking by taking you inside."

"And that kind of talk is what's scaring me. What's with all the secrets and mystery? Who are you?"

"I told you, I'm a wizard. I won't lie to you, you can ask me anything you want. Anything at all. After all, if you're going to marry me, you should know what kind of man I am. I'm not a good person, Penelope, even though I sometimes try to be. I already know I don't deserve you, and you sure as hell don't deserve the life you'll have with me. I'm dangerous, I get into trouble constantly, I have idiots for friends, a daughter who terrifies me because she is so beautiful and will be so strong one day, and you will put your life at risk many times by being with me. But this will happen, so please, trust me?"

"Well, when you put it like that, what choice do I have?"

We nodded to each other then got out of the car. Penelope was bemused beyond belief by her own actions. I mean, who did this kind of thing? Got picked up by strangers and went straight to their house after they told you they were basically insane?

"So, a wizard, eh?" she asked. "What, you do children's parties, entertain kids at bar mitzvahs?"

"Something like that, yeah," I mumbled, the words difficult, as if I was incapable of lying to this woman. "Come on, let's get inside." Penelope followed me down the street while I surreptitiously checked we weren't being followed, until we reached the front door. I unlocked it, went inside, then held the door.

Penelope glanced back to the street, shrugged her shoulders, and said, "Here goes nothing."

She didn't know the half of it.

One Small Step...

"It's... er... Nice. Comfortable."

"Haha, don't worry, this isn't where I live. It's just to house the Gates."

"I knew it! You're some kind of weirdo collector. You've got a whole house just to store your gate collection. That's it, I'm outta here."

"Wait, wait! Please?"

Penelope turned back to me, took her hand off the door, and said, "Gotcha." She smiled, and it was so beautiful. She was so funny. I adored her.

"You sure did."

"Arthur, what's the matter?" Penelope put a hand to my shoulder. "You're crying."

"Only because you're so beautiful. Funny too."

"Arthur, you are one very strange person, but thank you for the compliment."

"The Hat, they call me The Hat," I mumbled, then wiped my eyes.

"Who does?"

"Everyone. People in my world."

"Other entertainers?"

"I'm not an entertainer. It's difficult to explain to citizens, but you'll see."

"What's all this citizen stuff?"

"You know, regular folks. Normal people. Citizens."

"I don't know whether to be insulted or not."

"Don't be, it's a compliment. Please, come into the living room, sit, let me explain before your entire existence gets turned upside down. Once you come into my world, there is no turning back, and I need you to be sure. I don't want to scare you, but I must warn you. Once you come with me, you will never be the same again. You will look at the world with different eyes, will see things so differently, and your life will always be in danger."

"Sounds intriguing." Penelope's eyes sparkled in that way I was sure they always did when she was amused or excited. I could stare at them forever.

We sat on the sofa and I tried not to sniff so she'd notice. So, straight away, and I know I had a goofy look on my face, she asked, "Why are you snorting like that?"

"You smell lovely."

"Weirdo."

"Maybe."

"So?"

"So, here's the deal. Damn, I can't believe this is happening. I feel like I'm in a nightmare."

"Charming."

"Oh, it's not you. Actually, it is. You are amazing, and I don't know you. But I want to. I'm going to tell you things you won't believe, that you can't until you've experienced them. First, let me tell you a story about what I've been up to since last night. Don't interrupt, just listen, okay? Think of it as a story. Picture me as this hero. The scrawny, but handsome, hero."

"How else could I picture you?" Again with the smile and the sparkling eyes.

"First, Vicky and I went to a nightclub, and I hated it. Not my style at all."

"Nor mine. Ugh, all those sweaty bodies."

"Exactly. Anyway, we were there to meet a witch who had hacked into our bank accounts and stolen our money. Except she hadn't, but she kind of had. I'll get to that later. Well, things went wrong, and I ended up tied to a chair in an attic, and by morning... Er, you probably won't like this bit. I think I better give you more detail."

So for the next hour I told her everything that had happened, and more besides. She stopped interrupting after a while and just listened, open-mouthed, to my tale. I'd never opened up like this before, certainly never to a citizen. Let alone one I'd just met.

"And then I got out of the car, bumped into you, threw away your lasagna, and fell in love."

"That's quite a story."

"I know, and I'm knackered."

"Arthur, don't tease me. You're nice, and there's certainly something happening here, but I can't stay if you're going to play games."

I stood and began to strip.

"What are you doing?"

"I'm showing you." I lifted my shirt, pulled my combats down, and a voice from the pocket said, "Now we're getting somewhere."

"Quiet you, now isn't the time for your jokes."

"I didn't say a word," said Penelope.

"Sorry, I was talking to Wand. Um, I haven't told you about him, have I?"

"You talk to your wand? Ugh, what am I saying? You actually have a wand?"

"Yeah, when I have to. And of course I have one. Why wouldn't I?" I continued to strip and Penelope stared at my ravaged body. "Believe me now?"

"Oh my God, how are you still standing?"

"Because I am a man of steel, a wizard, and I'm stubborn."

"Look at your finger!"

"Gross, huh?" I waggled the pink nub and it retreated, like a turtle back inside its shell.

"What the hell?"

"Told you I was a man of magic." I grinned despite the pain.

"You poor thing. How did this happen?"

"Damn, I knew you didn't believe me. Okay, guess I'll have to show you." I dressed, then held out my hand. Penelope stood and took it carefully, noting for the first time what a mess of lumps and grazes it was. The finger seemed to grow at her touch.

"If I told you that I had one of a pair of magical gates in my kitchen, and when we stepped through them we would be transported to a barn in Cornwall, would you believe me?"

"No."

"But if I asked you to come with me, to have dinner with me and my family, in my true home, where there will be kids running around, my daughter, Vicky, and maybe a faery, would you come?"

"Um, that's rather intense for a first date, but I guess. At least I'd be safer."

"Great! Listen, what I said earlier, about your life changing, I meant it. About being with me being dangerous, I meant that too. That you might die, it's true. I know you don't trust me, but let me show you the Gates first. We'll go through, and then you can think about what I said."

"Arthur, I work in a shop, I live in a crappy little house, I keep doing the same thing every day. You're the most interesting thing that has happened to me in a very long time, actually, ever, and I think you are utterly deranged, but if what you're saying is true, then I'm in."

"Good. Great!" I led Penelope into the hall, walked her into the kitchen, and toward the arched doorway that looked like it merely led out onto the garden.

"I don't know why, but I'm scared."

"You should be. You're about to be ripped into a billion tiny pieces then reassembled through the power of magic hundreds of miles away. But don't worry, it's only excruciating for a moment."

"I appreciate the pep talk."

"You're welcome."

I don't know what possessed me, but I couldn't stop myself, and as we stepped forward I kissed

Penelope right on the lips. As we kissed, we were disassembled, the pain not even felt as I was so lost in the warmth and wetness of her lips. It felt so right, so perfect, that I didn't even notice when we were in the backroom of the barn.

We were still kissing, both of us lost to this special first time, but then Penelope gasped, which felt weird as she still had her tongue in my mouth, sprang back, and said, "Where the fuck did the kitchen go?"

"Told you, I'm a wizard."

Getting to Know You

"Yeah, but... but... Ugh, I thought you were trying to be funny or something. You know, impress me?"

"I wouldn't know how to impress someone. Um, the last woman I was with, it didn't end well. I killed her, remember."

"You said."

"But you came with me."

"I thought you were being metaphorical. You got her out of your life. It's how people talk now, how the kids talk. 'I killed him,' the girls say when they break up with their boyfriend."

"Ah."

"You're serious?"

Damn, maybe it was too soon for such stories. Definitely, but I was in this now, had to be honest. "I am."

"So, you're a girlfriend-murdering, trouble-making wizard with a magical portal and you killed three witches this morning, fought a super witch, got killed repeatedly, had a chat with Death, and... Anything else?"

"Oh, loads. But let me explain about my ex first. You see, she was a shifter, could change into a dog, a nice Collie actually. But she betrayed me to the vampires when I was trying to steal a warehouse full of magical artifacts from Cerberus, a super-secret organization that hides magical items."

"Obviously."

"Yes. When Candy betrayed me, and after loads of people got killed, I killed her for her treachery. Then I fought the original vampire, Mikalus, a man who I'd helped bring back by giving his centuries-old ashes to the vampires who resurrected him in my kitchen and threatened to use my daughter as a sacrifice. But Ivan, current head of all things vampire, and Vicky's brother, who also happens to be a werewolf, both of them actually, well, he stepped in and saved George. Now he's in charge of crime and vampires, but he's a good uncle, brilliant at babysitting."

Penelope stared at me open-mouthed.

"Um, too much?" I didn't know what I was doing. I was babbling like a fool, spilling secrets left and right as though all this made sense. I'd just told her enough to get her killed in an instant if any number of people found out. Plus, it was probably a bit of a shock. I mean, even as I said it, it sounded far-fetched. But damn, I led an interesting life, if a depressing one.

"There are vampires?"

"Yes."

"And werewolves?"

"Oh, yes. Vicky and Ivan can change once a month. You should see it, it's quite something. Actually, when I was tied up yesterday, um, last night, no, the other night, sorry, I suffer from insomnia, and get muddled. Did I tell you I'm a terrible sleeper? No? Sometimes I go into the sewers to work out with Beast. He's this huge muscle-bound dude who lives down there and puts me through one hell of a workout. He's—"

"Stop! Arthur, what are you talking about? I can't take all this in. It's too much. I don't know if this is a twisted joke and the cameras will appear, if you're just insane, or if I'm the one who's lost her mind. We just went through a magic portal!"

Penelope was beginning to lose the plot. She was pacing, and ranting, and looking flushed. She looked hot. But maybe I should have eased her into this? I couldn't though, she had to know, and right now, or this would never work. Not that I wanted it to. She was the last thing I needed. There was the memory of Candy and what I'd done. What if I killed this woman too? I couldn't bear to think about it. I could not risk it.

"I'll take you back. This was a terrible mistake. I'm sorry. I want to tell you everything, so you know, so you can make an informed decision, but I can hear myself talking and I know it sounds nuts. My life is complicated; this isn't for you. You live a regular life. You don't want to be dealing with vampires and witches and fae and werewolves and go through portals and talk to sentient sticks and see magic."

"Arthur, stop! That's exactly what I want. I, um, I didn't know I wanted it, didn't know any of this existed, was even possible. But if it is, I want in. Not because I am way overdue some excitement, although I am a woman in her forties so I most certainly am due that, but because, and I don't know why, this feels right. You feel right. We feel right. Us. Together."

"Great! Or, um, not great. You heard what I just said about Candy. I killed my last girlfriend. She betrayed me, sold me out, and in our world you know what happens when you do that."

Penelope stepped close. I felt giddy with her perfume and her very essence. She took my hands. "I would never betray you. Never."

I believed her.

Pouring My Heart Out

"So you have a genuine, for real, faery godmother? And not long ago you went to her home world, Faery, and rescued her from this mad woman who kidnapped her and your daughter?"

"And Vicky."

"Right, and Vicky. And Sasha's been trying to make up for causing the trouble ever since?"

"Yeah. You should see her, she is beautiful. Um, and so are you."

"You're so sweet." Penelope punched me playfully on the arm. I fawned like an adoring puppy. God, this was so terrible. "And you have extra lives? You know Death, you fought this witch woman earlier today, dug holes, buried people, thought you would die, and all that other stuff? How can you cope with it?"

"That's easy," I said, standing and stretching as boy did I ache. "I screw up, I fall asleep and crash cars, I get smacked over the head, all kinds of dumb stuff."

"I get the feeling you're anything but dumb. I get the feeling that you're brave and strong and a brilliant warrior and an exceptional man. I think you're kind, and love your family, and yes, you are a bit strange, but so is this whole situation."

"Um, yeah, maybe." I was getting distracted, because Penelope had stood up and was now very close.

Her eyes widened and she stepped back.

"Arthur Salzman, is that a wand in your pocket, or are you just pleased to see me?"

Look, I can't tell you how many years I'd dreamed of a hot woman saying that to me. Ever since I was a boy, ever since I decided to be a wizard and got my first wand. It's like the ultimate, utterly unoriginal, cheesy line, but as Penelope purred and I grew hot under the collar, I blurted, "Would you like me to show you?"

Penelope licked her lips and I knew I was utterly done for.

Cool Stuff That Never Happens in Real Life

Some time later, feeling giddy with an awesome post-hot-sex-in-a-barn high, and acting like a bit of a twat if I'm honest as nobody wants to see a man dance about like a fool because he's in love and can't believe he actually got to do it in the hay, we got dressed and I finally introduced Penelope to Wand.

"Penelope, this is Wand. Wand, this is Penelope."

"Pleased to meet you, Wand," said Penelope, smiling and looking ravishing with her tousled hair as she adjusted her blouse.

"Blimey, I can't believe you actually did it. You scored with a hot babe and you did it in a barn. You dirty bugger. So awesome."

"What did he say?"

"He said it's nice to meet you and you seem like a lovely lady," I said, glaring at Wand, then grinning like an idiot because I really did get to do it in a barn and she was super hot.

"What's this right on the tip?" Penelope reached out and touched the sigil near the top of Wand. He burst into life and white magic spurted from the end then he almost went limp.

"Hell, it exploded" screamed Penelope as she jumped back then checked her hand for burns.

"He isn't used to being touched by females, but he's never done that before. You okay, Wand?"

"Eh, what happened? What was that? I feel funny, all tingly, and if I had a stomach I'd say it's churning. Did I just shoot magic? That shouldn't happen. Arthur, this woman is a keeper. She's amazing. Electrifying."

"You think?"

"Sorry, what?" asked Penelope.

"Oh, I was talking to Wand."

"Right.

I switched to silent mode, or this would be too confusing. "She's perfect, isn't she?" I asked.

"Absolutely. You know this means trouble, loads of it? She'll distract you, she'll be on your mind all the time, and something awful will happen. You'll get yourself killed."

"I know. But I can't help myself. She's the one. And maybe I deserve a happy ending for once."

"Maybe." Wand didn't sound convinced, probably because I wasn't.

But there was a chance this would all work out, there had to be. After Candy, there was no way the same thing would happen again. I couldn't be that unlucky. No, this was my future, with her, and I was so upset about it because I knew it would complicate my life having a citizen involved in it. Not because anything bad would happen to her, for some reason I felt utterly confident she would remain safe, but because it would put me at increased risk and I wouldn't be focused. Plus, it was scary. I'd never felt anything even close to this before.

"You finished talking yet?" asked Penelope.

"Yes, sorry. Shall we go meet everyone? I'm cooking."

"Ah, the fabled lasagna?"

I stepped back, aghast. "Are you nuts? It's Sunday. Roast, with all the trimmings."

"Sounds perfect. Yum." Penelope licked her lips. We both stared down to a certain spot in my combats.

"Dinner can wait," I said, as I grabbed her and we rolled about in the hay a while longer.

Meeting the Family

"Welcome to the madhouse," I said with a grim smile as I opened the front door to my home and heat and noise hit. Neither of us went inside.

"How many children did you say you had?" Penelope asked nervously.

"Don't worry, only George the flame-haired girl lives here and is mine. The terrible twins are Vicky's. They come stay some weekends. Help George with the horses, hang out. They're little darlings, just like to play a lot."

"I do like children," said Penelope wistfully.

"They'll love you, everyone will," I said glumly.

"Hey, what's with the frown? You always like this? I'm not marrying a grump, you know." Penelope smiled, making a joke of it, but we both knew that this was real, that we were locked to each other like two perfect, final pieces of the most complicated jigsaw puzzle there had ever been.

Already it felt like we'd known each other years, yet I didn't know the first thing about this woman. I noticed how her brown highlighted hair caught the light and wondered how it was that something so ordinary could make my heart race.

"I do get grumpy," I admitted. "It's the lack of sleep."

"You don't need to worry about that anymore, Arthur. I will cuddle you all through the night and you can cry onto my chest and I will be there when you wake up in the morning. As long as it isn't after I have to get up for work. Work! Oh my God, I'm supposed to be in work. I totally forgot."

"That's what meeting a dark, handsome stranger does to a girl."

"I only started last week. I need to call them. I was only popping out on my break to get something for dinner."

"Do it quick, so I can introduce you."

Penelope made a hurried call. I didn't hear what she said as I was too busy daydreaming of cuddles and warm nights, then she tapped me on the shoulder and smiled nervously

We both took a deep breath, removed our shoes, then wandered down the hall and into the kitchen.

"Everyone," I shouted above the din, "this is Penelope. We're going to get married," I said glumly.

"Hi," said Penelope, and waved.

George dropped a mug of coffee, Vicky released a very sharp knife that clattered to the floor, the girls starting singing, "Uncle Arthur's got a girlfriend, nah, nah, nah, nah, nah," and I squeezed Penelope's hand.

We stood there, like a right pair of lemons, everyone staring at us.

"We, um, we met in town, and it was love at first sight."

"Hey, you could sound happier about it," Penelope chastised, her eyes sparkling at my misery.

"I told you, I'm bad news. This is awful, there'll be loads of trouble, and you'll hate me."

"I won't. I understand you already, Arthur. And remember what I promised?" Penelope moved closer and whispered, "You can get all the cuddles you want." She pinched my bum and I yelped with a stupid grin on my face.

"What's wrong with your face, Uncle Arthur?" asked one sprog.

"I think I'm happy, in a miserable, my life is over, kind of way."

"Is this your girlfriend?" asked the other sprog.

"I guess. We met when I made her drop her lasagna, so I invited her for dinner. This is like a tale of a princess meeting a handsome prince and they get married and live happily ever after," I said to the girls.

"You're so lame. That's for babies. I'm gonna buy my own stuff, marry a rock star. Girl power."

"Girl power," they both screamed, then ran out of the room and up the stairs. Judging by the smashing of steps, they'd put heavy boots on before they did so.

"Um, sorry about this," said Penelope. "I hope Arthur doesn't make a habit of bringing women home he says he's going to marry?"

"Nope, I can honestly say," said George, "that this is the first time it's happened. Hi, I'm George, his daughter."

"Hi."

They shook hands before George turned to me and raised both eyebrows, which meant it was very serious.

"What?"

"What do you mean, what? You just said you're going to get married."

"George," I declared, probably looking demented as my grin was hurting my face, "meet your future stepmom. I know, crazy right?"

"Of course it's crazy. What are you taking about? No offense, Penelope was it? But Dad, what are you saying? Vicky told me what happened, I saw her this morning, and she's been here a few hours now, I know what you've been through. You're concussed, exhausted, obviously lost the plot."

"I don't think he's concussed, and Arthur told me about the witches and the graves, all that. I think the exhaustion, the digging maybe, it's opened him up to something new. Plus, we click. Don't ask me why, I don't understand it either, and half of me thinks I'm going crazy, meeting a stranger and, er..." Penelope blushed scarlet and turned to me. "Care to carry on?"

"Oh my God," blurted Vicky. "You've done it. You did it and you just met. You pair of dirty, naughty—"

"It wasn't like that. It isn't like that. Penelope is a citizen, doesn't, or didn't, know anything about our life, about vampires and magic gates and shifters and fae, but I told her, and she believes, sort of."

"You told her about us?" asked Vicky, aghast.

"Yes, I did. I'm sorry, but she's family. She has a right to know."

"You just met her!" Vicky walked up to us, stopped in front of Penelope, and stood on tip-toe to vibe her properly.

"Are you on the level?"

"Yes. Look, I'm more terrified than I've ever been in my life right now. Apparently I was in the city not so long ago, now I'm in Cornwall, in a strange house, with a tiny woman squinting at me strangely and a room full of people who all know each other very well. I met an oddball man and had sex with him in a barn, twice, I might add." I wanted to high-five someone about that, but figured it best not to as I'd be left hanging. "And I honestly don't know what in Buster's name I'm doing. But I can feel it, know this is right, so I want to get to know you. All of you. And you should get to know me. I guess I'm going to be around a lot."

"That... That's... That was the bravest thing I've ever seen or heard," said Vicky, truly impressed.

"It sure was. I would have run a mile," agreed George.

"Coffee?" I asked.

Everyone said yes, and so it was, weird because it already felt utterly normal, a new woman was introduced into our lives.

What the hell was I doing? I didn't know, and most worrying of all, I didn't care. Penelope was normal, can you imagine it? I wondered what the catch was, for there surely was one.

"Right, I'm going to cook Sunday roast. I'm going to make it awesome, even par-boil the potatoes first. And I think I'll make onion gravy and I might even do that special thing I do to the cabbage. And how about parsnips? We could have butter on them, and I think maybe I'll use that new sieve I got. Hey, did you know that Penelope works in Tea Toweled? How awesome is that?"

"Who's he talking to?" asked Penelope.

"He gets like this when he's nervous. Dad will start patting your head soon, so watch out." George winked at Penelope. Damn but she was a great daughter.

"Does he always babble like a total idiot?" asked Penelope, turning to George, her lip trembling with amusement. Was she laughing at me? What was with this woman? She was a dream, she must be. Nobody was this utterly awesome.

"Pretty much, yeah." George shrugged as if saying wasn't it obvious I was an utter fuckwit.

"Usually," agreed Vicky.

"Do not," I said, getting up to begin dinner.

"You do. You say stupid stuff and you pat everyone's head."

"Do not. You do. You... you head patter." I reached out to pat George's head and say something soppy like, "You're such a good girl," but I didn't, because everyone was looking at me.

"Idiot," said George.

"Such a tool," said Vicky.

"I think he's lovely," said Penelope. Our eyes locked and we smiled. Vicky and George groaned.

Making Plans

While everyone got to know each other, and magic and evil and fae and wands and all that stuff were discussed at first hesitantly, then openly once I told Vicky and George that they might as well be honest, let Penelope have it full force and decide what she believed and what she didn't, I pottered about making dinner.

I cannot even begin to describe how mind-bending this situation was for us. Penelope had been thrust headfirst into a completely alien environment full of clearly insane people, but she handled it well. Maybe this was what it was like for citizens? They craved new experiences and jumped at the chance to experience another side of life. I didn't know. My whole life was one peculiar event after the other, but that was normal to me. I knew no citizens, no truly regular people, very well at all.

Once we'd eaten, Penelope insisted on helping clean up. She even told me off for missing a spot on the counter, which made me truly adore her, and she polished the tap and wiped the cupboard handles, which made me gasp in admiration and stand there drooling as she bent to do the bottom drawers. Vicky and George sighed and tutted at my appreciation of someone as obsessive compulsive as myself.

There was an awkwardness after that. Nobody quite knew what to do, what to say, and we'd hardly even discussed what had gone down over the last few days. To be honest, I wasn't even thinking about witches and cauldrons and the like, I was utterly obsessed with Penelope and she was all I could think about or look at.

Vicky retrieved the girls from the den where they were playing, brought them into the kitchen, and told them that they'd have to be up bright and early in the morning as George would take them back to the city.

"I'll do it," I said, "I have to take Penelope back then too."

Everyone stared at me, shocked.

"What?"

"Um, Arthur," said Penelope, "I think maybe everyone is surprised you're assuming that I'm spending the night here after only meeting you this afternoon." There were nods from everyone, even the girls.

"Yes, Uncle Arthur," lectured one smartass. "You're supposed to get to know people, then marry them, before they stay over. Everyone knows that." She rolled her eyes, already an expert at it.

"But you could always sleep on the floor, that's okay then, isn't it?" asked the other way-too-smart kid.

"Oh, that's all right," I told them. "We're basically married already." I turned to the women and said, "Sorry, I didn't think. This feels so right that it didn't cross my mind that Penelope would go home today. Actually, not ever. I want you to move in. Today. Now. Never leave," I blurted.

"That's it," said George as she stood. "I'm taking you to the doctor's. You've clearly got brain damage."

"No, I haven't. This is truly awful, I don't want this, it will cause trouble and Penelope is already in danger, but it's the way it is."

"You sure know how to woo a girl," said Penelope.

"I'm sorry. You've heard a little about my life, our life, you know this will be madness, right?"

"I do. But you're right. This feels normal. I hope it does for you too. I will stay, as just like Arthur, I honestly hadn't thought of leaving today. But George, I understand this is your home, that you don't know me. Maybe we should all take this a little slower?"

"No, it's okay," said George. "You're welcome. This is all just moving so fast."

"Damn right it is," I said. "But what can we do? We're in love."

We smiled at each other.

Everyone else groaned again, even the girls.

The Missing Link

"Okay, you two, time for bed," ordered Vicky, peeling the two girls from the various hanging or sitting positions they'd assumed on my aching body.

They didn't fool me, they often did this when they didn't want to miss out on grown-up stuff. I was a sucker for a cuddle, and I'm happy to admit it.

"Aw. We want to stay up and play."

"You can play tomorrow. Bed."

"But it's run around like nutters Sunday. Uncle Arthur hasn't tipped us upside down yet, either."

"Bed. Now."

"Fine. Can Penelope read to us too?" asked one with an innocent smile.

"Er, um, I don't know. Penelope might not want to," said Vicky.

"That would be lovely," beamed Penelope. "As long as your mum doesn't mind?"

"No, I don't mind."

After a kiss and cuddle, the girls and the two women headed upstairs, leaving George and I alone.

"Sorry about all this," I said, the lamest apology ever.

"Dad, this is a bit rushed, isn't it?"

"I know, and I'm sorry. I know I should check it's okay to bring someone home, not get your hopes up about anything, especially after last time. But, well, what can I tell you? This feels so right that I'm absolutely terrified. If I could get out of this, I would. I don't want or need this. I can't risk having my heart broken again. I assumed I'd die alone and bitter, not having a cuddle."

"It's that serious? You're that serious?"

"I am. So, what do you think?"

"I think she seems lovely. I think she seems like an average person. Normal. A citizen. And you told her enough to make her run a mile, so I guess she must be okay."

"She is so normal, isn't she? How awesome."

"Yeah, brilliant."

"What? Come on, tell me."

"Dad, she's a regular person. You know the life we lead. It's dangerous."

"I know, but for some reason, somehow, I'm convinced this will work out. There will be no surprises, she won't cheat on me, she won't betray us. And she won't die. Someone who cares about us. Is that okay?"

"Oh, Dad, it's more than okay."

George burst into tears and wept like a child. Things she'd kept bottled up for years came out. All the sadness, the loss of her mother, the regret over what she'd missed out on when she'd been alive, the disappointment about never having a mum who truly cared for her. And the fear of hope, for hope is a treacherous mistress and the sense of loss when it all goes wrong is enough to break you. So George cried because she dared believe there would be a woman who acted like a mother. A wife to me, the focus of our family, someone to take control of our wayward antics and maybe even rein us in on occasion.

Someone who would smile at us when we walked through the front door. Ask us about our day, be there for us, be our lifeline, our hope and maybe even our salvation, for we sure as hell needed saving.

It was scary for the both of us, as we answered to nobody but ourselves. To think there would be a woman living here who would be in charge of us, as undoubtedly that would be the case because we wanted that, needed it in our lives, was a terrifying proposition.

Then I began to cry too, and soon we were hugging and weeping, with fear, with regret for what had never been, and most terrifying of all, because we dared to hope.

"I found this woman creeping about upstairs," said Sasha, holding Penelope several inches off the ground, her fingers poised to rip her eyes from their sockets.

"Sasha, meet Penelope. Penelope, meet Sasha, my faery godmother and a little over zealous at the moment.

"Nice to meet you," stammered a terrified Penelope.

"Oh, hello, are you a friend of Arthur's then?" asked Sasha, smiling innocently.

"Um, yes. Can you put me down please?"

"Sorry, where are my manners? So, I shouldn't pull her eyes out and squish them?" asked Sasha sweetly.

"No, best not to," I said, wondering how long it would take Penelope to get her shoes on and run away.

Two's Company

The kitchen became very crowded very quickly. Once Sasha had released Penelope, and introductions were made, I was shocked she didn't ask to leave. But Sasha was, as always, intoxicating, and you'd do whatever it took to remain in her company. It was easy to forget just how enticing fae were, and Penelope watched her like she couldn't look away, which wasn't far from the truth.

Vicky returned after tucking the girls in, said hello to Sasha, and it all got a little too much.

"If you'll excuse us," I said.

"But you haven't told me anything about your new friend," said Sasha with a pout.

"All in good time. I'm sure these two clowns will tell you everything." I took Penelope's hand and whispered. "Sorry, this is a lot to cope with. Let me give you a tour of the grounds. We can check out the house later."

Penelope nodded with obvious relief. Who could blame her? She needed to get away from Sasha, as it was too much for a citizen to cope with for long. Sasha could do funny things to your head, and she'd been known to turn many a regular woman to little but a gibbering wreck, mind obsessed with one more glimpse of her, so best let them get to know each other slowly. Plus, there were simply too many damn women in the room, and it was getting ridiculous. It was a shame Steve wasn't here to even things out. He often came on weekends now to spend time with Vicky and the girls.

We said our goodbyes and went to get our shoes on. I gave Penelope one of my spare coats and we got out as quickly as we could. I closed the front door with a sigh of relief, and a huge smile now I was back alone with this adorable woman.

"We've got so much to talk about I don't even know where to begin," I said, scratching at my beard.

"We've got all the time in the world. Haha, I can't believe this is happening. It's so surreal I feel like I'm dreaming. What are we doing?"

"I've got no idea. But it feels right. Come on."

I led Penelope by the hand across the concrete yard. I showed her the barns, the various animals, and the storage rooms for all manner of equipment we used about the place. She seemed impressed by the scale of it all, and I guess if you were used to the city and a tiny house then this was like another world.

Whoever said money couldn't buy happiness forgot to tell you that it can at least make you more comfortable in your misery.

Wide open spaces, fresh air, and the responsibility of caring for animals goes a long way to keeping you grounded and appreciative of what the world is really about and what it has to offer if you just take the time to slow down and look.

"Let me show you the horses," I offered, feeling so happy I was fit to burst. This was like a dream come true, a missing piece I had always refused to acknowledge. I was walking around my own property with a partner by my side. It didn't get better than this.

"Do they bite?" asked Penelope with that twinkle again.

"Only me," I said grumpily.

"I love horses. When I was young, we used to go riding. I haven't done it for years. Heck, I haven't even seen a horse for years."

"Well, now you've got a horse whenever you want one. And you'll have to tell me about your family, your parents. I don't even know if you've got brothers or sisters."

"Not much to tell. And look who's talking. You're a bit of a mystery man yourself. Actually, haha, scrap that. You're utterly strange, your friends and family are nice but, um, strange too, and I guess everything feels too peculiar for me to accept any of it as real. I don't know what I'm doing. I think I'm losing the plot here."

"Hey, it's all right. I know this is a bit much, that we've gone a little nuts, but isn't that what everyone wants? For something crazy to happen and for the first time in your life to just go for it and see what happens?"

"Yes, of course. But, Arthur, you keep saying you're a wizard. I met a faery, there are vampires and werewolves and we went through a portal! Crazy."

Penelope was on the edge, that much was obvious. It was hard for me to put myself in her position, but even the little I could imagine made me sure she was close to breaking down. She wouldn't believe it, couldn't, as these things didn't happen, not to regular folk. My life was one big story to them, not real at all.

"Come on, let's just go look at horses. It'll ground you, center you, and you can laugh as they try to bite me while they let you stroke their noses."

"Okay." Penelope wiped her eyes and smiled. She was a brave woman.

We walked across the frosty grass on plastic mesh we'd laid for when the ground got too muddy, heading for the stable block.

The horses were noisier than usual, and I wondered why. Sometimes they got disturbed by animals, and sometimes when we went to check there seemed nothing wrong. They were scatty like that, and once one got spooked they all joined in. Horses were not the most stable of creatures in my experience. Maybe they'd heard us and were getting excited about some Hat teasing to come?

As we approached, the noise inside the barn grew louder. The animals were going wild, whinnying and neighing, and it sounded like they were kicking at the stalls. What had got into them?

Suddenly, the stable doors smashed open and horses scattered in all directions. I grabbed Penelope, and shouted, "Run back to the house. Right now," as I turned then dragged her away before she got killed on the day we met.

Almost Over

A terrifying vision in pink and PVC exploded from the barn on the back of a horse so black it was almost invisible against the dark sky. The sight was so nightmarish because it was such a crime against fashion. Selma was resplendent, or should I say repugnant, with a revealing leather basque, pink hair, and heels I would have assumed would make it impossible to ride.

Horses scattered in all directions, bolting with fear, not surprising given how Selma was dressed. Their breath was like white plumes of smoke in the frosty air now alive with their grunts and whinnies. They settled down quickly, controlled by cackling witches who's multicolored cloaks streamed behind them, tattered rags I knew to be an illusion to scare the living daylights out of me.

I glanced behind then kept running as riders encouraged their charges to speed up. Selma's voice sounded odd, off somehow, and then it clicked. I stopped running, knew there was no point and that getting to the house wouldn't happen.

"Whatever you do, don't try anything foolish. Stand beside me, but when I tell you to move, you move, okay?"

"What's happening?"

"We're under attack by devious, dangerous witches. I didn't expect them to find something out so soon, and I sure as hell didn't expect to meet you today. Do not say a word to them, understand? Nothing. And I'm sorry, this won't be pretty."

"Okay." Penelope didn't know what was happening, but I did. I'd screwed up, but for once I didn't feel completely responsible. Mabel had it coming and this was her reaction. Was I ready? No. Was I worried about Death? Not really. Why? Dunno. I'm funny like that at times, I guess.

The witches circled us as Selma stopped in front on her midnight beast.

"You can cut the act, Mabel. I know it's you."

"Haha, you see through my disguise?"

"Duh. Why bother dressing like that? What's the point?"

"After Selma's treachery I thought I would come and try to reason with you. Impersonate her and maybe get back what you have taken from me. But then I had a better idea," she cackled. As another rider pulled up, the Queen nodded to her and the woman waved a hand. Mabel's body morphed and she was back as the witch bitch I knew and disliked immensely.

"What, planning on winning me over with that outfit were you? Why'd you get her to put up the spell?"

"My sisters like to help, and practice is always good."

"Whatever."

"I see you, Arthur Salzman. I know your inner thoughts. You're the same as all men. You see a young girl in a sexy outfit and you lose your ability to reason. I was going to seduce you, get what is mine that way. But horses, oh, I do love horses. They like me too. It's a witch thing," she added.

"Blah, blah. So, what do you want again? I forget." I was trying to keep a shaking Penelope behind me, but it was little use as there were witches all around us now. I was going to lose this before it had even begun.

I am such an idiot. But how was I to know this would happen? How was I to know Mabel would be on my case so soon, and here of all places? And how was I to know I would meet Penelope?

"It's not here," I said, sounding so convincing that I almost believed it myself.

"Oh, it's here all right. I can smell it, taste it." Mabel pulled on the reins and the horse stopped circling us.

"Where's Selma?" I snapped, not in the mood for this at all. Plus, worn down to the bone, and weak as a kitten. What was I going to do? How could we escape? Mabel was stronger than me, that was blindingly obvious. Without some fast thinking, and faster acting, I was done for. Sasha was gone, would probably turn up when this was all over and offer her help too late, but everyone else was still inside.

Right on cue, George came rushing down the field, looking freaked then angry when she saw the mad witches riding her horses.

"Stay in the house," I shouted, but George kept on coming. "I said go back to the house. Now!" George shook her head and marched forward, ignoring the witches that were barely controlling the horses, angry eyes focused on Mabel.

"Ah, George, isn't it?" asked Mabel with a smile.

"Yes. You're on my horse. They are too." George indicated the others with a nod of the head.

"I told you to stay inside," I said gently.

"And I don't like people stealing my horses." George was defiant, and she looked scary. Red hair almost burning as her anger increased and so did her overall color.

I'd never seen her like this, but it was as though she could burst into flame at any moment. She'd been learning her craft, and fast. These damn witches would be the death of us all. I decided that if I survived I would reevaluate what I knew about them, and tread a little more carefully in their presence.

This would get messy very quickly unless I did something. So I did what I had to do.

"Fine," I sighed, "you win. You get down, let George sort the animals out, and I'll give you what you need." I bloody well would as well.

"That's more like it," said Mabel, grinning with a self-satisfied smile that made me regret not doing my best to kill her back at the Residence. Not that I could have, but still.

Mabel dismounted with surprising grace and the others weren't half bad either. With a nod from Mabel, they led the horses back to the stables and the Queen held out the reins for George, grinning at her. "The offer is still open, you know. You may join us, learn from us."

"I think I'm doing fine on my own," said George, taking the reins carefully and leading the stallion away after a few protests from the beast.

"Now, you will return what you have stolen."

"Why is it so important?" I asked, my curiosity getting the better of me even now. "I know for a fact that Selma believed you were going to use the cauldron to do some mad witchcraft, somehow use it to destroy Ivan. But I don't believe it for a second. What's the deal, eh? Why so much riding on a damn cauldron?"

"You really are a stupid man," noted Mabel. "You think I would tell one as young, and as untrustworthy as Selma my plans? Nobody knows. That is how you keep secrets. They knew I was to use the cauldron, but not how. What makes you think you deserve the answer?"

"Oh, just curious. After all, I think we know each other pretty well now, right? Just between us," I whispered. "Promise I won't tell."

"Arthur, I'm scared," said Penelope, gripping my hand tight.

"Don't worry. Go back to the house, wait for me there. Go with George, now." I nodded at George as she returned. This was the perfect way to get them both away. No way would George leave Penelope here, so she had to go too.

"I'll take you," said George, then she nodded at me. I released Penelope's hand reluctantly and turned to Mabel.

"Will you let them leave? Your fight is with me, right?"

"As you wish," she said dismissively.

I watched as George literally dragged Penelope away. What she was thinking I had no idea, but it wouldn't be anything good. I'd blown it good and proper now. After seeing the kind of crap that happened on an all-too-regular basis she'd be off, no matter how we felt about each other.

"Now it's just us," I said.

"Just us."

"And what was it you wanted again?"

"Don't play games with me, Arthur, I am not in the mood. Return what is mine or I shall kill you then I will go into that house and kill everyone you care about. Who is the woman? Penelope?"

"Just someone I met. But c'mon, I think I know you well enough to know you wouldn't really kill them, would you?"

"No, probably not," she admitted. "But I have been known to change my mind. After all, I had every intention of killing you for your intrusion, but look at us now. The best of friends."

"Yeah, besties, that's us."

"So, will you retrieve what is mine?"

"Retrieve? Why, my dear Mabel, it's right here."

And with that I disappeared.

Thinking On My Feet

A gentle bubbling and gurgling filled my ears and darkened my soul as I reached from behind one of Mabel's crones and slit her throat. She dropped dead before she knew what had happened. Witches screamed and shouted, panic setting in, but I twisted the Teleron I held tightly in my hand before anyone had a chance to come wag their finger at me and tell me I wasn't going to get any supper.

Again, I vanished, then was next to another woman, further away this time as none of them were keeping still, which was most inconsiderate as the last thing I wanted was to be melded into a witch for the rest of my life. She whirled as my blade arced, her momentum forcing the knife deeper than I'd have liked. It felt gross as the vibration of the steel hitting her spine right through her throat sang up my arm.

I was away again, appearing behind the last woman who was turning this way and that, trying to anticipate my attack. I whistled and she spun, magic flaring from the tip of a very nice looking wand carved from a red wood I didn't know, but she missed by a fraction and I was upon her, blade already stained with her sisters' blood. I slashed hard and fast, was gone before the blood spurted.

"Surprise," I whispered in Mabel's ear as I appeared right behind her. She hadn't moved a muscle since I began my disappearing act.

Mabel turned her head and smiled. "I'd heard you had one, but didn't believe it. That is a fine artifact you have, Arthur. Would you care to sell it?"

"Hmm, let me think about that. Nah, I'm good." I disappeared, then returned a safe distance in front of Mabel several seconds later, my infinite bag slung over my shoulder, compact yet uncomfortable, weighty yet not weighing a thing, and I almost keeled over backwards until I got used to carrying such a strange item once again. It threw me off balance every time, but I reckoned I needed it now, for it contained something important. Something that had to be explained, maybe even returned if this night was to end with all my important, and even not-so-important, bits intact.

"Let's see what the fuss is all about, shall we?" I said as I reached into the bag.

"What are you doing, you stupid man?" said Mabel, her patience clearly wearing thin.

"I'm getting what you came here for. Do not move," I warned. "One step and I'll be gone, and I will destroy it. You understand?" I glared at her, my face stony, making sure she understood I wasn't messing about, that this had gone on long enough. I'd had a gut's full of the whole bloody business. Hell, I'd only done this to stop the killing, but it was already out of hand. How many dead witches were there now? This was ridiculous.

I wondered again if I should have just left Ivan to deal with it, left him to kill the bloody lot of them. I think maybe I should have.

"As you wish."

"What is wrong with you? Why are you so obsessed with destroying Ivan? And what is with this cauldron? I know magic, and I know artifacts, and there is absolutely nothing that this cauldron could do that you couldn't find another way to accomplish. Whatever it does, you could go after Ivan without it. What's the deal?"

Mabel stared at me but remained silent. If that was how she wanted to play it then fine.

"Well? Answer me."

"You are correct. In fact, it was just an idea, the cauldron. But now, well, it's the principle, isn't it? You stole from me, and that isn't nice."

I remained focused on her, the lights from the stables shining bright, lighting up the whole area. The horses were still noisy, but safe, and at least nobody could sneak up on me. But I wasn't about to look down and give Mabel a chance. Again, I said, "You move a muscle and I'm gone. I will destroy it, and then you. Understand? I may not have much magic inside me, but I can still kill you. You let me live earlier, but you also killed me many times and would have carried on doing so. I showed your women respect even after that, buried them and gave them peace. You let me live because of it. You have morals, you have forgiveness of a sort, so don't push me. I will crush you."

Mabel nodded.

I reached into the infinite bag and grabbed hold. As I pulled my arm out, so the bag expanded, the edges growing fuzzy as space and time and who knows what else rearranged themselves to accommodate this truly magical item. I tried not to think about how it worked. I'd done that in the past and it made my head hurt too much.

Nonetheless, I continued pulling and grinned as I yanked out my prize. It had been easy to take. During the confusion at the house when Vicky had smashed the wall down, I'd grabbed the cauldron in the chaos and stuffed it inside. I hadn't had the chance to inspect it, but I had it. Now Mabel wanted it back. I knew she'd find out, but my plan was to go to her, tell her to keep the peace and I'd return it. No such option now, and I guess it wasn't the smartest of moves. But I'd promised Selma I'd try to get it, and she was sure this held the key to stopping Mabel, so what choice did I have?

"Ta-da," I said with a grin as I pulled my prize out from the bag. It felt bloody heavy, much heaver than I'd remembered.

"A chain?" asked Mabel, frowning. "Don't test me."

I glanced down at the thing in my hand. "Damn, wrong item. That's the problem with infinite bags, it's a bugger to find anything. Hang on, be with you in a jiffy." I reached in again, deeper this time, so deep I worried I'd fall in and be lost for eternity. I rummaged around, all manner of oddities rearranging inside to get my attention. Next out came a furry rabbit that I hurriedly shoved back in; it was one evil beast and no mistake.

Next was a ladder, the first few rungs of metal enough to tell me I had the wrong item, then it was an anchor, but that didn't come out very far as it was from a very special ship and hardly useful when not at sea. Then I grasped warm metal, a curved handle, and I knew I had the right thing.

"Don't move," I warned again as I pulled out the cauldron. The handle creaked as the body of the cauldron swayed back and forth as if pleased to be away from the horrors that lurked within.

Mabel's eyes widened but she remained still. I placed the artifact down on the grass and removed what appeared to be hay from the inside. Good for protection I guess. As I removed the large lump of dry grass, several items tinkled in the bottom of the cauldron. Mabel gasped, I risked a glance down, and there in the bottom of this black bowl were a handful of very shiny pink things.

"Bones? Painted bones?" I asked, not quite sure.

"None of your concern," snapped Mabel.

I tried to figure this out, but couldn't. What were a load of bones, finger bones by the looks of it, maybe a complete hand, doing in the cauldron. And why were they so pink? They were almost luminous.

"Oh no, tell me this isn't them?"

"That depends on what you think them is," growled Mabel, looking anxious as all hell now.

"It's Kinky Bones, isn't it?"

Too late, the bloody things sprang at me and wrapped tight around my throat.

I was going to die at the hands of a set of seriously pissed off bones. Not just any bones, but the Kinky Bones. This wouldn't be nice.

A Kinky Surprise

Everyone thinks of witches as having a certain look, acting a certain way, and doing certain things. I had to adjust my opinion after what I'd been through, but there was still a way about them, a set of traditional values that passed down the many generations, and they all acted and dressed alike for the most part. The deeper you went, the more similar they were. Same with wizards. Yours truly being no exception apart from more handsome and skilled than the other scruffy muppets.

Then came Kate, better known as Kinky Bones, short-lived queen of the witches, but never, ever to be forgotten. She came from nowhere, blasting through the ranks of the old, outdated crones, and became one of the first witch queens of the modern era. She embraced the new sexual freedoms of the age, flaunted it, got a reputation the witches disapproved of mightily; she didn't care. Her exploits became legendary, her sexual conquests and perversions shocking both then and now.

She temporarily did away with many of the old ideals, strove for newness, for fresh ideas, for the witches to change and embrace the modern world. This was back in the nineteen twenties, the roaring twenties quite literally for some, including her, for she went too far and paid the ultimate price, with fire.

Kate was burned alive, not by persecutors, but by her own kind. She was too far ahead of her time, certainly too wild, and the old-timers, the witches who'd been around for centuries, wouldn't stand for her meddling and her ideas. She wanted to make the witches into something they weren't, to bring them into the limelight, show off, be proud and in control. Sounds like someone else I knew.

Kinky Bones was powerful and wasn't afraid to show it. She killed numerous sisters who stood against her, and when the old queen died she eliminated the competition in any way she saw fit then took control. She dove headfirst into the heady times of the twenties, embraced the partying and the modern fashions, the new dances, music, and drunken revelry with a wild abandon that shocked most, delighted a few. There was chaos in the witch world for the few years she ruled, until she met her demise. But even death didn't stop her and her obsession with all things perverted and decadent, and chaos followed her to the grave and beyond.

This now dead queen had magic like no other before her, and her death did little to destroy such potent energy. It had to go somewhere, it had to be transformed or it would build and catastrophe awaited, so she became an artifact in her own right. Her corpse refused to burn properly. When the fire died down she still stood, half burned, body intact, hair still there, clothes gone, a macabre smile on her face.

But witches were used to such nonsense and they had their ways. Bury them deep, and far away, and forget, that was their answer, but not this time. Something wasn't right, in fact it was so far from right that for a month nobody would go near the corpse of Kinky Bones. She remained tied to the stake, not rotting, not feeding the worms; even the birds failed to peck out her eyes.

There was something else that kept the witches at bay.

Kinky Bones was pink. Maybe from the flame, maybe from the magic she'd held inside, or maybe she'd always been pink and nobody had known because she always covered up and wore gloves. Her skin shone with an ethereal luminescence, almost dayglo it was so bright, and it terrified the others.

Finally they had an answer. For some strange reason they chopped her up, thinking that would be the end of her and the strange magic that surrounded her and danced above and around her body. But no sooner had she been dismembered than the pieces came together again, and the next day she was whole.

Exasperated, she was boiled, then skinned, until, after several weeks, and a lot of lime, potions, and spells she was nothing but a skeleton. She was pulled apart, and apparently it took two horses to do it, and her bones divided amongst the leaders of the witches.

But bad things happened to those who owned her bones, and nobody was prepared to take on the macabre inheritance when those tasked with safeguarding the artifacts died. So she was scattered across the world, young witches tasked with taking the pieces far away and throwing them into the deepest oceans, into volcanoes, placed underground in caves where nobody would find them.

For even her bones were pink, and they became known as the Kinky Bones, just like the woman. Over the years the tales grew wilder, but nobody owned up to keeping any of the bones, for anyone who did would meet an untimely end. There were stories about some of the deaths, none of them nice, of how the bones sent their owners mad, that they would come alive and destroy them, or consume their magic, although when they were found there was never any sign of the bones having moved, only strange markings on the corpse like they'd been battered or choked, strangled or worse.

But it looked like Mabel wasn't bothered by any of that, and she cackled as I stumbled back and landed hard on the ground, five separate digits joined together and strangling me. It wasn't possible. There was nothing connecting each small piece of bone, but a hand it was, and it was annoyed with me for some reason.

"You woke her," cackled Mabel as she strode forward and stood over me, watching as I died.

I would have said, "Ah, so this was your plan. It wasn't the cauldron as such, but what was inside. You were going to let Kinky Bones loose on Ivan, knowing nothing could stop them if he was the focus," but I couldn't, because I was struggling to breathe, so instead I just said, "Argh," or something.

Mabel laughed, a seriously worrying full-on witch cackle, while I flailed about and grabbed at the bones slowly squeezing the life out of me.

As I died, I couldn't help but wonder why this was her chosen way of dealing with Ivan. Then I understood. It was a cruel way to die, as vampires aren't easy to kill, what with the whole regenerating thing. But this, this unstoppable set of bones, it would keep on going, kill and kill again, keep on squeezing as Ivan died and his body refused to do so, fought back with all the vampire strength it could muster. Eventually he would succumb, and Mabel wouldn't have to be anywhere near him.

It was a clever idea, hands-off so to speak. I'd die, come back, die all over again, and like a repeat of my last encounter with this insane woman, it would be easy for her, hard for me. Except, this time my luck would run out.

Sometimes it sucks to be a wizard. I was trying to impress my girlfriend, and as I watched her horrified face, staring around at the bodies yet nonetheless running to me along with George, I knew I'd probably, make that certainly, blown it in a typically epic Hat way.

Grr

Artifacts, by their very nature, are serious and strange objects. Some are sentient, others can be unruly, most are unpredictable, all are dangerous.

The same can be said for wizards. Especially ones who see their new, and soon to be ex, girlfriend and their darling daughter running headlong toward if not certain death then certainly maiming and misery. Plus, I didn't really fancy them having to go out like I was. Being killed by a perverted set of pink bones is not classy, it's downright disgraceful, not to mention embarrassing, so I struggled for all I was worth, not that I was worth much.

Mabel may have thought I was a weakling, that my actions didn't live up to the hype of my name, and so far she'd been right. But this time was different. I was ready and I may not have been as able as I would have liked, but I knew what I had to do and how I'd do it. I had to get into that zone, that place where magic came from, the Quiet Place, and I had to do it quickly. What I'm really saying is, I had to get my mojo back.

You can secure magical energy in numerous ways, and Mabel knew this as well as me. She would have thought I'd maybe got a little but not a lot, but she didn't know what I'd been up to today since I left her, would have assumed I'd rested, tried to recover. I hadn't. I'd been meeting Penelope then having sex in a barn with a stranger that felt like a best friend.

There is a special place where magic always resides, and that's the emotion of the human heart, and sex. Sex magic has been used since the dawn of time, long before humanity understood that this natural yet most sacred and special act is more powerful than any time spent in the Quiet Place. Sex, the act of forging new life, of connecting so deeply with another human being, is a true magic. After all, this immensely complicated series of perfect connections from the entirely physical to the most transcendent is how you create a human life, and nothing is more amazing or wondrous than that. And I, not to boast or anything, but let's face it I was over forty and over the hill, and utterly knackered before I met Penelope, had done it twice.

What could be more apt when dealing with the pink bones of a sex-obsessed witch?

Inside of me was a chance of life, a kernel of deep-knotted energy forged by the power of emotion and the act of sharing my body with another. The stirrings of life force, of an awakening as the body struggled and tried its best to create another human. A teeny-tiny Hat. That power was stirring. Partly through the act itself and the power it brought to you if you only focused on the wondrous biology going on inside you, but just as much through the emotion that made sex more than a simple yet pleasurable way to spend a few seconds—um, I mean minutes—but something deeper, and much more special. Much more magical.

Hat power of the most primal kind.

Digging Deep

My emotions were running high, and I knew from experience that there's power in emotion. It isn't something you can force, will into being when the time isn't right, that's what settling down in the Quiet Place is for, to access the universe and let its truth enter you.

Just as potent, debatably even more so, is the energy you can harness from inside when your body is thrumming in time to something wondrous, when you're on the right wavelength. It's one and the same really. The underlying nature of the universe at work. I was, after all, a human being, a creature so miraculous, made up of things that by rights should be called magic, that I was a true marvel. Something unbelievably rare. A sentient creature in a universe of almost utter emptiness.

With Penelope on the scene, I was full to bursting with emotions of all kinds, and our little tryst had stirred up deep and powerful chemicals, a furnace fed by the fires of creation itself. I knew I could call on this in my time of need. Call it the body's innate sense of self-preservation because it knew there was a chance to procreate and continue the Salzman gene pool, call it having a reason to live, call it what you will, but I centered myself even as I faded away. Death was standing on an empty beach, waiting for me, as I let magic consume me.

Wand vibrated in my pocket like he was having a stick seizure, my body thrummed with the immense potential it contained, all that energy stored in a tiny flesh-prison, and we both burst into life simultaneously.

One of us burst in a more literal sense than the other. Wand burned a hole right through my pocket and my hand automatically snapped out to grab him as he shot skyward. The warm wood felt like shaking the hand of an old, dear friend, and we said a silent hello to each other.

"You dirty devil," he said, and I could picture him grinning.

"I am, aren't I?" I said silently, my throat being squeezed so tight I was losing focus.

Having had many a near death experience before, and not as worried about it as those who only got to experience it once, I stayed as calm as I could and focused my will. This would be a delicate operation, no blasting wanted or required.

I let a spell form, the words unnecessary, just the memory, a feeling of the complete system wrapped up into a tiny ball of pure intent, and energy streamed down my arm and into Wand, who flared bright and joyous at the return to form.

He vibrated so fast he was a blur, but that may have just been the lack of oxygen to my brain. The sigils flared bright, he spasmed once, then twisted my wrist until his tip made contact with a pink finger bone trying to work its way through my throat.

To say it was electric is an understatement. It's like saying attaching electrodes to your balls makes them tingle, and as the energy expunged through Wand and tore at the fingers, my heart stopped for a moment under the onslaught.

A reassuring thud, thud, thud, signified I wasn't dead yet, and the easing around my neck told me we were onto a winner here, so I pushed deeper, sliced Wand across the bones like an amateur playing the xylophone, resulting in a cacophony of wood on bone worse than a woodpecker having a seizure.

Magic flared in earnest.

Bright and beautiful, Wand's power was unleashed in an extravagant display that shook my teeth loose and made the hairs on my ears retreat inside for safety. The Kinky Bones made a last-ditch attempt to pierce my skin but our power was too strong and the hand tumbled away to the ground. I wasted no time clambering to my feet and assuming a suitably impressive fighting stance. My knee hurt from bending it, but I looked awesome so it was all good.

All of this happened so fast that George and Penelope still hadn't quite reached us, but it would only be a second and they'd be here.

"Get back," I screamed, then muttered under my breath and a sigil on Wand shone like a blood moon.

Red energy crackled, disrupting the night sky as it blasted the ground at Mabel's feet and she was lost to a shower of earth and sod as a seven-feet-wide and deep hole exploded right where she stood.

George and Penelope pulled up short at the chaos and I shouted again, "Go back, I can handle this." George and I made eye contact and I nodded to her. She did likewise then grabbed Penelope and dragged her away even as she called out to me. Me, she was calling for me. That was sweet.

With renewed vigor and determination, I let loose again with another blast of violence designed to destroy not Mabel but the ground, forcing her to retreat and reconsider her actions.

She stepped back, but she wasn't panicking, and she even smiled as I held wand aloft, ready to go at it again.

Then something grabbed my foot and I knew why she was so damn smug.

Kinky Bones gripped my shin hard and squeezed, the pain immense as bone ground against bone. I hopped about, shaking my leg, looking less than awesome now. Mabel cackled as she advanced.

I lowered Wand and used him to prise the bones away from my leg, but no sooner were they off and laying on the ground than they regrouped into a skeletal hand and launched at me, this time going for somewhere much more delicate and definitely less bony.

Have you ever been grabbed in the nether regions by a set of imperishable magical bones renowned for being part of a powerful witch who was as kinky as they come? No? It was a first for me too.

The bones did something weird to that place between a man's most important bits and my bum, and I wasn't sure what exactly was happening, but I knew I didn't like it. Fingers reached up and did unspeakable things to my limp, shrunken member, and it was right about then I may have yelped and clawed frantically at my molester as the hand gripped tight and kept on squeezing.

"You won't be a man for much longer," laughed Mabel as she took another step forward and pulled out a familiar object from her pocket.

"Seriously? You're going to shoot me again?"

"Why change what works?" she said with a smile as she aimed.

The Queen squeezed the trigger.

This was becoming annoying.

An Aha Moment

The hand did something particularly disgusting involving one finger forward, one back—which wasn't as nice as it sounds—and I gasped as I doubled over, timed to perfection more through luck than sheer awesomeness, and the bullet sailed past.

"Wand, sort that out will you?" I hissed as I grabbed the bones in my left hand and flung him at Mabel with a throw that would make any cricket bowler clutch his head in shame for my pathetic ability.

"Be a pleasure," he said, following up with a happy, "Whee," as he flew at the Queen.

Mabel's eyes widened as Wand shot at her, streaming through the night like an angry comet. He hit the gun's barrel dead center and Mabel's hand spasmed then caught fire as the metal melted and her skin sizzled.

She screamed and dropped what she could of the gun but it was molten now, most of it wrapped tight around her hand, melding to flesh and bone, her hand utterly useless. She screamed and screamed again, unable to stop wailing, but I had my own problems to deal with. Namely, the perverted hand fondling nether regions in a way-too-intimate, but less than arousing manner.

Wand hovered there like a, well, like a hovering stick, as I shouted, "I didn't know you could do that."

"Neither did I," he replied, sounding pleased. Which you would be, wouldn't you?

"Do what?" screamed the Queen, staring at her hand in horror.

"I was talking to him," I said, now not the time to get into it.

Wand shot back and I reached out and grabbed him like I'd thrown a boomerang that had actually come back like it was supposed to.

The bones were playing up again and I gasped and almost fell as they clutched tight and something began to tear. Oh no, this wasn't good. Penelope wouldn't want me to be broken, I didn't want it either.

"I have a plan," I croaked to Wand.

"And I like it," he replied, sounding too damn cheery by half.

"Ready?"

"Yup."

I smashed down onto the bones with more force than I'd intended, and although it did the job, I knocked myself over and fell flailing into the frosty grass. It felt nice, the iciness easing the fearsome burn. As the bones scurried across the grass, regrouping for another assault on my neck now I was an easy target, I rested Wand on the ground then released him.

He swept this way and that in front of the bones and they grabbed onto the shaft and clung there, trying to squeeze the life out of him. Fully loaded with a complete hand now forming a tight grip along his length, he set off like a rocket towards Mabel and smashed into her mangled hand.

The metal shattered, and so did the bones and flesh beneath, and the whole thing fell to the ground with a dull thud. The Queen's eyes clamped shut before she leaned her head back and screamed into the night sky as she waved her stump around, the wound already cauterized.

But Wand wasn't finished yet, and he darted forward and impaled himself on the stump, burrowing deep as Mabel let loose with a primeval wail of utter agony mixed with terror.

I clambered to my feet and moved forward, watching as Wand burrowed deeper until the Kinky Bones made contact with the witch's flesh. The bones swayed this way and that, as if sniffing out fresh flesh, and then the entire hand leaped forward and grabbed tight around Mabel's forearm.

"Here, boy," I said, then whistled.

"You cheeky blighter," laughed Wand as he pulled free with a sick squelch then angled back to me. I caught him with a now practiced ease and blew on the end, as much to get the goop off as to cool him down.

As I moved to stand in front of Mabel, I watched as the Kinky Bones shifted on her forearm, then crawled down even as Mabel pleaded to get it off her and clawed at the bones to no avail. The hand jumped forward and snapped onto the end of Mabel's stump.

"Okay, are you going to say it, or shall I?" I asked Wand.

"You do it. You deserve it."

I readied myself for the worst line I'd ever uttered, smiling despite myself, and said, "That was handy."

Wand groaned, but chortled nonetheless, and as Mabel screamed yet again and ran around battling at her new hand and then dropping to the ground and thumping the bones against the mangled mess of her own ruined hand, I suddenly had a moment of clarity.

Why wasn't she doing something about this? Why was she just smacking about, hoping it would release itself?

"You can't do magic on your own, can you? It's true. The Kinky Bones drain the owner's magic. You're almost a citizen."

Mabel looked at me with pure frustration and a deep sadness before the tears fell. She hung her head and her arm went limp. She'd given up, admitted defeat, and could do nothing to stop this. Queen Witch without magic.

Downer.

The Truth

"But you're a witch," I said softly, watching as the tears fell. The Queen was silent now, her screams spent, but as she looked into my eyes she whimpered like a puppy waiting outside the supermarket for its owner to return.

"Help me, please?" she pleaded, staring at her alien hand.

"How can you not have magic? How are you Queen if you can't use it?" I was certain of it now. It explained so much, especially the gun.

"I don't have to tell you anything!" spat Mabel, bitter and mean even now when she was pleading for help.

"Suit yourself." I turned my back on her.

George and Penelope, unable to contain themselves, came running across the field; no way would they return to the house this time.

"Dad, are you okay?" George flung herself at me and I hugged her then backed off and held her at arm's length.

"I'm fine, just shaken up. Damn, that was a close one."

"Arthur, you... you... you used magic! You're a wizard!" Penelope blurted, looking as confused as Vicky in an adult clothes store.

"I know. I told you I was." My knees buckled and I almost fell but George and Penelope caught me and held me upright.

"Sorry about this. It's a bit much, I know." I glanced at the corpses, the ruined hand on the ground, and at Mabel herself. She was on her knees, whimpering with pain and humiliation.

"A bit much? You killed them, you used magic, you... And your wand, it..." Penelope stared in horror at the stump on the ground then at the dead bodies, then at Mabel, and I think something must have finally clicked into place. The horror of it all. As I watched Penelope, saw her take it all in for the first time as the adrenaline slowed, I understood. I'd lost her.

She was seeing it for what it was, seeing me for who I was, and it wasn't a pretty sight. I was blase about the whole thing, wasn't unduly affected by the death, it being such a constant, but my heart went out to Mabel for the mess she was, for what she'd made me do to save myself and those I loved. But I understood Penelope's reaction, because this was terrible. People were dead or maimed, everyone had been in danger, and it wasn't right.

Penelope's eyes glazed over as shock set in.

"Help me, please," pleaded Mabel as she held her hand up and the fingers bent.

"You brought this on yourself. What was I supposed to do?" I said.

"It will kill me. Please?"

"Like you wanted it to kill me? The way you intended to use it to kill Ivan? You've got no magic of your own, and you were going to use this to eliminate him. What then, eh? Think you would have been safe having so much power? Ah, so that's it. You wanted the power to hide your lack of ability. With so much control, you'd never have to get your own hands dirty again. You could use your people, nobody would expect you to get involved personally." It was a hell of a way to hide a secret, but at least she thought suitably epic.

"It went so slowly," she whispered. "I searched for the Quiet Place but I couldn't find a way in. I can't access the magic I've spent a lifetime immersed in. The Kinky Bones want power. They talk to me, tell me to do things. If I let them take Ivan, I will have my magic returned. Argh, help." Mabel clutched the bones as the fingers went nuts bending and wriggling as she tried to stop them.

Then the hand bunched into a fist and smacked her square on the nose. Blood spurted as she screamed, and cartilage snapped but the fist kept on hammering at her as her head whipped sideways and she fought for control.

The Queen slammed her arm into the ground but it made no difference, and the hand acted more viciously each time she did so. Mabel was exhausted, muscles strained at her neck, her face was a bloody mess as she got punched repeatedly, and she gave up trying to stop it. I grabbed her, yanked on the forearm to stop the fist connecting, but there was too much power, too much strength, and it broke free and continued to punch and slap.

"Cut it off, please, cut it off," yelled Mabel through broken teeth, her lips split, blood pouring from her face in multiple places.

"Go get a knife," I said to George as I grabbed the arm again and pulled as hard as I could. "Penelope, go with George and stay at the house."

Penelope nodded numbly, then turned and walked away as George ran as fast as she could.

"Why all this, Mabel? Why were you going to do it? The truth."

"To have control. I thought I could regain what I'd lost. I'm weak, everyone would find out sooner or later. I had to do something for me, but for my sisters too. We would have glorious power, be feared and respected, and we could rule. Men don't deserve the power. They ruin everything. And the hand, it wanted me to do this. It's done things to me, to my mind. I know it, but I can't stop it. Can't stop myself."

"You got that bit right," I said, straining to stop the fist battering her to death, my own muscles screaming with the effort.

"Why did you lose your abilities? I know for a fact it isn't just the hand. It can't be, magic doesn't work like that." I asked, but I wasn't sure I really wanted to know the answer. I'd heard of it happening before, but rarely, and there was always something momentous behind it.

A life-changing event that broke the connection, sometimes permanently, with the Quiet Place. You could blame artifacts, say they sucked it out of you, but you had to give in to it. Mabel had been strong, she shouldn't have given up like this.

"I lost something precious, and then I was alone. Couldn't gain access. Something broke inside. The hand called, promised me power if I gave it some of my own. It promised great things if I would help it for a while." Mabel would have said more, I'm sure, but I couldn't keep hold and the Kinky Bones smashed into her mouth, completely ruining her lips and knocking several teeth right out.

Mabel spat blood and teeth onto the grass and shrieked then laughed. A manic, soul-wrenching cackle of the damned and disgraced. She'd lost it, was on the other side now, deep in the throes of madness.

Where the hell was George?

I spied her running at us, but when I turned back the bones were wrapped tight around Mabel's throat. She'd be dead before George made it. I readied myself, drew on what little strength I had remaining, and pulled Wand out. No reaction.

"Wand, wake up," I shouted as I shook him. Nothing. He was spent, his actions too much for both of us. We'd called on something special and powerful but it was used up, and the source of that power, the connection with Penelope, was gone. Penelope had been broken by a single day in my presence, and the magic had gone along with her.

I grabbed the bones, tried to prize fingers apart, but it was no use. I stared into Mabel's eyes as she gasped then stopped breathing. A few seconds later the bones relaxed and the arm went limp, fell across Mabel's chest as she keeled over and lay in the grass.

"Got it," said George, panting as she held my Santoku cleaver out for me.

"Get the cauldron," I mumbled. "And the hay that was inside."

George looked at me quizzically, then at Mabel, and said, "Oh." She dropped the knife and ran to do as I'd asked.

I picked up the cleaver, took a deep breath, then chopped the bones off as best I could. It took a few goes, and it wasn't pretty, but I got it done.

George placed the cauldron down and held the hay. "What now?"

"As soon as I throw the bones in, put the hay on top. Then we put a bloody good ward up, okay? I don't know what the grass does, but I'm guessing it's there for a reason."

"Okay."

I scooped the bones up on the cleaver's blade and dropped them inside the cauldron. They rattled around, awareness returning, so George hurriedly covered them. They stilled, so we wasted no time, and together we formed a ward to stop them being removed or escaping. It would do for now, until I thought of something better.

I stood with a groan and said, "Come on, let's go back to the house."

We walked arm in arm away from the massacre of the Kinky Bones.

Blew It

Penelope was standing at the open doorway next to a concerned looking Vicky.

"Are you okay?" she asked.

"Fine. Kind of."

"Take me home, please," said Penelope, her face blank, her body almost limp.

"Let me explain first," I said, already knowing the answer.

"I just want to go home." Penelope began to cry.

"Okay, let's go," I said.

"No, George can do it."

With those words, my heart, which I'd been so careful to protect, was broken. I knew I should have just given Penelope her shopping and got the hell away as fast as I could. It would never mend from this.

I nodded, resigned to a lonely future.

Penelope followed George to the car.

She never looked back. She never even said goodbye.

Frosty Reception

"So, are we cool?"

The witches gasped, all thirty-three of them, and then I pulled Wand away from the mad old bint holding on to him, her other hand holding another witch's and so on and so on, the mad, wild women weaving around the house and into the grounds like a bizarrely dressed snake.

"She wanted to kill Ivan, betrayed her sisters, killed them, and used the Kinky Bones," said the witch closest to me. There were murmurs of agreement.

"I know that," I said. "What I want to know is if we are cool? Wand showed you what happened, best he could anyway, so you know I had no intention of killing her even after she shot me dead repeatedly. So, I'll ask again, are we cool?"

The witches stopped moving, were as still as statues, and remained that way for several minutes. Then they broke from their freaky witch communal gossiping, however they did it, and began babbling all at once.

This was the last thing I needed. We'd brought Mabel and all her dead cronies back with us, George and I, and then she'd made calls and gathered the witches for the big news. It hadn't gone down well and I'd nearly been killed within seconds, but I told them I could show them what happened, and they let me. Now here we were.

"You may go," said the ancient crone beside me.

"Good." George and I moved to leave; the stench of patchouli was becoming overpowering and I was starting to have visions.

"Wait! What about the cauldron, and the Kinky Bones?"

"Spoils of war," I said, marching out with George beside me.

"Be careful," warned several women, which was nice of them.

"That went well," I said with a smile once we were clear of the madhouse.

"Yeah." George frowned.

"What?"

"They'll be a nightmare now, bickering and fighting to decide who's next queen.

"At least they won't be trying to kill us," I said, trying to remain upbeat when all I wanted to do was hide away and write love letters to Penelope that she'd never open because she hated, maybe even abhorred, me for what I'd done.

"I guess."

We left, went home. I had things to do.

Caveman

There's something primeval and indescribably satisfying about a fire. Ever since mankind first learned how to tame this most magical of elements it has been a constant in our world. It signifies life, warmth, advancement, and safety. A way to keep the beasts at bay, to protect your family and ensure your survival.

More than that, fire creates a sense of place, a focal point, somewhere for a group of people to gather, to cook and come together. Not only are the flames mesmerizing, but a simple fire can bring people closer in so many ways. From preparing the earth, gathering rocks to form a circle so you don't burn your house down, to collecting wood, it creates jobs to be done, giving each person involved a sense of satisfaction and the knowledge they have contributed.

Which is why, as I squatted in front of a large circle of stones out in the field well away from the stables, where so much had gone down the night before, I felt immensely satisfied as I stared into the flames. I felt like a cowboy from the old wild west, out on the trail, exploring the new frontier. Like a caveman protecting his family, or a lone warrior ready to fight off the dragons that would destroy all he loved.

Still, it was over, and I was alive, if less than fighting fit.

My knees hurt and I wasn't sure I'd be able to stand back up, but nonetheless I remained where I was and leaned aside to grab a long stick and poke the embers. That's another thing about men and fires. You have to poke them with sticks. I don't know what it is, but it's an unwritten law, like the only time a lot of blokes cook is when it involves a barbecue. Outdoors and primal, ancient urges and callings goading us into action. Or maybe it's because cooking burgers is a lot easier than making lasagna, and people expect it to be burnt anyway so you're onto a winner.

The fire sparked as I wiggled the stick, and the fresh wood I'd added caught, flames licking around the short lengths and adding to the heat.

Above the fire I had put together a large metal tripod that had been rusting in a barn for a while, one of those impulse buys that then just gathers cobwebs, but tonight it was getting use. A long chain hung from the center and was perfect for hanging up a pot to cook. It was adjustable, and I'd decided slow cooking was the best option for the meal. It gave me the excuse to remain out here for hours, contemplating the flames and the cycle of life and death, how nothing truly died, was merely transformed from one element to another.

Now it was dark, and I'd turned off the lights at the stables so the only light was the one I myself had created. I stirred the murky, thick contents of a meal that was almost ready. It smelled great, but I may have been biased.

I was aware of footsteps approaching, but I didn't turn, just continued to stare, and poke about so sparks danced high into the void. Flames licked the pot before dying down, causing the stew to bubble angrily for a moment.

"You came back," I said, turning to see Penelope standing there, her arms crossed to ward off the chill of the night air.

"George came and got me."

"I didn't think I'd ever see you again. After yesterday," I added, in case she'd forgotten.

"I didn't think I'd ever return. Arthur, you have to understand, what happened, it was a lot to take in. Things like that don't happen in my world. You killed those women, you murdered them."

"I know what I did," I snapped, a little harshly. I was a fool for thinking I could ever have a future with someone like Penelope. And she was right, I'd murdered them, and I felt nothing but sadness for it. Not guilt, not regret, just sad that I'd killed yet again and it hardly affected me now. This was the worst punishment of all, to know you were a monster but wish you weren't.

"I wasn't accusing you, just trying to explain that I've never seen anything like that before. I've never even seen a dead body."

"I've seen plenty," I mumbled, then prodded the fire.

"Does it hurt? To kill people? Does it hurt inside?"

I turned to face Penelope so she could see my face. "It hurts because I feel nothing when I do it. If someone tries to hurt me or my family, I will destroy them. Do you understand? This world is different to yours. This world is violent and dangerous and we are dangerous people. We don't answer to anybody else, we don't play by the rules others do. We have our own, and they are costly if broken. We all know what we signed up for, and accept it. We kill and we try to survive. Those women knew exactly what the risk was. But yes, it hurts because I think maybe I'm numb to it now. It used to tear me apart, and in some ways it still does, knowing what I've done, what I'll do again, but does it break me, make me fall apart? No. It just aches in my heart for the man I've become."

"I don't think you're numb inside." Penelope squatted beside me and put an arm on my shoulder.

"I've blown it, right? We had this amazing day together and now I've blown it. I understand, I know this is way too much to take in, too much to handle. But thank you for coming to tell me in person, that means a lot."

"Arthur, you are so dense. I haven't come to say goodbye. I've come to say... Well, I've come to say I'm in." Penelope beamed at me, that sparkle of amusement in her eyes.

"You want to stay with me? Be involved in all this?"

"Arthur 'The Hat' Salzman, I fell for you the moment I saw you. There you were, this scruffy, strange man with a nice hat, looking like the world was about to end and it was your fault, telling me you were going to marry me and you could cook, and I fell for you. Then you said you were a wizard. I didn't believe you, of course, but now I know it's true. Look, my life is average, I'm average, you aren't. I'm the lucky one here, to get to spend time in your world, see the other side. This is a true gift you've given me, to let me in, see magic and fae and meet you and George and Vicky and Sasha and all the rest. I feel honored. I want in. I want you."

"You mean it?" Penelope nodded and I smiled at her as my heart leapt and my spirits soared into the emptiness. I couldn't be this lucky, surely? Looks like I was.

"There's just one thing," she said, breaking eye contact and looking nervous, maybe even afraid.

"I knew it! You're going to tell me something truly horrible. Are you dying? Do you have to leave for years? Something worse?"

"No, I was just about to say that I always sleep in the nude, and I know some people don't like that. Will it be a problem?" The glint in her eye was back; she was teasing me.

This felt so right, so normal, that I wanted to cry. Instead, deadpan, I said, "Guess I'll just have to get used to it."

"Guess you will." Penelope took the stick off me and poked the fire.

"What you cooking?"

"Wait and see."

Dinner Time

Penelope and I stood staring at the fire, arms around each other's waists. It felt just about perfect.

We turned when we heard the loud chatter of everyone else.

The twins, allowed to stay up late because this was a special occasion, special because everyone was alive, ran forward then began dancing around the fire like trainee mad witches, while Vicky warned them to be careful in that screechy mom-voice she'd perfected over the years. Steve followed behind her, encouraging her to let the girls have fun and winning brownie points for sticking up for them.

George and Sasha came next, both brightening the night with their beauty and the faery dust that fell. Sasha's silver dress, tight as her skin as always, reflected the light of the fire, making her look like a flaming bronze statue, and behind them came Selma, dressed in too much leather and yet not enough of it to cover much of anything.

"Looks like we're almost all here," I said to nobody in particular.

The night was filled with laughter and voices, but there was an edge to it. Hardly surprising after what had happened, all we'd been through.

"Who's hungry?" I asked, smiling at the sight of family and friends.

Everyone by the seems of it, judging by the rubbing of bellies and the call for me to dish up, so I poked the embers, making the fire crackle and the thick stew bubble. I reluctantly released Penelope and moved over to the folding table I'd set up with everything I'd need. This was so perfect. I hadn't expected Penelope to come, but I'd prayed for it. For once, seemed like somebody was listening. I picked up the ladle and returned to the fire where everyone gathered around.

"Wait," said Vicky. "That isn't the... It is, isn't it?"

"I don't know what you're talking about," I said innocently.

Selma moved forward and inspected my cooking pot. "You're using the cauldron? Are you mad? It's Mabel's original cauldron. And you know what was in it?"

"I sure as hell do. I've rehomed the bones for now, Mabel's dead, Kinky Bones won't bother us any more, and well, it's a nice pot for cooking in. It's made for using, that's what cauldrons are. They're just pots."

"Yes, but I do believe a witch's pot has magical abilities," said Ivan as he appeared from out of nowhere, his aide by his side.

"Bloody hell, you scared me to death," I said, scowling.

"Sorry we're late."

"Don't worry about it. Now that we're all here, I want to say something." Everyone stared at me, and I felt uncomfortable, verging on stupid, for what I was about to say. I'd say it anyway.

"Go on then," urged Vicky, one eye on the girls in case they decided to burn the world down or that today was the day they would become the rulers of the universe, which they very much planned on being at some point, maybe in a few years.

"Penelope and I are going to be married, and I know you all think it's nuts, and we do too. I figured after yesterday, and I'm sure everyone who wasn't here has heard all about it, that we should waste no time." Penelope smiled and took my hand and squeezed tight. I was kind of pushing my luck, but I knew it was this or nothing.

"I've already wasted enough time," said Penelope.

I made eye contact with Ivan. Vicky had told him what we'd done, and why, and he was surprisingly grateful for us avoiding it turning into a full-scale war.

"I assumed Penelope would never return to our world of utter madness, but she has, and I'm so happy. So, please be kind, and don't forget she's new to all this." I cuddled Penelope tightly and she blushed at the attention.

"Arthur, I'm pleased for you," said Selma, "but you can't use the cauldron and you sure as hell can't cook in it."

"Why not?"

"Because... because it's not the done thing. It's for potions, secret stuff," she said nervously.

"Don't be daft, it's just a pot now. What could possibly go wrong?"

Famous last words, right?

Turns out, we had a very nice dinner. We ate, we chatted, we laughed. Nobody tried to kill us, and nothing exploded.

And the cauldron and its contents? Let's just say it's gathering cobwebs and leave it at that.

For now.

The End

Book 8 is Ash Addict.

Get author updates and new release notifications first via the Newsletter.

Read the Dark Magic Enforcer series for more magical mayhem.

30748209R00206

Printed in Great Britain
by Amazon